Letters from the Mountains

Patricia Román

CHAPTERS

Acknowledgements

Thanks to Lorraine Mace for her deep-edit plotting skills and all-round common sense, to Eleni Kyriacou for her meticulous dotting, crossing and wheedling out of anything extraneous, and to the beta reading team at The History Quill for their support and encouragement. Huge gratitude also to Jesus Bordera of Txto Editorial for helping me understand the ins and outs of Spanish publishing and to my husband for his unconditional support in ways that only we know how.

Praise for Letters from the Mountains

"An interesting, evocative novel with some lovely descriptive passages"
(Eleni Kyriacou, author of The Unspeakable Acts of Zina Pavlou)

"This is a valuable book, with characters that are familiar, three dimensional and authentic"
(Katie Isbester, Claret Press)

Letters from the Mountains was shortlisted for the 2022
Flash International Novel prize.

To the people of Andalucía whose past suffering was the catalyst for creating this story.

The author has adjusted the Spanish lyrics describing the Andalucía flag from its original. This was done to fit the rhythm and style of an English narrative whilst maintaining the authentic spirit of its message.

Part One

1. Exile

Andalucía 1957

B ar receipts, bus tickets, nameless fluff, Ernesto rummaged through his pocket, pulled out the envelope and squinted at the date. Was it '47 or '49? Hard to tell. He studied the address, stained with grease from an oil-soaked sardine he'd devoured to stave off his hunger, and marked with drips of tawny rum that looked like blood. The whole thing was illegible. Perhaps agitation would yield up its secrets so he shook the envelope against his ear. But there were no rattles or jangles or dislodgings of documents. Just one sheet of fine paper like a whisper he couldn't quite hear. He traced a finger across the indentations where rough string had compressed the heap of envelopes into a single, almost impenetrable bundle. Not just one letter but ten, each the same size and each written in the same immature hand.

He'd left the others in his room, prising just one from under the string because ten mysteries were too much for a single evening when he'd rather just sit at this table enjoying his drink. But here it was, an envelope of unknown origin and undisclosed contents that ensnared his curiosity. He rapped it on the Formica-top so hard that the noise seemed to echo across the square, then, draining the last drips of his favourite rum, he called the barman over and relaxed into his chair. But the question disturbed him like an annoying wasp. Who had written these letters and for whom? And why had Juan given them to him, shoving them into his hands saying

'Here, Ernesto, take 'em quick and keep 'em safe. No one'll bother you – seein' as you're a stranger.'

Of course Juan was right. Who would be interested in a man with no history? A man with no life? He sighed and shoved the envelope back into the pocket of his overcoat, eager to ignore it. Those letters were nothing to do with him. He was keeping them safe for a friend. Yes, that's it; a favour to old Juan.

The fresh drink flowed down warm and easy as it always did at this empty hour when it calmed his nerves but had not yet rendered him into oblivion. With his guard down, melancholy slipped in and he fixed his eyes on the haze of rainbow colours arcing over the fountain and weighed up his situation. In Cuba there were tree-lined squares like this, and tall buildings with geranium-filled balconies like these, and tables full of people drinking just like they were now. With such familiarity all around, shouldn't he feel at home? But this wasn't home. This was a landing place, a holding bay for his emotions, and oh how he missed the sparkle of Havana, its scattered light, its glittering ocean. He shook his head because Juan was mistaken. Back in Cuba he *was* no stranger. Back in Havana he *did* have a life. That was before coming here of course, before all the blood and the lawyers and their demand for commitment; before the end of his old life and the beginning of this new unrelenting end.

Havana, August 1955

It sounded like a pig squealing after its throat had been cut. So he'd gone to take a look, and that was the biggest mistake of his life because Silvio was there, and beyond him, wedged between the urinals, was a man convulsing, wound pulsating, eyes rapid-rolling, almost dead.

The man's blood came oozing towards him across the urine-soaked floor, circling his suede loafers, rising over the thin soles, breaching the nap. He watched the bright-hot blood coagulating on the ice-cold tiles forming ruby-red crusts and he dared not move and break the seal. He saw a knife abandoned on the floor and his knees began to tremble. What should he do? 'Help!' he shouted but his cry came out weak and helpless and no one was there to hear him. Silvio had vanished too. Where the hell had he gone? Someone was coming.

'Ernesto, don't just stand there,' a voice behind him said. Get out the way!'

Then another voice shouted 'Call a doctor!'

By now the man had stopped moving and everyone went quiet.

Two hours later Ernesto left the police station, exhausted by their questions and disappointed with his answers. 'I didn't see anything' he said. 'I couldn't think' … 'I just froze' …'I didn't know what to do.' … 'No, sir, I didn't see who did it.' … 'I've told you all I know,' until finally they released him to the barren night.

Outside, Arsenio was waiting in a new Chevrolet Bel Air. 'Did you tell them it was Silvio? he asked.

'I didn't know. I mean, I…I didn't know what to do.'

'Well did you, or didn't you?'

'No, boss, I didn't.'

'Thank Christ for that. My son's an idiot.'

Arsenio dropped him outside his apartment and Ernesto listened to the retreating hum of the V8 engine bouncing off the tall buildings then fading to a satisfying silence that soothed the residue of his trembling. He trudged up the stairs pondering the impact of his lies. Of course he'd seen Silvio stab the man - two, three, four times in fact. Even as high as a kite, stumbling and mumbling, he'd plunged the knife in like a professional. Ernesto sighed, knowing he should have told the police – should have explained that he'd been in his dressing room, heard them shouting and gone out to see, and that he'd just stood there and watched it all happen. *Yes, officer. I saw everything!* But of course he didn't tell them that. Instead he'd kept his treacherous little mouth shut because Arsenio was top dog. Arsenio paid Ernesto's wages. He'd never find another job on the island if he testified against his boss`s son.

Ernesto fumbled his way through the darkness, threw his bloody loafers in a corner and eased himself under the warm sheet, careful not to wake Belle. What would she think when she found out he'd lied? Would she recognise his feebleness? Would she finally see him as the weak little man he knew himself to be?

Next day, the banner headline of the Havana News declared *MAFIA MAN MURDERED* and the following day *SILVIO VALDÉS ARRESTED*. By the end of the week lawyers had named their reluctant witness as *MUSICIAN ERNESTO COSTA*, and a week later there were threats to his life. *WITNESS IN HIDING*, the banner said. By the 19th September 1955 the prosecution's prime witness had fled the country. *COSTA GONE!* shouted the headline. And that's what he'd done, fled, abandoned Belle, run away. But what else could he do? How could he betray Arsenio by testifying against his son? But then how could he not? If Silvio escaped jail, then the Mafia would seek him out for thwarting justice or even suspect him of killing their man himself. Either way he would be dead.

Ernesto took another gulp of his ill-advised rum. A bell tolled for evening mass and through the descending gloom, chairs scraped against cobbles as people hurried off to worship. Three workmen remained, whispering over their drinks, shoulders hunched, foreheads touching. One raised his head and a whiff of fermentation from the distillery rose from his clothes.

'Should have been given a penalty,' he declared before recoiling into the dense conversation of his comrades. More whispering followed until another man raised his head too. His shoulders were broad, his neck thick and Ernesto wondered if he was a weightlifter.

'Expecting rain,' he said.

Ernesto sighed. Two years of these lacklustre conversations. Back home talk was fertile and strident, with simultaneous chatter about everything from the going rate of the dollar to national politics and, of course, the Mafia. Here though, discussions were dull and subdued as if no one had a serious opinion about anything. But then he remembered that having opinions was dangerous and taking a stand even worse. That's why he'd escaped wasn't it? To avoid taking sides. Yes, he decided, being a stranger with no obligations was easier, smoother, lazier even, than having to commit.

He shoved his hands in his overcoat pockets hoping to find physical solace in the gesture, but his fingers fell on the mysterious envelope. Not this again! He shook his head, took another swig of rum, and through a fog of alcoholic confusion the two dilemmas seemed to merge as one. How could something so small feel so immense? How could this letter, so thin and fine, feel so massively important? And how could his one, seemingly innocent decision to investigate a man's cry in a gentleman's toilet, have such devastating consequences? He shook his head again. It was getting to be a habit, almost like a tic. But the question had come back and he was asking it again. Why had Juan given him such an unwanted responsibility? And how could such a flimsy communication, written by a child, trigger such adult consternation? He didn't like it one bit. He'd toyed with steaming the wretched things open in the communal kitchen, but one of his fellow lodgers might have come in and asked what he was doing, or, even worse, reported his activity to the authorities. As a stranger in their country, that wasn't a good idea. So he'd left it. Better not to know, he told himself. Better not get involved.

A young family settled at the table opposite and he heard the woman say in a tight voice, 'Sit quietly, children. Mind your manners.' The girl was holding a doll and the boy was under the table, pushing his toy tank so hard it clattered across the cobbles towards Ernesto. He thought about ignoring it but the boy looked anxious so he bent to retrieve it.

'Here,' he said offering it back.

The woman whispered 'thank you,' but when he smiled she looked away as if engaging with a foreigner was taboo. The husband ordered drinks.

'That man's got funny hair,' the boy said.

Another sigh. Back home no one saw him as an outsider. Back home he blended in, not just for his looks but for his easy-going nature, happily listening to the robust declarations of his friends, admiring their convictions without commenting himself. They called him *el indeciso* – the ditherer. And they were right, always on the side-lines, watching, listening, but never making judgements, forever on the fence. Ernesto tried to shrug it off but here it came again, the burden of his error, lying to the police, escaping, abandoning Belle. He couldn't bear it. He shook his head, desperate to dislodge his anxiety, desperate to exorcise his indecisive nature, but there was no point in denying it. Life was so much easier when he didn't have to decide between one action and the next.

A lorry pulled up, its tyres groaning as it settled half on, half off the pavement.

'Five barrels, amigo,' Ernesto heard the barman shout from the interior. 'There's a party here tonight.'

There was a time when he loved to see people enjoying themselves, their whoops and cheers and the odd drunken stumble lifting his spirits as they swung to the Big Band Combo of Arsenio Valdés, Ernesto riffing at the back before coming under the spotlight to perform his solo. Now though, he'd left all that behind, the razzmatazz, the casinos, the drugs and the Mafia. Always the Mafia.

He ordered a coffee to combat the booze. The father read his paper. The mother sat upright supervising her children, their eyes straying towards him across the narrow space. Ernesto sat back, tired of their childish scrutiny. He closed his eyes, retreating into his private domain, imagining the tremor of a mouthpiece pressed against his lips, a tuning slide moving effortlessly in his hand, the warm air advancing smoothly through a labyrinth of tubular brass. Making music was his only refuge, the place where his world still made sense, where his convictions were real and where neither the Mafia nor Arsenio could find him. Making music felt like a satisfying truce. After all wasn't it this that had enticed him here in the first place? Without music he'd wither and die so where better to escape to than a country that shared his love for melody and song? But there were limitations. Here, guitars were hung back on walls by midnight, musicians asleep in their beds, performances done. In Havana, music was like an old friend moving in and out of people's homes any hour, day or night. The staccato chatter of guiros and claves, the deep murmured rhythms of the double bass, the wild shouting trumpets and the long drawn out call of the trombone. They wafted out of every window in every street, and if people weren't sitting down listening, they were dancing in the streets, in the bars, in their bathrooms. They said babies danced to the rhythms of a Cuban rumba from inside their mothers' wombs. And it wasn't just the music. 'Let's go somewhere they speak our language,' he'd suggested to Belle. But she'd stared at him as if he'd offered her poison. 'Oh Belle you had your chance, 'he said opening his eyes and stirring a spoon through his now-cold coffee, the dark liquid creating a swirl that seemed to have no end. A twilight mist had settled on the table. He wiped the moisture away with the side of his sleeve, and looked around. The workmen had gone, the family departed, the bar was deserted. Just him.

He emptied his glass, staggered across the road and let himself into the block that housed his apartment. Well that's what the landlord had called this L shaped room with one window overlooking the street and a kitchen and bathroom down the hall. It was all he could afford but at least he was alive, thank god, and still making music, if only in the confines of this lonely room. His head was spinning as he opened his trombone case and pulled out Juan's bundle of letters, pushing the one stained with rum and oil, back into its resting place with the other nine. 'Tell no one about them,' Juan had instructed, and he hadn't. Then he squeezed the whole package into the side pocket of his case and flipped the clasp shut with a short satisfying action that suggested he was done. If the letters were important to someone, it certainly wasn't him.

Next morning he lay in bed with a dry mouth and a heavy head, anticipating the overtures of another day. Two years and these sounds still seemed fresh and reassuring, still full of hope. Surely something good would happen soon? First came the glissando rumble of shutters rising on Juan's shop below, then the dull tympanic thud of morning papers slammed onto his counter, followed by a customer's high pitched greeting and Juan's bass-line mumbling back. He liked all this, the routines, the noisy predictability. It reminded him of his extended family back home, parents, uncles, aunts, and cousins, all sharing the same space in a disharmony of daily sounds that was almost orchestral. He rolled over and waited. In a few minutes a cyclist would navigate the cobbles, their wheels rattling with vibrato, and later still Paco would knock loudly on his door as if bashing on a high-hat, or he would shout up from the busy pavement with that hoarse voice that sounded like grit.

But until then he would stay under his blanket and think of the beautiful and now unobtainable Belle.

'Oh Belle, why didn't you come?' he called out to the room, staring at the ceiling, visualising her face. But of course no one answered. Instead a cold draught wafted in from the stairwell, scurrying under his door, raising dust off the un-swept floor before releasing it silently onto the bare wooden boards. In the end he pushed the thin blanket away and leapt out of bed, not daring to stay longer in case the memory of Belle's extraordinary being ensnared him as it usually did. He opened the window and saw the sun filtering through a morning mist, making the buildings shimmer with translucent light, but it would take another hour before the full blast of sunshine reached his window, prodding its angular rays through the frail glass and penetrating his tiny room so there was nowhere to hide. He leaned out into the fresh air where rows of orange trees fringed the street. These treasures were young when he'd first arrived, held up with stakes to prevent them from bending in the breeze. Now though they'd grown to the height of his window and stood almost unaided and bulging with fruit that looked mature enough to eat. He reached across the dark green canopy and twisted an orange away from its stem. It felt firm in his palm. He dug his thumbs into the surface, opening up the arched and dimpled peel and remembering the texture of Belle's skin, the way he would pass his hand gently across her thigh. He sighed and the loneliness within him almost made him weep. He pulled away a segment and placed it on his tongue, but it was bitter and hard, not succulent as expected, so he threw it in the grate. Things here were not always what they seemed.

2. Paco

Ernesto looked at his watch. Just enough time to practice before Paco arrived. So he stood under the central ceiling light, feet slightly apart, and took a deep breath. Inhale two beats, exhale three, inhale two beats, exhale three. He swapped it around. Inhale three beats, exhale two, and so it went on until his lungs were relaxed and ready. Then he moved into the corner where his trombone lay dismantled on a shelf. He pressed the bell to the tuning slide and carefully pushed the mouthpiece into place.

"It's time fella," he said as if addressing an old friend and taking a deep breath, he raised the instrument to his lips, blowing long and hard to make the instrument vibrate. Oh how he adored that first, virgin sound. Then, with his lips tightened, he began the buzzing exercises that always preceded performance; short, sharp, repetitious. After that the scales were easy. He could play them in his sleep. Sometimes he did. Then the arpeggios, and as those first undulating notes hit the air, memories of old applause echoed back, forcing him to close his eyes, remembering. People used to say he loved that 'bone more than he loved his women, and Ernesto was inclined to agree, except perhaps for her.

There was a loud bang on the door, rattling its hinges.

'You in there, Nesto?'

Ernesto sighed, positioned his instrument back on the shelf and opened the door. Paco was leaning against the jamb, panting with the effort of climbing the stairs.

'You're early,' Ernesto said, annoyed at the change to his routine.

'Morning, Cubano. Come on let's go.'

'I'm practising.'

'To hell with that. I'm thirsty.' Paco slapped him on the back in such a friendly way that Ernesto didn't protest. They went downstairs, footsteps echoing down the stairwell that separated Ernesto's cool private world from the heated bustle of the street. Paco stamped his heels staccato across the cobbles and Ernesto made long strides in his loafers. They pushed through the ragged throng of children coming back from morning school and Paco steered him towards the bar.

It wasn't like the bars back home. New to the country and eager for company, Ernesto had wandered into the square and encountered the narrow doorway covered with bullfighting posters. He'd pushed it open hoping to find warmth and friendship but instead, photos of matadors emerged from the gloom, their frames stained yellow with age-old nicotine. Old men sat alone drinking rough sherry and muttering in the darkness. Leftover food from the night before lay abandoned on a sawdust floor. A warren of back rooms led to the far end of the interior, where a door was propped open to the street, the only chink of illumination in this new world full of confusion and squalor. The toilet was a tiny space under the stairs, with a curtain for privacy and a hole in the floor to squat. That was the first and last time he'd entered the bar. Ernesto and Paco preferred to sit outside in the sun.

'I'm done in,' Paco said shoving his feet on the chair beside him.

The barman came out, blinking into the unforgiving light, and put a jug of strong black coffee between them, with two bottles of spirits. Ernesto noticed he was even paler than usual, emerging from the darkened bar like a troubled mole dislodged from its natural habitat.

'Here you go, Cubano,' he said, pushing Ernesto's favourite Havana Rum across the table. 'Beats me why you drink that stuff.' Then he turned to Paco. 'Can't he drink something decent?' he said pouring a glass of the local sherry. Paco raised it like a challenge and leaned in close to Ernesto's face.

'You should've come last night, Nesto. Told you there'd be plenty of women.'

'Yes, but what sort of women, Paco?

'Who cares?'

'I do!' Ernesto snapped back. 'And look at the state of you.' His shirt was half out of his trousers and his eyes were bloodshot and narrow. It was obvious he'd been out all night. Paco shrugged as if he didn't care and Ernesto smiled. How different they were, not only in attitude but also their looks. Both musicians, both middle-aged, but Ernesto was tall, stretched thin like his beloved trombone while Paco was short, with a rounded belly like his guitar. Their hair was different too, his all curly and short, Paco's long and straight and flopping over one eye. In fact they differed in most things, especially their attitude towards women.

'You want to be careful you don't get the clap, my friend, if you haven't already,' Ernesto said, repeating his usual advice.

'Well *you* won't get it that's for sure, you bloody hermit.'

Ernesto sipped his coffee as Paco rolled an untidy tube of black tobacco. His friend was right. Ernesto wasn't interested in women, not now, not after Belle. And hadn't he chosen to come to Spain for that very reason? Not only to escape the threat of death or destitution but to live in a place where women were still chaperoned in public and where they dropped their gaze when they passed him on the street? Not that he wanted to subdue them, it wasn't in his nature, but in this city women were meek and less assured than back home and that made him more relaxed. Besides, he liked the lack of crime, the respectability, the self-control, the way society was well ordered, how people went to church and no one broke the rules. But as usual he kept these thoughts away from others, especially Paco.

'Did you play last night?' he asked

'Of course! Those bitches loved my bulerias, ' Paco said, licking along the paper's delicate edge.

'You're too uncontrolled my friend. What happened to the pure rhythms of flamenco?'

Paco lit the newly-formed cigarette and took a deep draw before releasing it with his response. 'I tell you, man, these foreign girls, they're something else.'

Ernesto sighed. He'd heard it all before. So ignoring Paco and the pungent smoke that hovered between them, he stretched his long legs over the pavement and watched as a warm breeze disturbed the newspapers outside Juan's shop then shimmied through the orange trees, rippling like water until it reached the end of the street. He followed its wake down to the junction where the fountain was throwing rainbows of light into the heated air. This was a favourite meeting place for tour groups to take photographs, but few visitors came up to where Ernesto and Paco were sitting. Sometimes they made it half way, to the Gentlemen's Outfitters, peering through the canopied window at sober waistcoats, felt trilbies and braces woven in the colours of the Spanish flag, but they rarely ventured further. Perhaps the peeling paintwork and rusty verandas meant this end of the street was dangerous and its inhabitants unrefined.

But then what was this? Coming up the street was a vehicle he'd never seen before. He squinted into the sun to get a better look and as it drew closer he recognised a car he'd only seen on hoardings -

a new town car. According to the advertisement it was going to revolutionise motoring, but he doubted it. This thing was short and stubby with squared-off wheel arches. An ugly contraption with no grace at all, he thought, recalling Arsenio's sleek, new Chevy Bel Air that he'd witnessed before leaving Havana, with its large front grille and chrome profiles sparkling under the street lights. An impressive coupé in two-tone blue. He sighed, remembering his old life, the one he'd abandoned, the one that had passed.

Paco left and Ernesto crossed the street to collect his newspaper. Juan was sitting in his usual place staring at a brand new television propped up on a pile of old papers.

'Lucky you, having one of these,' Ernesto said.

'Yeah, 'cept everyone wants to watch it,' Juan mumbled, prising himself up from his chair and stretching to switch it off.

'Need a hand?'

'Leave me be, I's alright,' Juan said and Ernesto didn't argue as he tucked *The Chronicle* - always *The Chronicle* - under his arm and went to leave.

'I'm leaving too,' Juan said pulling down the shutters and not mentioning the bundle of letters he'd forced into Ernesto's hands the week before. Ernesto didn't say anything either, just watched the old man shuffling off down the street in his worn-down slippers. Ernesto turned to go and bumped straight into a broad-shouldered man who seemed to have appeared from nowhere. The man grunted something unintelligible and walked away before Ernesto could apologise, then he frowned. He'd seen that man somewhere before - in the square from the night before - the one who looked like a weightlifter.

Ernesto returned to his room wishing that, like Juan, he could take an afternoon rest but knowing he could not. Whenever he closed his eyes, blood came rushing into his vision, great pools of congealing blood. And Belle came too, staring, reprimanding, holding him to account. Too many feelings were lurking in his heart. Too many doubts were lodged inside his head to allow for a peaceful sleep. The window to his apartment jutted over the street and by now those early morning rays, so harsh and singular, had given way to softer, communal beams that permeated his shaded room giving it a comforting midday glow. He positioned his little table next to the light, unfolded *The Chronicle* and spread it carefully onto the surface. Somehow, moving his palms gently across the print and turning each page with his delicate bony fingers gave him great satisfaction and just like his music, calmed his mind. This was how he finished his mornings, reading his favourite newspaper as the light from a softly climbing sun threw dappled rays onto the ink-blackened page. He liked this broadsheet. It reported satisfying perspectives on his chosen country, a world full of the certainty and stability that his old country now lacked. Things were happening over there, things he didn't like - disruptions that he considered unnecessary, dangerous even. Any minute now he was expecting events to turn nasty and when he looked at the International section, there it was.

FAILED COUP IN CUBA

At 10 a.m. 13 March 1957, a group calling themselves the Student Revolutionary Directorate (SRD) stormed the Presidential Palace in Havana in an attempt to assassinate President Fulgencio Batista. The attack ended in failure leaving Havana radio station, already seized by the rebels, unable to report Batista's anticipated death.'

Ernesto sighed with relief, remembering the cool sophisticated Batista, always with some beauty on his arm as he strolled into the nightclub. Once, after Ernesto had performed his solo, Batista had walked over to the stage, shaken him by the hand and given him a huge tip. Surely the man was no threat to his people? But even so, that group – who were they? - the SRD, had risked their lives. Those kids had wanted him dead. Ernesto stared into the sky. Was Batista a scoundrel? Surely not? Were the students right to rebel? Ernesto didn't think so. But as usual he wasn't sure. As usual he didn't know what to think. Then he realised what bothered him most was Belle. What would happen if revolution came? No one would sympathise with a nightclub dancer who fraternised with the Mafia. A small cloud pranced across the sky, followed by others cavorting in line as if mocking him. He shuddered. 'Why didn't you come with me, Belle? Why?'

3. Beneath

A May-time sun came flooding in. Ernesto jumped out of bed to open the window and close down his dreams, or were they nightmares? He was never sure. He peered outside. Here was safety, here was the day. But last night had confirmed the opposite. High on the Crow's nest, mast lurching in the wind, sailors below, one of them holding a barrel over his head, another battling the sea. That's how his dreams were, always above, always watching some apocalyptic scene down below. They were so real and so frequent that he named them his 'watching dreams' as if he, a tall thin stranger, had observed the local inhabitants by day and pressed them into unwitting action by night.

This morning, too exhausted to listen to Paco`s boasting, he finished his coffee and crossed the street to collect his paper, and saw the same broad-shouldered man leaving Juan's shop.

'Nice morning,' Ernesto said hoping for a connection.

'I suppose so,' the man said then lumbered away leaving Ernesto smiling at the man's reply. It had been brief but at least it was something. Ernesto frowned. Hadn't he seen this man somewhere else today? But where? Then he realised. That's my sailor, the man in this morning's dream, the man lifting barrels over his head just like a weightlifter would. He frowned, wondering if his mind might be a bit out of control, as if his observations by day had penetrated too deeply into his subconscious at night. Then he collected his paper and scurried back to the safety of his room, like some street dog protecting its loot from the pack. Once again he positioned his table under the window, opened up *The Chronicle* and smoothed it out as he always did. A month had passed since the unsuccessful coup in Havana and all was quiet. Thank goodness the rebels had backed off. He flipped to the local news where photographs of smiling parents with sons and daughters, gleamed from the page, boys in sailor suits, girls in white dresses, their gloved hands clutching bibles, rosaries dangling from immature fingers. Everything as it should be he thought as he turned to the centre page and saw a large photograph of General Franco in military regalia with a caption beneath it. *El Caudillo, His Excellency the Head of State, our illustrious Leader, General Franco.* Ernesto smiled. Why did the press call Franco by three different titles like a priest referring to the Holy Trinity? Did they think he was God? He studied the round face, the heavy eyelids, and the small stature familiar to everyone. His portrait hung in every town hall in Spain, every library, every school, and almost every home in the land. Perhaps not Paco's he decided, adjusting his thinking. Ernesto had once asked him,

'Why do you hate General Franco so? He's done you no harm.' And Paco had looked at him through a haze of black cigarette smoke, with what looked like scorn.

'If you don't know by now, my friend, then you never will.'

'Well I quite like the man,' Ernesto had responded but already Paco had squashed his cigarette butt into the cobbles and was walking away, head down, blocking him from further intervention. Their conversations were often like that, cut short before either of them could truly explain what was in their hearts.

Ernesto studied the man in the photograph. He liked Franco almost as much as he liked Cuba's Batista. The two men were masterful, even if Batista was a lothario who loved the high life and Franco ruled his people with a moralising fist. Ernesto admired both men for their firmness and dedication, and how they provided jobs for their citizens and a sense of immovability that made him feel safe. But most of all he liked their singularity of purpose and ferocious strength - two characteristics he lacked. These men weren't like him. They were strong where he was weak. They were resilient where he would yield. 'It's true,' he spoke aloud, addressing the room as if it were a critical friend. 'After all I left didn't I?' and the room seemed to agree. He sighed. There was no escaping his cowardice, leaving Havana, unable to tell the truth for fear of reprisals, abandoning Belle. It was part of who he was, and although he couldn't be like his two heroes, he told himself daily that his music was compensation for his flaws and that this was surely enough?

Then he noticed the date, July 18th. So General Franco will visit the city on the National day of Spain. Every year on that day, Batista would send a cablegram to honour Franco's victory in the Civil war, and Spanish dignitaries would fly to Havana to take part in official celebrations over there, no doubt attracted by the city's nightlife and opportunities for illicit romance. Ernesto nodded in recognition. There were connections between the two countries that transcended national boundaries, so that even the Atlantic Ocean seemed like a tranquil lake that one might navigate with nothing but a cultural oar.

He remembered the year when Belle dragged him to Havana Cathedral to hear the Te Deum and to watch Batista celebrate mass with the Spanish ambassador. Dear wonderful Belle, she'd tried so hard to improve herself, but they'd criticised her, saying she was too pushy for the colour of her skin and he closed his eyes for a moment remembering her jet black body and the curve of her sumptuous thighs. If she'd been white or even mulatto like him, self-improvement would have been approved. His colour was acceptable, desired even. At the height of their passion Belle would whisper 'mulatto' in his ear as a sign of her love and he would burrow himself in her gorgeousness. But out in the real world things were different. Her identity card said it all. Below the photograph, stark and dark against the white background, appeared the word 'BLACK'. He sighed. How could she hope to better herself when the authorities labelled one colour inferior to another?

He opened his diary and wrote in the date of Franco's visit, promising himself that in three months' time he would be out on the streets, waving the Spanish flag in one hand and the Cuban star in the other. But then, in a moment of surrender, he closed his eyes imagining both flags flapping, pulling him from left to right, stretching, wrenching and tearing him apart. He opened his eyes and stared at the clear blue expanse above his head. There was one small cloud hanging there and in that slip of a moment he conceded. That's me, he thought. I'm in limbo, floating between one land and another. Between two lives, neither of them resolved, between people who held convictions and him with none. How he wished he could have been braver in that toilet, grabbed Silvio to stop him, made a citizen's arrest even. But what did he do? Nothing! He shook his head to remove the pain, to remove the image of that dreadful blood surrounding his loafers, like twin islands in a gruesome sea, sticky red liquid congealing and hardening into a crust. He shrugged. What was the point of picking at old scabs? So when Franco came to town he would smile, he would mingle and he would force himself to feel happy with his lot.

Another month passed and Paco was drumming his fingers against the table as if practising a musical flourish, whilst Ernesto sat quietly nursing his rum. That was the other difference between them. Paco's stubby fingers were never at rest and his head would jerk from side to side as if dodging bullets, whereas, despite his inner worries, Ernesto could manage a whole morning sitting quietly with his hands immobile in his lap. There were more things too, Ernesto nodding slowly as if counting a beat, Paco tapping his feet frantically on the pavement as if ready to take flight. Perhaps it was something to do with their instruments. The temperament of flamenco guitar was that of the *Zapateador* the stamping dancer, snatching and clapping across the floor, whereas his trombone needed nothing more than his long thin fingers pushing the slide forward and back, his lungs easing out the air, sending it forth in harmonies that ran together like water.

Today it was obvious that something was wrong. Ernesto leant forward.

'What's up my friend?'

Paco pushed a hand through his mass of black hair, seeming to weigh up whether to reply. But as he opened his mouth, the barman appeared with a bottle of rum and slammed it down between them.

'Here, Cubano. On the house, take as much as you want.'

Paco jumped at the man's voice then set his mouth firm, seemingly no longer willing to answer Ernesto's question. Ernesto frowned. Had the barman just censured their conversation? But he didn't pursue it. Instead he stirred the rum slowly through his coffee wondering what secret could be so serious that they had no intention of revealing. He sighed, feeling like the outsider he still was, then finishing his coffee, he crossed the road, bought his newspaper, tucked it under his arm and trudged up the stairs to his room, weary at the thought of losing his friend Paco to some unexplained preoccupation.

In his room, he pulled the trombone case off the shelf, removed the bundle of letters from their hiding place and inspected them.

Here was another mystery he was unable to fathom and it felt as if the whole city was excluding him, keeping him at arm's length, preserving him from the truth as if he was too stupid to understand. He studied the bundle carefully to see if there were any changes. Perhaps the string had made deeper indentations, perhaps the paper was looking a little yellower, but apart from that they remained the same as when he'd last inspected them two months ago. And Juan was right. No one had come looking for them in his apartment because he was anonymous, someone to be overlooked like a dead fly in a spider's web. Ernesto sighed and pushed the bundle back inside the case, closing the lid with a firm push, figuring it was easier to ignore them than have even more unanswered questions bringing him down with their uncertainties.

By early July, large banners were hanging over balconies and tall poles stood at attention along Main Street. A few days later, flags were attached and unfurled in a blaze of yellow and red that altered the landscape of the city. Paco spat on the floor.

'Bloody eagles.'

'Eagles?'

'Look, there in the middle.' He pointed to where a large black asymmetric bird form had been added to the Spanish flag. 'The symbol of Franco's regime,' he said.

The barman was hovering again. 'Keep your voice down,' he warned.

Ernesto looked along the street and asked. 'And the Andalusian flag? Why are they not flying that too?' There was a long silence while Paco and the barman exchanged glances then they roared with laughter making him feel foolish. He didn't ask again.

Next evening Paco guided Ernesto down a side street where the pavement was so narrow they had to walk in single file.

'You first,' Paco said, 'I'll keep a look out from behind.'

They stopped at double doors that stretched to twice his height and above, carved in stone, was an ornate crest. Paco pushed open a smaller door within the entrance and immediately the odours of damp mortar, spent tobacco and ancient fermentation hit the air.

'What is this place?' Ernesto asked.

'Used to be a bodega belonging to the Dominguez family,' Paco answered, sighing with what seemed like relief as they stepped inside and closed the door on the world outside. The interior was opaque but as his eyes adjusted, Ernesto saw that the ceilings were high and the walls were bare stone. In one corner was a wooden bar and now, hunched over upturned barrels that served as makeshift tables, he could see several men. Their movements were disjointed from years of drinking the local sherry and their eyes seemed ransacked of reason. Poor souls he thought. In Cuba people drank a lot but never morosely. Over there was joy. Over here seemed bleak.

Paco beckoned him.

'This way,' he said moving to another doorway at the back, and into a smaller room even darker than the first. Oil lamps lit the corners where men and women were smoking and laughing in such an animated manner that Ernesto smiled. What a contrast to the gloom outside. He scanned the faces and recognised the weightlifter, or was he that sailor from his dreams? He was with the other two men he'd seen in the square when they had talked so glumly about football and the state of the weather. Now though, they were smiling and laughing so he raised his arm in greeting but not one of them responded. Ernesto shrugged as he took a seat. What more could he do?

Paco jumped onto a small stage and tuned a guitar before stepping up to a microphone to make an announcement.

'Tonight I dedicate this song to my dear friend The Cubano, in the hope that when he hears it, he will understand.' He raised his glass towards Ernesto and now, with Paco's endorsement, the three men, and those around them, raised theirs too.

Paco's voice was surprisingly rich and mellow.

A green flag unfurls

Like a wing of delight.

Emblazoned with a sash

Of winter dawn white.

She brings us assurance

By day and by night.

And grants us the courage to

Continue our fight.

When he'd finished Paco came over.

'So what do you think?'

'I didn't realise you could sing so beautifully, Paco.'

'No, not me. The words, Nesto? Did you understand them?' He pulled up a stool and leaned in. 'The other day you asked why there were no Andalusian flags in the streets. Well after our civil war this bloody government banned all regional flags, especially the Andalusian one, us being such rebellious bastards. But rest assured, my friend, our flag is still here in our hearts and on our tongues too.' He tapped his chest and waved his arms at the men and women still singing. *A green flag unfurls. Like a wing of delight. Emblazoned with a sash. Of winter dawn white.*

That night, Ernesto lay in bed wondering at that windowless room tucked away in the body of the building, unseen but surely the beating heart of the whole neighbourhood. He'd listened to talk of valour in the civil war, and overheard conversations that would put most of them in jail. And the weightlifter and his two companions? How wrong he'd been about them. Of course their words, delivered under the light beams of the city were different to those expressed in the darkness of that room hidden in the back of an old bodega. Of course their conversation in a public square had been trivial and sterile. Who knows who could have been listening to their talk of revolution and a return to a republican state? He sighed with incomprehension. What could be gained by being stuck in the past, unable to accept the conclusion of a war that finished nearly twenty years ago? Why couldn't they let it go? And what about Paco? His face had lit up talking of revolution. Surely this was dangerous? But Paco's singing had been exquisite and Ernesto slept well that night, with no waking dreams to disturb his rest, knowing that perhaps, in time, his friend would reveal himself as much more than the person he pretended to be.

4. The visit

By the second week in July, leaves on orange trees were curling in and their tips turning brown. Saharan dust lay on everything from the geraniums on balconies, to the table outside the bar, where Ernesto and Paco were sitting. Paco had reverted to his public self.

'Good night last night, Nesto,' he said, winking.

'Spare me the details, I don't want to know,' Ernesto said turning away and stretching his legs out across the pavement. He watched a group of tourists wandering up from Main Street, cooling themselves with their new fans and patting their pockets to check they hadn't been robbed. A heat haze was rising off the cobbles, distorting his view. Then through the shimmering light, a solid, dark shape appeared and it seemed to be gliding along the pavement like a military tank on manoeuvres. Ernesto stared, trying to decipher what he was observing, and as it slid past the gentlemen's outfitters, moving out of the heat haze and into the unhindered air, he realised that it wasn't a single object but another group of strangers huddled together as if they were one. He frowned. Something was odd. They didn't amble in a disorderly manner like tourists did. They didn't stop to look in shop windows. They didn't wear sunglasses or sandals or straw hats, but formal jackets and ties. Their feet moved in unison and each had a small identical moustache.

The barman came out to watch. 'Franco's men,' he snarled and put his hand on Paco's shoulder. Both men had stiffened. Ernesto counted, one, two, three, four, five, all walking towards the door to Juan's shop. One kicked it open and shouted something he couldn't hear. Then a pile of newspapers was dumped onto the street. 'Better get going,' the barman whispered. 'Use the back exit.' Paco stood up, his chair falling noisily to the ground.

'Bye, Nesto, got to go,' he said, and dashed into the bar. Ernesto stood too, imagining Paco running through those gloomy rooms, past the old men and the disgusting toilet and towards the bright-lit exit at the rear. He picked up the chair that Paco had abandoned and stared at the two unfinished coffees on the table in front of him. What's going on? he asked the air. By now the men had vanished. Ernesto crossed the street to find Juan sitting on the floor of his shop, with his head between his knees. He was shaking and the television was blaring above his head. Ernesto stooped down to retrieve one of Juan's slippers lying in the corner.

'Christ what just happened?'

'Nothing. I's alright. Leave me be.'

Once again Ernesto knew better than to interfere. He took a *Chronicle* off the rack, put the money by the till and went to leave. But then he noticed the pile of newspapers in the gutter. They were all the same publication, *The Monkey* and each of the front pages had been slashed with a knife. He didn't approve of this paper. It was full of exaggerated stories about people being tortured or dispossessed and littered with bad spellings, but he couldn't bear to think of any newspaper being vandalised like this. One by one, he picked them up, shook off the dirt and left them stacked neatly in the doorway. Then he tucked his beloved *Chronicle* under his arm and climbed the stairs to his room, wondering if perhaps the country he had adopted as his own contained more dangers lurking within it than he had previously realised.

On the 18th of July Juan's shutters rolled up, newspapers were dumped on the counter and a cyclist rode by on the cobbled street. Ernesto lay in his bed listening to these familiar sounds and thinking of Belle as he always did. Last night she'd come to him in a dream. He was on the mast looking down. Of course he was. He was always looking down. The sea was wild and so was she, riding in hard on a white horse. He heard an orchestra performing *The Ride of the Valkyries*, as clear as if they were in his room. He was playing too, high up in the crow's nest. Wave after wave of phrasing, on and on he played, and Belle was riding. And now she was swaying, leaning over him, moving. *Mulatto* she cried with such undulating passion that, for a moment, he refused to open his eyes. But then he saw a knife and it was covered in blood. Drip, drip, drip, and the sound of a man shouting, and it was coming from below. He opened his eyes, realising it was real, the rise and fall of someone asking a question then demanding an answer. Ernesto pictured the group he'd seen the day Paco had dived into the bar. He remembered their dark suits and identical moustaches and the pile of *Monkey* newspapers lying in the gutter. 'Franco's men,' the barman had said. Ernesto jumped out of bed, dressed quickly and ran downstairs. When he arrived Juan was sitting on the floor again, nursing a bruise on his forehead.

'What happened?'

'Best not to ask, my friend,' Juan said, keeping his head down to exclude further conversation. Ernesto didn't push for an answer. Instead he nodded at Juan, so unwilling to share his secrets, and strode over to the bar, desperate for an early morning drink to settle his nerves. In the back of his mind he wondered if those men had been looking for the bundle of envelopes he was harbouring just above their head in his room upstairs, the ones that Juan had told him not to open. If so, they were getting close. He felt himself shiver in the July heat. What had he got himself into? And more importantly, how could he get himself out? He shook his head, more out of habit than negation. What could he do? Whatever the old man was up to had certainly upset the authorities and he didn't want to get involved. *Don't ask,* Juan had said and Ernesto agreed. Better not ask questions about things that didn't concern him, after all, it wasn't his fight and if he didn't get involved then he wouldn't get into trouble.

Paco joined him, throwing himself moodily into a chair and silently rolled a thin cigarette, hardly touching his drink. Moments passed with the silence between them getting fatter, hotter, filled with discomfort that Ernesto could hardly bear. Recently, what conversations they'd had, were restless and incomplete. Paco hadn't mentioned his flight through the depths of the bar to avoid Franco's men, and Ernesto hadn't asked him to explain. Somehow bringing it up seemed a step too far. Paco drummed his fingers on the table whilst Ernesto sipped half-heartedly at his coffee; two friends together but so far apart. Eventually Paco yanked back his sleeve and looked at his watch.

'Bastard Franco's due in half an hour.'

'I hope he comes in one of his classic cars.'

'I couldn't give a toss what he comes in as long as he gets here,' Paco said.

'Maybe a Chrysler or a Pontiac,' Ernesto mused. 'Or even a Cadillac?'

'Christ man,' Paco snapped. 'What is it with you? First with your trombone and now your cars?' Ernesto was barely listening. He'd changed his mind. In Cuba, casino bosses favoured big, brash American cars, but not Franco. He was far too serious for that.

'Perhaps the Hispano-Suiza Pegaso Z-102 or something traditional like the K6T cabriolet, with the roof down so the crowds can cheer him as he passes?'

Paco looked at his watch again. 'Should be there by now. Come on, drink up.'

They walked towards the square, to a hum that grew deeper as they approached.

'Sounds like the whole city's here,' Ernesto said. As they turned the corner he gasped. In the apartments that lined the vast square, every balcony was crammed with citizens leaning over to get a better look. Blinds had been rolled up, windows opened and ceiling fans whirring to fight off the July heat. On the ground, people stood in tight groups clutching flags, jostling for better positions. Some perched on benches, or climbed onto lampposts and for once the police did nothing to stop them. People clutched white handkerchiefs they'd brought to salute their General and held decorated fans that they flicked and vibrated. Paco and Ernesto moved into the crowd, keeping their legs braced against the swell. With the handkerchiefs waving, the fans fanning, the flags flapping, and the crowd heaving, it seemed that the whole city was pitching like a ship on a sea of expectation, just like in his dream. The motion made Ernesto feel sick but he was excited too. Finally he'd see the man he so admired in the flesh. But of course he said nothing of this to Paco.

An orchestra started something loud and boastful that Ernesto didn't recognise. Everyone turned as one. A large motorcar had just arrived and was moving between them, splitting the crowd, then another with darkened windows. But it was the third that carried El Caudillo and everyone waved as it slid past. Ernesto was surprised. It wasn't the open-topped K6T he was expecting but the heavier J12 with a solid roof, smaller windows and a deep engine roar, a brute of a car except for the delicate squeal of its white-walled tyres sliding over the granite ground.

'That's *our* car,' Paco snarled, 'the one our Republican leaders used before that bastard got his hands on it. Had to get it reinforced in case we tried to assassinate him.' Ernesto could see that Paco was right. The Hispano-Suiza J12 bodywork was riveted in multiple places and the rear was sloped to prevent an assault. Now the crowd moved forward, straining on tiptoe to get a better look. Being taller than all of them Ernesto had the best view and he watched a bodyguard step out of the second car and stride towards the J12. He opened the door and Franco's wife, Carmen Polo, emerged wearing a necklace of pearls. The crowd gasped and Ernesto sighed, imagining that row of creamy white beads around the deliciously dark neck of his beloved Belle. How elegant she would look too. The bodyguard moved to the other side. El Caudillo appeared from the cavernous interior, adjusting his military uniform, smoothing his medals. How much shorter the man seemed in real life. Then the city's mayor stepped forward to shake the Generalissimo's hand and the crowd gasped in unison as hundreds of doves were released into the air, fluttering above the flapping white handkerchiefs like distant cousins, before moving off and merging with the bright blue sky. How wonderful!

General Franco turned to a veiled statue in the centre of the square.

'Damn it. What's going on? I can't see,' Paco said from his shoulder.

'He's pulling on a rope,' Ernesto explained and the veil fell to reveal the newly-cleaned figure of Miguel Primo de Rivera. The crowd clapped and Paco muttered under his breath.

'Idiots, it's just another bloody dictator.' He tapped Ernesto on the elbow. 'I'm off now. Goodbye my friend and thank you.'

'Thank you for what?'

'For being you, with not a bone of unkindness in your body'
Then he threw his arms around Ernesto for what felt like longer
than he should, and turned, walking away quickly, forcing his way
through the crowd to the edge of the square. Ernesto frowned.
What was that all about? He watched as Paco positioned himself
under the clock tower, looking small and fragile against the might
of this municipal building as, once again, Paco checked his watch.
Did he have a rendezvous? Two men arrived and greeted him.
Ernesto squinted into the light to see who they were. One was the
weightlifter and the other was a much younger man with a similar
stature to Paco. The three seemed to be nodding as if in agreement,
then the weightlifter slapped them on the back and left. Ernesto
watched, intrigued. What was going on? Paco and the younger
man waited a few moments then moved into the adjoining street,
and before they faded into the shadows Ernesto noticed they both
had the same gait.

Who was that young man? And why was the weightlifter there
too? But with no answers, Ernesto turned back to the square. El
Caudillo was steering his wife towards the car. Was he leaving
already? The crowd were quiet. The bodyguard looked anxious. A
chorus of angry shouting broke out, fists were raised and amidst all
the handkerchiefs, Ernesto saw a hand holding a pistol. Someone
shouted, *Long Live the Republic*. There was a shot. The bodyguard
threw himself forwards. Someone was down. The crowd lurched.
Ernesto kept his eyes ahead. The J12 was moving off with General
Franco and his wife inside, and three protesters were being dragged
away by a group of men in dark suits. *What just happened? Did you
see? Who was that person shouting?* the crowd asked as they began
to disperse.

Bewildered, Ernesto went to the bar to think. *Long Live the
Republic!* someone had shouted, but surely - that question again,
after twenty years, wasn't it time to let things go? And that pistol.
Was it an attempt to assassinate the General right there in the

square? If so, who would be so foolish? Or so brave? The barman brought him a coffee.

'No rum today' Ernesto said. 'I need to think.' He sat with his head in his hands pondering not only the pistol in the square but the finality of Paco's farewell. What did he mean *not a bone of unkindness in your body?* It wasn't true. He'd let people down - Belle mostly. And after that he'd escaped when he should have stayed and stood his ground. At least those protesters had stood up for what they believed in, just like those rebels in Cuba a few weeks ago. At least young people had courage. Not like him for Christ's sake. Not him, a carcass of a man eaten up by fear. And why had Paco acted so strangely? And who was that young man with him? He shook his head and called the barman.

'I'll take that rum now, a full bottle,' he said. Sometimes life had to be obscured rather than confronted. He finished his coffee, grabbed the rum and crossed the street. Juan was watching television, his bruise a dark purple. *The Chronicle* was already laid out on the counter so Ernesto tucked it under his arm and, bottle in hand, went to his room where he moved the table under the window and spread the newspaper out as he always did. Here at last was security. Here he could relax.

UPDATE ON THE GENERAL'S SCHEDULE

Following an assassination plot on our illustrious leader, the General El Caudillo has moved his entourage to the Dominguez estate for a private luncheon before returning earlier than scheduled to the El Pardo Palace in Madrid.

Ernesto frowned. Something didn't add up. This was the morning edition so the paper must have known in advance about an attack in the square. And perhaps Franco's security men had known about it too because they certainly acted as if they did. He shook his head. This looked like trouble and he didn't like conflict and he didn't like change. He preferred a simple life where people were nice to each other and where music eliminated any sorrows lurking in the corners of his soul. He folded *The Chronicle* away, tired of all this political intrigue, and opened the bottle. Just one for now he told himself. But two glasses in, he fetched his trombone and lay on his bed, hugging it to his chest and inviting music into his head. Jazz today, up and down and in and out like an un-metred poem. He imagined himself with his old band, playing a mixture of bebop and croon, watching everyone enjoying themselves, swallowed up in the mood as much as he. How he loved all that and how he missed it, he thought, allowing the memories to swim in and out of his mind. Yet the events of this morning wouldn't leave him. Something odd had happened, something he had seen but not fully understood.. But what?

Heat and the morning rum dulled his senses. Against his will Ernesto closed his eyes. Sleep was something to be resisted. Sleep was the enemy, bound up with truth. Giving in meant letting go, allowing his dreams to open up the gaps he tried so hard to close. Today though, he couldn't resist that drag into slumber. A few moments later Belle was driving a Pegaso sports car, dressed so elegantly with a pearl necklace around her neck, while a thousand doves fluttered over her head. But the beads were too heavy and she tore them off. There was blood everywhere too and the engine stalled, Belle let out a scream and the doves flew away. There was a vibration and Ernesto heard the shot of a pistol. It was aimed into the air. Was it? Yes of course it was. He'd seen it hadn't he? So *that* was it. That's what he had been trying to fathom. The pistol wasn't fired at El Caudillo, but in a different direction, into the air.

He sat up shocked, knowing he had seen something important, knowing that he'd been given a truth he did not want to possess. 'No. That can't be true,' he declared to the room, but inside he knew he was right. The whole thing had been staged and because he was so tall he might be the only one who had seen it. Now, wherever he looked in his solitary room, the pistol hovered, demanding his attention and whenever he closed his eyes it was there too. He reached for the rum. Here was evasion, here was denial and with the covers pulled tight up against his chest, he poured another drink.

5. Loss

The empty bottle rolled under the bed leaving a trail of sticky brown liquid across the floor. He opened the window to a veil of mist that had settled over the city, trapping in the untamed heat.

'Christ I feel rough,' he said, and the room replied with creaks and groans as if it too had been drowned in alcohol from the night before. He staggered down the corridor surprised at his poor coordination. He hadn't drunk a lot, surely? But his head pulsated as if he was going to die. Reaching the safety of the bathroom he leaned over the sink and let a stream of cool water run over his cheeks and into his eager dried-up mouth. The ancient lead pipes juddered making his headache worse. He rubbed his fingers through his mass of curly hair. What happened last night? Something, but what?' he said out loud, trying to recapture his thinking. But the more he tried to grasp it, the more it spiralled away.

After cleaning himself up, Ernesto emerged into the too-bright street. Paco hadn't called today, so he went to the bar and ordered a single coffee without the dreaded rum. The barman looked miserable.

'Seen Paco?' he asked,

'No. Have you?'

'No but...'

'But what?' Ernesto asked, remembering Paco's last farewell.

'Not sure. Maybe it's nothing.'

'Tell me.'

'Just that there was a bit of trouble on the Dominguez estate.'

'And you think Paco was involved.'

'Maybe,' the barman said then returned into the darkness of his bar, and Ernesto rested his damaged head in his hands wondering what Paco had been up to now.

The midday heat grew like fur, wrapping itself around the town, until even the lampposts seemed to sweat. Clouds grouped and swelled and turned a little darker and the air pressure hurt his ears. He had to lie down so he lumbered across to Juan's shop, grabbed *The Chronicle* and tramped up the stairs to the safety of his room. Spreading the paper onto the table he squinted at the headline.

ASSASSINATION THWARTED

Yesterday a band of youths attempted to assassinate our illustrious leader but only a single shot was fired before General Franco's bodyguards seized the perpetrators and marched them away. Later a spokesman for the General, reported that 'El Caudillo and his wife Dona Carmen were both well and enjoying a hearty meal at the Dominguez estate.' Ernesto read it twice. 'A single shot was fired.

'That's it,' he shouted to the room 'that's what I couldn't remember.' His conclusions from the night before rose up like an unsuppressed fever - the young man raising his pistol above his head – yes, above his head. Not at the General but above his head. Why would he do that? And the bodyguard who rushed over, had he been expecting it? Last night's drink had erased that uncomfortable truth. Now though, in the savage heat of a sober

50

day, he understood that the whole thing had been a deliberate act of illusion.

Through the window the dark clouds continued to accumulate, rendering him unable to think. He sat on the edge of the bed and the edge of his nerves, hoping the clouds would burst and that a storm would finally clear the air. But they didn't. Instead, a firm breeze came up from Africa and pushed the clouds away revealing the ever-present startling sun. 'I must find Paco,' he announced to the room. He was talking to his room a lot recently. Did this mean he was going insane, talking to the space as if it would provide him with answers? Yet going mad was better than going nowhere. 'I must find Paco and discover what happened at the Dominguez estate.' But his friend didn't call that day or the next. In fact like the impending storm that didn't arrive, all week he waited in vain for Paco to bang impatiently on his door.

Ernesto got worried. He went to the same spot in the square where Paco had hugged him. He remembered the flags, the handkerchiefs, the motion of the crowd and his feeling sick. Then he stared into the darkened side street where he'd seen him last and realised that Paco hadn't just departed. He'd completely disappeared. He went to the bar.

'Where is Paco? What's happened?' The barman shook his head. Ernesto ordered double rum - to hell with another hangover, and leaned into the barman's face. 'You said there was trouble at the Dominguez estate.'

'It was nothing.'

'What do you mean it was nothing? You said there was trouble.'

'Well I was wrong. Alright?'

Ernesto knew better than to insist. The man seemed scared to speak. Instead he drank his rum, collected his paper and went back upstairs, plonked himself under the window and started to read. He scanned the headlines, studied the articles, searched the missing persons section but there was nothing. He stared at the photographs of others who'd gone missing too, images he'd not taken seriously before, but he saw them clearly now, men with haunted looks and women with defiance in their eyes, and read one of the captions. *'Eduardo Gomez, 49 years, distillery worker, went missing May 1955. Modest reward offered by his wife and daughters.'* Ernesto frowned. Did Paco have family? Would they be searching for him too? And then, to his shame, he realised he knew nothing about Paco's personal situation. Did he have brothers or sisters or parents? And were they searching for Paco? He shook his head as if to release his guilt. He didn't know the answers to his questions because he'd never bothered to ask. How could he have been so incurious? How could he have been so unkind? He tried a different approach. There was a pile of old newspapers in the grate, stacked ready to fuel a winter fire. He searched through them now in case he'd missed something about the Dominguez place but there was nothing there either.

Another week passed, then another. How could someone disappear so completely? He waited, hoping for that knock on the door, and for his short, stout friend to appear from nowhere and drag him to the bar for a drink. He remembered, almost with affection, the way Paco's black tobacco wafted across the table and got caught in the back of his throat, and even forgave him the way he squandered his talents to impress the ladies. Then he remembered that night at the meeting room when another Paco had emerged, the one who had sung of his beloved Andalusian flag, the one who sang from his heart. That's where I'll find the answer, he told himself. I'll go to the meeting hall and ask there.

Ernesto took a seat at the same table he'd shared with Paco, raising his hand to greet everyone as he had before. But they blanked him again as if he was still that stranger and it felt like a knife stabbed through his heart. Sweat dribbled down his back. Why were people so hostile? A man and woman jumped up on stage and stood at the microphone. They sang together, two youthful voices, plaintive and spare with a melancholy so gentle that Ernesto surrendered to the feeling and thought of Belle and her exquisite voice and how everyone in the nightclub sat up and listened. But then he remembered how angry she'd been. How she'd screamed at him 'Go away, leave!' He'd walked all the way down the Malecón, cars full of revellers passing him by. He'd walked until dawn lit up the ocean, trying to decipher her grief. Why was she so infuriated? Why was she so tense? He knew he'd let her down, that he should have testified, that he should have been braver. But it was more than that. Poor Belle, always trying to be more than life allowed, but it hadn't worked; it could never have worked. Oh Belle, you should have come with me or I should have stayed with you.

A voice broke through his daydream. He looked up. The weightlifter was standing over him.

'Why you here, Cubano?'

'I'm looking for Paco.'

The man pulled up a stool. His thick neck glistened with sweat.

'Well you're in the wrong place for that.'

'Why? You all love Paco. Surely you'd know, more than anyone, where he is?'

'But would we tell *you*? The man looked scornful.

'Why not? I'd do him no harm.'

'Well we don't know that, do we? You came in here with him one day, and then he disappears.'

Ernesto began to tremble. This man looked as if he could lift him up with one hand and plunge him to the floor with the other. 'It's nothing to do with me,' he said twisting his bony fingers into his palms.

'Well like I said, we don't know that. You could be a spy, or a watcher. You know what I'm talking about don't you? Them that watches and listens and goes behind people's backs and denounces them.' He studied Ernesto's face. 'You look surprised, Cubano, but you've heard of denouncements haven't you? It doesn't take much. Criticise the church or the state, or have a spat with a neighbour and someone'll tell on you. There's plenty of people with an axe to grind and plenty of bastards willing to put you in a cell.' Ernesto frowned and shook his head but the man was determined to make his point. 'You think the world is simple and nice, but it ain't, Cubano. I'm tellin you it ain't.' Ernesto felt a flush of annoyance. He looked around at the drinkers pretending not to listen and tried to sound firm.

'Two years I've been here trying my best to fit in and after all this time you still don't trust me?'

'As I said, first, you ain't from here so we don't know you, and second because you keep going on about how great our leader is and I'll tell you…' he paused as if checking the words he was about to say, 'there are those what might agree with you but there's plenty here that don't.'

'How do you know what I think?

'Cos I'm one of them watchers. See you in our neighbourhood, carrying that fascist paper you read. Hears you in the square too, going on about our "dear" leader Franco and everything he's done for us. So I *do* know what you think.'

'Well what do you expect me to say? El Caudillo seems popular here. What about all those handkerchiefs waving in the square?'

The man scoffed. 'Looks is deceiving, Cubano, you'd be surprised.'

'You mean that big welcome wasn't authentic? The man ignored the question.

'If you're looking for Paco you won't find him here,' he said frowning so fiercely that deep grooves appeared across his forehead. Then he pressed his empty brandy glass to his cheek and waved across to the waiter for another drink. Ernesto stiffened. He didn't like this man's manner. He was either mad or drunk.

'Well if you won't tell me where he is, I'll look for him myself.' Ernesto was surprised at his own ferocity and the man was too. His forehead softened.

'Look, something happened over on the Dominguez but we don't know what. Maybe they took him, maybe they didn't. But if he's escaped, he'll be in the mountains, not here, not in this city.'

'Took who? You mean Paco? Why would they do that? And who's they? And what mountains are you talking about?

'Look, Cubano, give it a rest. Besides you need to look at your own country instead of here. Not going well for your Batista is it?'

'How would you know?' Ernesto snapped back. The waiter had placed a double brandy on the table.

'Told you. I listens. Hears it off them sailors in Cadiz, the ones sailing in from Havana. They say your Batista's finished, that the Mafia are leaving and a mighty revolution's comin over there, as well as....' His words tailed off.

'As well as what?' Ernesto asked, but the man had stopped talking and was tipping back his glass. Then he slammed it down between them as if to conclude their conversation   and wandered back to the bar. Ernesto got up to leave as two sweet voices came drifting through the room. *A green flag unfurls, like a wing of delight, Emblazoned with a sash, Of winter dawn white.*

That night Ernesto dreamed of Paco wandering aimlessly in some deserted landscape, separated from everything he loved. Then the dream switched to Belle. She was on stage and he was on the lighting tower looking down at the double mound of her charcoal coloured breasts. He saw men seated below her and each held a brandy glass close to his cheek. Belle was singing half-heartedly but it wasn't her voice the men were listening to and it wasn't her dancing they were applauding. This time she was sliding her clothes to the floor, moving to the insistent slow hand-clap of excited, yearning men. Ernesto watched her hips sway to the music. *No Belle, no!* The pain was ferocious. He woke up and leapt from his bed, opened the window, and rubbed his eyes to drive the image from his head. But the moon was shining in, too dazzling, too bright. He started to cry. 'Oh Belle, my love I should have stayed.' Then he rolled back into bed and curled up tight, telling himself it was nothing but one of his ridiculous dreams.

6. Urania

There'd been a shift in the night, as if his thoughts had moved around and come to rest in a different order. I've been drifting, he told himself, enjoying a simple life in a land I thought I knew. But with brutal honesty, the man in that dark meeting room had reminded him he was a stranger, not to be trusted with a nation's intimate fears. And those newspaper captions too, full of mourning for the missing-assumed-dead. All this time he had been too blind to see their pain, too deaf to hear their cries. He'd thought life was easy in Spain but it wasn't.

And these weren't the only things troubling him. His own country was on the point of war. '*A mighty revolution*' the weightlifter had said. If so, then Belle was in trouble too. '*Collaborator! Traitor!* That's what they would call the woman forced to dance and sing and god knows what for the Americans. But were they really leaving? How could he know if this was true? Then he remembered what the man in the meeting room had said. *Off them sailors in Cadiz, the ones sailing in from Havana,* and Ernesto knew what he had to do.

The ship was due on Thursday and he needed money to travel to the coast. So he pulled his trombone case off the shelf. Alongside his instrument concealed within the green velvet interior, was the compartment containing those letters he'd been so determined to ignore. He ignored them again now, lifting his instrument and pulling out a purse containing the fruits of his busking. It wasn't much. Who wants a trombonist in the land of Flamenco? He sighed. These savings were supposed to be for his return trip home and in a couple of years he would have enough. Oh well, he thought, taking some for today's trip. What's another year of waiting?

Thursday came. 'I'm off to the harbour,' he declared to the room as if he'd just made a binding contract from which he must not falter. Then he packed his trombone into its case - perhaps the city of Cádiz would be more sympathetic to his musical skills, and took the next bus out of town. By midday he'd reached the port of Santa Maria and bought a ticket for the Vaporcito, the little steam ferry that would take him across the bay to Cádiz. He settled below deck where the sea spray wouldn't affect his instrument case and the cross winds that bothered the bay wouldn't dislodge his resolve. A couple sat opposite, the wife looking down, knees pressed together under her skirt, her husband staring directly at Ernesto as if he'd never seen anyone his colour before. They ate their sandwiches and whispered about him as if he wasn't there but he didn't give in to their prejudice, it wasn't worth it. Instead he ran his slim fingers across the bench and felt the multiple layers of marine paint applied over decades, giving the woodwork an unintended roundness that calmed his mood. The ferry trundled along the river mouth on its way out to sea, the engine whining and grumbling beneath his feet. He peered through the grubby window. All along the bank were jetties leading to fishermen's warehouses and on the water, small fishing craft tied around capstans on the harbour wall, bobbed up and down in the ferry's wake. Ernesto felt the boat rock a little and heard the engine whir like a flautist warming up, as it pushed out into the cross currents of the bay. Then he felt the change in frequency - more like an oboe, deep and resonant, as it set its course across the sea. Soon they were out into the open expanse where winds were wilder and the spray hit the windows with surprising force. Thank goodness he had chosen to sit inside.

It wasn't long before they were approaching the harbour and beyond that, the city itself with its erratic jumble of rooftops and multitude of turrets reflecting the sunlight. How he loved Cádiz, a city unrepressed, a city of rebellion, a city of dreams. It was also the birthplace of his favourite Spanish composer Manuel de Falla and thinking about that made him happy too. Then on the horizon he saw the Urania coming in, the same ship he'd arrived on two years earlier. He remembered how he'd encountered people laden with suitcases asking what in the name of god he was doing entering Franco's Spain when, to escape his tyranny, they were going in the opposite direction. But he'd dismissed their comments as hysteria. Besides, they didn't know that Ernesto was escaping too. The Vaporcito started to make its turn, coming in sideways and disturbing the harbour water then banging against the wall and rebounding slightly before stabilising into its docking position. Further out he saw the Urania dock too. How small the steamer seemed against this vast transatlantic ship, and how small Ernesto felt against the task he was about to undertake.

He waited by the ship and watched as thick ropes were thrown down and tied around capstans. Passengers disembarked, business men first, probably there to sell tobacco and rum then a few tourists, followed by nets of cargo hauled out of the hold and dropped onto the harbour floor awaiting customs. An hour passed until the engines made their final revolutions and funnels exhaled their last plumes of steam, leaving an insubstantial trace in the afternoon sky. A few deckhands emerged - Dutch, Italian - no use to him, then more sailors, more languages, and finally the sound of his beloved Cubano issuing from someone's lips. It was soft and inviting and a wave of nostalgia rolled over him. Two years spent listening to the harshness of Andalusian Spanish, enunciated in short, sharp, aggressive breaths and now this Caribbean lilt, the arch of the voice, the anticipatory lift like a soft ocean wave as if something good was about to happen. He'd forgotten how wonderful it sounded, reflecting the positive way his people loved to live. Two boys and an older man had come down the gangway. The boys strolled off but the older man approached with an outstretched hand.

Ernesto spoke first. 'Hello my friend, buy you a drink?'

'Sure. I suppose you want to know about your homeland?' Perhaps he'd noticed Ernesto's closely curled hair and mulatto skin. Ernesto nodded and took the man to the harbour café where he ordered two rums. The man wasted no time. Revolution was apparently on everyone's lips.

'People think we're a bunch of amateurs but we're not, not now we've got that Argentinian with us.'

'Who?'

'Che Guevara, that's who. Him and the Castro brothers training us up in the hills.'

'I've read something about that here,' Ernesto said remembering those old *Chronicles* stacked in his grate. 'But they write about revolution as if it's a disease.'

'Scared it'll happen in Spain too,' the man said clutching his rum. Ernesto noticed how his fingers were like sticks, and his knuckles stood out like burrs. This man had hunger in his belly and sadness in his soul, so he ordered a sandwich and when it arrived he pushed it across the table.

'So what about the ordinary people? What's happening to them? The papers don't tell us.' The old man swallowed and pushed his empty glass across the table. Three rums later he couldn't stop.

'Things are looking grim. Those Americans pay good money for a youngster. Got two daughters misself, twins coming up thirteen; breasts like mangoes. My woman tries to keep 'em pure but there's no income. Why d'you think I work the ships? Got to, haven't I? Else they'd be forced to do sex shows like them poor buggers from the countryside, so hungry they'll do anything. And I means anything.' Ernesto frowned as the man leaned forward. 'Boy on girl, boy on boy, girl on girl, all in the back rooms of them casinos, Americans looking on, stuffed up with cocaine. I fears for my two daughters but what can I do?'

Two hours later the Urania had shut down completely, lights out, momentum gone, conversation spent. Ernesto walked away from the harbour leaving the old sailor crying into his rum, no doubt lamenting his twins, but also his Cuba, and what it had become. The journey back was much slower. A wild wind had entered the bay, whipping the sea into an angry froth and delaying the return crossing until late in the night. Finally he sat in the last bus home, clutching his unopened trombone case against his chest. How could he have busked after meeting that man? How could he have brought the instrument to his lips after what he had learned? As the bus juddered along the highway, he closed his eyes, contemplating the moral collapse of his old country, that poor man's twins and his people so desperate they would do anything for money. No wonder a revolution was being prepared in the hills. He thought of Belle and wondered if, like in his dreams, she'd been caught up in the lasciviousness of it all, or would she have resisted? It was hard to tell with Belle. She had a stubborn streak, he knew that, but at the same time she was eager to please. Belle had been an enigma then, and even now he still didn't know what to think now.

The evening was closing in. Pale ineffectual lights came on inside the bus, casting a liverish glow over the brown plastic seats, making him feel sick. He closed his eyes and drifted off until the bus stopped somewhere in the countryside to pick up four agricultural

61

workers, their clothes covered in dried earth, their bodies stooped from toil. They fumbled for coins and as the engine idled Ernesto saw that one was shorter than the others, with hair that flopped over one eye just like Paco's. Oh my friend I'd almost forgotten about you, Ernesto thought and immediately felt shame. How could he be thinking of Cuba a thousands of miles away, when his Paco had gone missing right under his nose? He shook his head, disgusted with himself for such insensitivity and yawned with the pressures of the day. Then he turned his head towards the window of the stationary bus. Outside, the lights from the windows were casting chequered patterns across the grass verge and beyond that he saw an arch made of iron with ornate letters above that spelled out DOMINGUEZ.

Now Ernesto was wide awake. Wasn't that where Franco had gone for his lunch? And didn't the barman say there'd been trouble there? Something to do with Paco? The engine revved. The bus jerked forward. It moved away. He rushed to the back window trying to keep the gateway in view. There was a long drive stretching up into the darkness and at the end of it a single light coming from a house on a hill. Was Paco in there? They were speeding away now. The light was receding, removing, retracting. What could he do? He had to know. Up front, the workers laughed off their day with a joke and a song. He moved towards them. Perhaps they would know if Paco was there. But then he remembered he was a foreigner. What if they didn't like strangers asking questions? They were young and strong and he was middle aged and weak. Perhaps they would attack him just for a laugh. Or what if they knew where Paco was and would tell the authorities that a stranger was asking? Reluctantly, he returned to his seat. All day he'd been determined and strong, but tonight in this weak, insubstantial light, cowardice triumphed once again. Besides, what *could* he do? Paco was gone and that was the end of it. Outside, the blackness returned. Ernesto slumped in his seat. He was fragile, he was spineless and he hated himself for it. He wrapped his arms around his body and curled up tight listening to the men's confident singing, as the bus entered the city, arriving at its terminus in a darkened square.

Walking slowly back along his street, two neighbours rushed past without greeting him. The gentlemen's outfitters was shuttered and bleak. Across at the bar, tables had been stacked and pushed into the shadows and any sign of humanity cancelled by the night. He sighed, wanting someone to say good evening or wave at him from across the street. Then he noticed a light in Juan's shop and remembered he'd missed his *Chronicle*.

'You sold out?'

'No, here, I saved it for you.'

'Why are you still here?'

'Oh you know, this and that,' Juan said without explanation. Ernesto wasn't in the mood for mysteries. He was disappointed with his day and turned to leave. But then he noticed under the counter, a copy of *The Monkey,* the same paper Franco's men had slung into the gutter. He pulled one out.

'Thought these had been banned ages ago,' he said looking at today's date.

'Well there is still people what likes it,' Juan retorted, perhaps defensively. But then his tone changed. 'You want one? Might do you good reading some'at decent instead of that propaganda you got tucked under your arm.' Ernesto hesitated. He hated the look of the thing. 'Go on, take it. No charge.'

'Ok thanks,' Ernesto said despite himself. The last thing he wanted was a confrontation. Besides, the unusual warmth in Juan's voice was the first kindness he'd received all day. How could he refuse?

Upstairs, Ernesto moved the table under the central light and spread out both papers, overlapping them to make them fit the surface. What a difference in their appearance. *The Chronicle* crisply printed with sharp black outlines and a magnificent crested banner spread along the top. The other so absorbent that much of the print had blurred onto an illegible smudge and a headline incorrectly spelt *LOCAL HERO DISSAPEARS*. Ernesto snorted his disapproval. What amateurs! He threw it in the bin and turned to the Chronicle. It spoke of food shortages and a reminder for all foreigners to renew their registrations with the local police. Ernesto made a note to do so and turned the page in search of anything more interesting. Finally in a section below communions and baptisms, he read,

TERRORIST DETAINED AT DOMINGUEZ ESTATE.

After weeks of speculation we can finally reveal that on July 18th an enemy of the people was arrested whilst attempting to assassinate our great and illustrious El Caudillo. The terrorist was apprehended in possession of a 1916 Mauser rifle similar to those issued by the defeated Republicans but totally ineffective in these modern times. A spokesman for the General dismissed the attempt as the half-cock delusions of a failed agitator and mediocre marksman trying to overturn the most successful and peaceful period in the history of our great nation.

He read it again recognising the Dominguez estate that he'd passed today and that the barman had mentioned in relation to Paco. But this couldn't be about him, surely? Paco was no sniper. What did he know about guns? Nevertheless he pulled *The Monkey* out of the bin and took his time reading the misspelt text below their inaccurate headline.

LOCAL HERO DISSAPEARS (Report by The Monkey's Mouth)

They got our Paco. Someone ratted on him that's for shor. Some conniving bastard's informed the orthorities. Skilled marksman, they rekon he could take a man at 500 meetres. His wife Dolores Torres cried all night sayin' she mite never see her hubby agen.

Ernesto's thoughts were racing. Our Paco? Do they mean *My* Paco? Skilled marksman? He's a guitarist not a shooter. And a wife? He has a *wife*? What about all those women Paco boasted about? If he's married he must be a serial adulterer! He shook his head incredulous at what he was reading then spoke to the room as if Paco was standing right there beside him. Who are you my friend? Just like Belle, you are a mystery. I didn't know what to make of *her* then and I don't know what to make of *you* now.

7. *Dolores*

Ernesto was neither in nor out of sleep as the shutters from Juan's shop rolled up and a bicycle juddered across the cobbled street, each sound reaching into his unconscious and pulling him into the day. He rolled over and yawned, enjoying this morning routine until the sudden uncomfortable facts from yesterday ruptured his ease. The plastic seats, the liverish light, those dusty workers, and finally the two newspapers telling him a truth he was reluctant to accept. He got up and went to the window, remembering the revelations he had read the night before. Could any of them be true? He had to know. Dressing quickly, he glanced at his trombone lying fully assembled on its shelf in the corner. The case was still open from the night before when he'd replaced the remains of his money into it, ignoring those damn letters. With so many mysteries piling up he couldn't even bear to look at it. The trombone glistened in the morning sun. Why aren't you going to play me? it seemed to ask. But how could he indulge his pleasures at such a moment? So, for the first time in his professional life, he abandoned his morning practice, grabbed *The Monkey* and ran downstairs to the bar.

'Open up,' he shouted, banging sharply on the narrow door.

'Steady, amigo, what's the problem?'

'Paco's the problem. Did you read it?' he asked, waving *The Monkey* in his face.

'Of course I did. Everyone round here reads it.'

'Well is it true? Is Paco really a sniper? Has he been arrested? And do you know where they've taken him?' Ernesto could hardly believe his torrent of questions, nor the force with which he expressed them. He sounded like a confident man.

'Well you seem in a hurry.'

'Just tell me please.'

'They found him alright, setting up his rifle behind the chapel. Police turned up and arrested him. Someone must have told 'cos they knew exactly where to find him. Good thing his nephew escaped though.'

'Nephew?'

'The two of them planned it together, made a pact.'

'What pact?'

'You'll have to ask Jorge about that.'

'Jorge? Who's Jorge?' This was too much to take in. Ernesto slumped down at a table and took a deep breath. He thought about the young man he'd seen in the square, the one with the same stature as Paco, the one who had disappeared with him down a darkened street. Ernesto's head was reeling. The barman was talking.

'Don't reckon you'll find Jorge anytime soon. He's gone underground that's for sure, especially now they got Paco. Chances are he'll talk.'

'You mean torture? Is that what you mean?' Ernesto was desperate. 'Well what about his wife? He *has* got a wife hasn't he? Does she know something?'

'Maybe. Hard to tell with them two.' Then he started writing on an old receipt. 'Here Cubano, if you really want to know, go and ask her yourself,' he said handing Ernesto the address.

Dolores Torres lived across town in a new apartment block close to the main road. It was a dismal building with narrow concrete walkways and anxious-looking people watching from balconies. Her flat was on the fourth floor and despite the newness of the lift, he thought he could smell urine.

'Who are you?' Dolores snapped as she peered around her front door. 'And what d'you want?'

'To know about Paco,' he replied softly, trying not to cause offence. But she had already looked him up and down and caught his accent.

'Not from round here are you?'

Ernesto ignored the question. 'I'm trying to find out where they've taken Paco. I assume you know.' She shook her head then pressed her hands on her broad hips in defiance, and he saw how her fingers were red and her knuckles were calloused from too much domestic work. Ernesto was beginning to feel sorry for her. 'I only want to help,' he said smiling to sweeten the air between them. To his surprise; she stood aside and let him in.

'Well for a start I don't know where he is. You need to talk to that Jorge boy and don't ask me where he is neither 'cos I haven't a clue.' She folded her arms across her vast chest as if that was the end of it. But Ernesto insisted.

'Well at least tell me what made him do a thing like that, trying to kill the General?'

'The old fool! Fifty-two years old and still banging on about the war. As soon as he heard the General was coming he started bringing strangers into the flat and talking politics again. Told him to stop 'cos you never knows whose listening.' She pointed over to a table covered in a patterned oilskin. 'Then he starts polishing his old rifle right here in our kitchen.'

'But why does Paco hate the General so?'

'Don't we all,' she scoffed

But its more than that, I'm sure.

'Well, something happened way back. That's all I know,' she said wiping the sweat that had collected on her forehead.

'Surely you must know more. He was your husband.' Ernesto was still finding all this hard to believe.

'Look I'm not getting involved but you heard of Sauce del Valle?'

'No. What is it?'

'It's a village in the mountains. Well it was.'

'And?'

'Well him and this Jorge decided to get their own back, but it didn't go right did it!'

'What didn't? Please, you have to tell me.'

'Well someone snitched on them.' She folded her arms again. 'Could've been Jorge himself.'

'Why would he do that?'

'I don't know, but he didn't get arrested did he?' She seemed agitated now and would no longer look him in the eye. 'Look, you'll get your answers up there in Sauce del Valle, not down here where we're all too scared to speak.' Then she pushed him out, slamming the door behind him.

Back in his room Ernesto placed himself carefully across the surface of his neatly made bed, its counterpane unruffled by sleep, and extended his legs, feet wide apart and arms outstretched until he filled the rectangle with his extremities. He looked up at the ceiling, then down at the floor. Nothing moved. All was still. He let his eyes meander across the middle space, observing mildly, the tired armchair, a wardrobe full of old clothes, the hinge still broken because he hadn't fixed it. He looked across to his trombone unemployed in the corner, imagining the buzzing vibrations on his lips and the phrases he might play. But he didn't have the appetite to make beautiful sounds. *The Chronicle* was on the table under the window next to today's copy of *The Monkey*. This time he'd paid for it himself, handing over the money sheepishly at having purchased such a thing, and he couldn't be sure but did Juan smile at his little victory? Neither paper had been touched. Instead they both lay in the soft unobtrusive sun, their texts unread, their contents undigested. Ernesto lay unmoving. His whole being had closed down, unable to take in the enormity of what was happening. Instead he gazed at the cobwebs in the corner and tried to clear his mind. But every twist and turn ended with the same conclusion; Paco deserved to be in prison. There was no way around it. People called him a hero but he'd done a terrible thing, planning to kill. 'Why do that?' he asked the room, 'why assassinate someone who was building reservoirs and installing factories? There was even talk of an oil refinery near the coast that would bring jobs to the area. Unlike the playboy Batista, these people should be grateful for a strong leader like Franco on their side. Maybe they were disappointed that they'd lost the civil war all those years ago but why be obsessed with old disputes? Oh Paco what have you done?

He recalled the day of the General's visit, crowd waving, handkerchiefs fluttering above their heads, and the wonderful J12 arriving. He tried to focus on the nephew. The barman said they had a pact, and Dolores hinted at revenge. What did all that mean? He saw again the moment when the weightlifter, Paco and his nephew had met under the clock and checked their watches. Did they have a plan? Then there was that shot he knew to be fake and the General being whisked away. Did they already know the General and his entourage were not going to stay in town as originally planned? Yes that's it, he declared to the room. They must have known Franco was going to the Dominguez estate instead. But how? And then it all went wrong. Why?

He gave up. There were no answers to his questions. So he looked over at his trombone case, and in his head he imagined the bundle of letters, sitting there inside the green velvet compartment waiting to be opened. His fingers began to twitch as if anticipating the day when he might just do that. But no, that would be wrong he thought and diverted his eyes to his trombone glinting in the leftover rays of the sun. He tried to distract himself by closing his eyes and remembering how he'd been summoned to the Cuckoo Club at short notice. It was gone midnight but they were expecting a special guest and would Ernesto come over and play? He'd arrived breathless, wondering who the guest could be, and found Frank Sinatra leaning against the piano. They exchanged nods and Ernesto received the sheet music for *I'm Getting Sentimental over You*. Sinatra's voice was like liquorice and Ernesto played his heart out that night and now he lay there on his bed, going over the lyrics of that song and letting his mind drift from the mysteries he was encountering in Spain to the mysterious Belle thousands of miles away in the Caribbean seas. He sat up and with the song rolling around in his head, looked again at his trombone. Should he play? But the melody was as smooth as honey, not bitter and disjointed like his thinking. How could he play something so rounded and complete at this moment of fragmentation?

8. Jorge

Next morning two newspapers lay unopened on his table and the trombone remained un-played, on the shelf. An unusually cold September air was beginning to bite so Ernesto grabbed his overcoat and closed the door on his dormant room. What else could he do? It was as if he'd put all his questions into a box, labelled it 'unanswered' then pushed it aside because none of it made sense. He crossed the street searching his wallet for enough money to pay for a single coffee and rum then settled at the table he used to share with Paco. After a few minutes a young man approached. His chest was broad and his face round, framed by that familiar straight hair flopped over one eye. He was short too and even before he sat down, Ernesto knew who he was. The man put out his hand.

'I'm Jorge. Good morning.'

'Isn't it dangerous, you being out in the city?'

'In this neighbourhood I am safe. The barman keeps his eyes open. Besides unless Paco has talked, only a few people know of my allegiance with my uncle; you and the barman and perhaps my aunt. I observed you at her flat and I have come here to enquire what it was that she said, and also because I have a message for you from my uncle.'

A message from Paco?'

'Yes but first report to me what my aunt said.' Ernesto smiled. This young man had an air of confidence and a formal manner of speaking that didn't fit in around here, where men grunted into their drinks, or said nothing at all. There were other contrasts too. His eyes looked friendly but his thick eyebrows formed a heavy ridge across his forehead making him scowl. Was this the face of an assassin? He took a different approach.

'The barman said there was a pact between you two.'

'Yes, we had a pact, but I don't want to talk about that. Did Dolores tell you where the police have taken him?' Ernesto shook his head and immediately Jorge's shoulders dropped, his inner control apparently gone. Ernesto warmed to him. He could only be in his thirties at the most. So young, so worried.

'I think we both need a drink,' Ernesto said calling over the barman. 'On the slate,' he added remembering the few coins he had left in his pocket. Jorge grasped the glass and threw back the rum.

'God in heaven what's this?' he wailed and Ernesto laughed.

'You'll get used to it' he said ordering another. Ernesto tried to be kind. 'Look, don't worry about Paco. The worst they can do is charge him for poaching or trespass. And from what I see, anyone can enter the Dominguez estate. There's no fencing along the road so you could wander onto their premises without even knowing it.' This wasn't quite true, he thought, remembering the sign on the metal arch he'd seen from the bus, but instinct told him that this youth needed reassurance.

'Yes I suppose so.'

They sat for a while contemplating Paco's situation until, after their third rum, Ernesto broke the silence and asked his question.

'I've been thinking. Those boys in the square with the pistol?

Was that something to do with you?' Jorge looked surprised.

'Yes, sort of. But how did you know?

'Never mind. Why did they do it?'

'I was in the locker room at college and overheard a man promising them money to cause trouble. Said it was just a prank, something El Caudillo would enjoy. The man said they could collect their payment from the General himself at the Dominguez estate that afternoon. When I told Paco, he realised that the General would be off his guard, not expecting trouble out there in the countryside because no one knew he would be there. Except *we* did so we devised our plan.'

'You mean you planned an assassination,' Ernesto corrected him.

'Well yes, but you don't know...'

'Don't know what?'

'Oh nothing. You wouldn't understand.' Ernesto didn't press the point. It was enough that Jorge had seen his disapproval and blushed.

'So what *was* your plan?' he asked.

'We left the square as soon as that shot was fired. I had an old Seat ready and we made it to the estate before the General arrived.'

'Really? Before the J12?'

'We calculated Franco would take his time waving to the crowds. The man can't resist his moment of adoration, so we were already setting up the rifle when he arrived.'

'I see,' Ernesto said, struggling to imagine an alcoholic Paco holding a gun steady against his cheek. 'The paper said he was a sniper but surely he didn't know how to handle a gun?'

Jorge looked offended. 'My uncle is the best sniper in the world. Everyone knows that.'

'Who? Paco?'

'Yes,' he whispered. 'My uncle eliminated dozens of fascist in his time.' Ernesto shook his head. This couldn't be true. But even if by some strange chance it was, then why didn't he tell him? Why didn't Paco boast about that instead of his women? He felt his eyes sting as he held back the tears. Why hadn't Paco share his real life like Ernesto had shared his? He felt hurt but then he remembered that his friend was missing and probably in a police cell suffering unimaginable treatment. He shook his head again, angry at himself for thinking so selfishly and angry too, at Jorge sitting with him so apparently free. He became suspicious.

'And where were you when the police arrived?'

'Paco sent me to the car for more ammunition and when they grabbed my uncle, I bolted,' he said, more blood rising to his cheeks.

'And how were you both planning to escape once you'd shot the General? His sarcastic tone wasn't lost on Jorge.

'Look I realise it was foolish but...'

'It was more than foolish. It would have been treason and murder. What were you both thinking?'

'I know, I know.' Jorge put his head in his hands and Ernesto spoke more quietly now.

'So do you know where they've taken him?

'No idea. I daren't ask myself but have you enquired at the meeting room? Those men might know.'

'I tried,' Ernesto said, and then he remembered the bus. 'Look, I saw four men come off the Dominguez estate last week. Probably travel on the same bus every evening. Why don't you catch it yourself then you can ask them whatever you want?'

'That's it! Well done, Nesto. Can I call you that? Uncle always did.' The mood had changed. Jorge was fired up. His eyes twinkled with compassion. 'Come with me, Nesto. Keep a watch in case I'm in danger. Besides I could do with an ally and a friend' Ernesto squirmed in his seat.

'Me? No I don't think so.' Why should he get involved with those men? 'No,' he repeated 'not for me.'

'Never mind. I'll go on my own,' Jorge said without hesitation and started to leave.

'Wait!' Ernesto said pulling him back down. 'What about Paco's message?

'Not now, Nesto.'

'You promised to tell.'

Jorge sat and rearranged his expression.

'Well, he said you were his only true friend, that he's sorry he couldn't tell you stuff because you were innocent and to keep playing that 'bone.' There was a pause.

'Is that it?'

'Yes, that was all he said but I could tell he liked you – said you never think badly of anyone.' Ernesto was disappointed. He'd expected a proper message, not this. Jorge was still talking.

'I'll meet you here same time tomorrow and let you know how I fare.'

Ernesto nodded and watched Jorge walk away with a rum-induced stagger, keeping under the shadow of the balconies until he reached the fountain and disappeared out of sight.

Ernesto appeared in the old man's doorway.

'Thought you weren't coming,' Juan said gruffly, handing him *The Chronicle*. 'Was about to close.'

'Things on my mind,' Ernesto answered.

'What about *The Monkey*?' Juan said holding it up.

'Not tonight.' Ernesto wasn't in the mood for blurred text and propaganda.

'You should read it,' Juan said. Ernesto sighed. All he wanted was to lock himself in his room, and think about the message Jorge had just given him. He didn't want an argument on the merits, or not, of a political paper of such poor quality. Juan insisted, the back of his bony hand pressing against Ernesto's chest.

'Take it; on the house.'

'Go on then.'

Now four newspapers were spread on the table, each undisturbed, each unread. Ernesto bit into a piece of dry bread. He hadn't eaten properly for days but this would have to do. Crumbs fell onto his now untidy bed. He flicked them away onto the rag rug at his feet and they disappeared into its deep unshaken tufts. Ernesto didn't care if he made a mess. He was beginning to realise that the world was much more complicated than he had thought. Paco a potential assassin, Paco a communist, Paco married, maybe even dead? And what about Jorge? *Come with me* he'd said, asking for his support. But Ernesto had declined. He'd let him down just like he always let everyone down. 'Not for me,' he'd said. How weak and fearful was that? And how shameful now that Paco was in custody? Where was the bravado of yesterday when he'd set out for Cadiz? Where was the determination that had taken him all the way to the coast, across the bay and into the harbour? He took a deep breath to fill the vacuum he felt inside then let it out in a huge sigh. Those plastic seats had won. That sickly yellow light inside the bus was shining inside his head. Ernesto closed his eyes to block it all out and soon surrendered to a premature sleep. He was on that mast again. Ropes held him down, too weak to move, too feeble to make a difference. Paco was crouching in the distance with a rifle but then the world went black as if he'd just been shot.

It was already dark when he woke so he switched on the light above the table, too restless to resume his sleep. Which newspaper to read; yesterday's or today's? Finally he folded the older ones, put them neatly into the grate, and reached for today's *Chronicle*. There was a headline he had to read twice to take in.

MAN DIES IN POLICE CELL

Paco Garcia, a well-known agitator and failed assassin, suffered a heart attack whilst in police custody. A doctor confirmed the death as natural causes. His wife Dolores Torres has been informed.

Paco dead? He read it again. Paco dead? Yet somehow he already knew it. In his dream and in his heart he'd already acknowledged that horrible truth. He felt sick, he couldn't breathe. He ran out into the street and across to the bar.

'Is it true?

The barman nodded. 'Just seen it myself.'

'Are you sure?'

'Afraid so.' The barman was opening a fresh bottle of rum. 'Here Cubano, take it! You need it.'

'He grabbed the bottle and moved to his favourite table, where Paco had once sat chatting, smoking, smiling, boasting, and above all, alive. Ernesto dropped his chin to his chest. 'Paco dead,' he repeated and the barman nodded again. What else could either of them say? The evening moved relentlessly on. Every now and then Ernesto raised his head to bring the glass to his lips and by midnight the barman put a hand on his shoulder.

'Time for bed, Cubano.'

In his room Ernesto took today's copy of *The Monkey* and squinted at the headline. There it was, right across the top in blotchy capital letters. Why hadn't he seen this before?

PERISHD IN POLICE SELL

Comrayds, our Paco is dead. From natural causes? -my arse. He was shot - murderd - and now we've lost a marksman, husban and comrayd-in-arms who's perishd at the hands of this brutal govunment.

Ernesto's stomach churned and his head began to spin. He went to the window and leaned out for fresh air, but it was heavy with droplets of inevitable rain. He shouted into the night, 'Paco why didn't you tell me your plan? I could have stopped you, you foolish bastard.' The wind picked up. He tried to close the window but couldn't turn the latch. He peered at the stars almost hidden now by purple cloud. The atmosphere was thick and the pressure hurt his ears reminding him of Havana, where a sudden charge of lightning would flash across the sky and rain would plummet from the grey-lit heavens, turning the streets to mud. He didn't like what was happening, it had to stop. His friend was dead. Belle was across the ocean. He was alone. He shook his head and blinked his eyes. There'd be no more reality for him tonight. No more remembering. He threw all four newspapers into the bin and yanked at the window until it finally closed. For a moment a waft of air pressure blocked his ears and he shook his head. 'No more remembering,' he told the room. 'Not tonight.'

He went to the corner and picked up his trombone. With his sleeve, he wiped away three days of dust and neglect and put the instrument to his lips. Drunk as he was he knew exactly what to play, something from his student days at the conservatoire. Feet apart for balance, long arms stretching the tuning slide back and forth, he moved as if man and music were one, and the elongated notes of *Mozart's Requiem in D Minor* emerged into the heavy air. He had to imagine the trumpets and the bassoons talking above and below him, and the violins soothing his pain, each note undulating through his body, rising and falling, marking time, waiting for rain as he played a lament for his departed friend,

9. *Sauce del Valle*

The storm arrived at midnight, rumbling in from the south like an overloaded lorry. Minutes later clouds discharged their cargo across the city; a dense, impenetrable deluge, pounding the ground with unsparing force. For hours it pummelled the rooftops and scuttled down drainpipes in a cacophony of noise from which, at first, Ernesto did not wake. Rum had rendered him unconscious but the urge to visit the bathroom was too compelling. He staggered there and staggered back, to hear the wild discordant water lashing at his window, battering the glass like bullets. Then he remembered Paco; shot dead and undone. He started to cry, lightly at first because men don't cry. Besides it was only the residual alcohol stirring his emotions. But then he was a child again, letting out uncontrollable howls that shuddered through his body like a disquiet baby in its mother's arms. If only Belle were here now. She would know what to do; stroke his brow, whisper in his ear and ease his pain.

By morning the city was exhausted. Leaves, heavy with rain, released their burden, falling in syncopated rhythms on the pavement below. Gullies, filled with night-time water, now began to ebb, making the drains stink. Ernesto crossed the damp street to repay the barman for his borrowed rum and as he counted out the few coins, he realised that if something didn't turn up soon, he would have to raid those precious notes he'd accumulated for his trip back home.

They met as arranged. Ernesto wrapped in an overcoat to ease his hangover and Jorge still wearing the clothes he'd worn the day before. They asked for a jug of water. It seemed only right to keep things simple. Ernesto spoke first.

'You know then?'

'Yes,' he replied. And with the exchange over, they sat in silence for several minutes until Ernesto broke it.

'Look I need to understand. Why did you try to kill the General? What drove you both to do it?'

At last Jorge seemed willing to explain.

'It's a long story but if you're willing to listen, it needs to be told.'

Ernesto nodded. What else could they talk about now that his friend was dead?

'Have you heard of Sauce del Valle?'

'Dolores said something.'

'It was a village, high up in the cork forests.'

'Was?'

'Yes. A beautiful place with a bakery, a bar and a new church that the adults helped to build. They were so proud of that little church that they put a sign on the front, just underneath the bell tower "Constructed by the men of our village. 1923." Up on the hill was a windmill too, where farmers took their cereal crops to be milled into flour and down by the river were hundreds of willows. When I was a child I called them the crying trees because of the way their branches fell into the river like tears. The valley was huge and very fertile with houses dotted right across the land, each with smallholdings where villagers grew vegetables and tended their goats. They all had a donkey or a horse. Some even had cars.'

Jorge stopped talking while Ernesto removed his coat. It seemed his story required no distraction or interruption. But there was no chance of that. Alcohol still ran through Ernesto's veins, making him disinclined to speak. Instead he nodded to signal he was ready for Jorge to continue his story.

'My grandfather was a carbonero – selling charcoal to the villagers. My grandmother was a seamstress and my mother made baskets. We lived together in the family house although my father was often away. He worked for the new socialist government, liaising with the unions and advising ministers. They said my father was clever and that he would go far. His brother Paco, my uncle, wasn't interested in politics. He'd studied classical guitar in Granada.'

Ernesto interrupted. 'Classical. Not flamenco?'

'Yes that's right and he *made* guitars too. Set up a workshop in the house adjacent to ours.'

Ernesto raised an eyebrow. 'Paco made guitars? Surely he didn't have the patience?'

'My uncle was different then, quieter, gentler, more willing to show his feelings, said he wanted to feel the music as soon as he started to carve the wood.'

'I understand,' Ernesto said, unconvinced.

'I used to love the smell of cedar wood curling away from the plane as he carved out the sound boards.'

'So what changed? What turned him from a man of music into a revolutionary?'

'It was my father who persuaded Paco to join the resistance. Working for the government, he knew what was going to happen, that Franco would step in as soon as he got the chance. When the unions started arguing and government factions split the party, of course Franco seized it, taking over huge swathes of the country by force. Papa gave my uncle a rifle and told him he had to defend the Republic against Franco and his fascist ideals and as soon as Paco picked it up he understood. To him it was just another instrument; something made from wood and metal that you held to your body to make it speak. Within weeks of intense practice he was an expert marksman.'

'But Jorge that was twenty years ago.' Ernesto took his glass and gulped down the water gratefully. 'Why should that matter now?'

'Let me finish, Ernesto. I told you my story was long.' He took a drink too and then began again.

'It was a while later, on the 31st of October 1936. My mother and I were half way up the hill, going to collect flour from the mill. First it was only one plane circling, and then others came behind it. When my mother saw them she grabbed my hand and dragged me to the top of the ridge. We could see the village down below and all of a sudden a neighbour's house exploded and stones flew into the air like fireworks. The boom came seconds after, echoing around the valley. Then more bombs came, pounding the earth one after the other, on and on, exploding with a terrible sound that made the willows shudder below. For a moment the bombs stopped and in that awful silence the screaming came, echoing up that hill with eerie magnification. Villagers were running towards the church trying to take cover. But the bombing started again and they blasted that too. Now the whole village was ablaze and black smoke filled the sky so we couldn't see. Eventually the planes left and my mother and I crouched on that hill waiting for the smoke to clear. She led me trembling towards the village and told me not to look. But of course I *did* look, and it was terrible. I remember the people as colours, soot-black clothes ragged and torn, faces covered in grey dust, white legs and arms exposed, with gashes of bright-red blood showing through, some bodies torn apart, unrecognisable. And I remember the silence; a horrible silence that seemed to fill the void like a scream. Then I heard the whimpers of the injured cutting through and we went from house to house searching for survivors. We went to our house but it wasn't there anymore. The walls were demolished, its stones scattered about in the orchard, blown there like bubbles. My parents' bed lay mangled in a corner and the door to the kitchen stove was hanging off its hinges. My mother went into the salon and I heard her gasp. When I followed she did nothing to shield my six-year-old eyes. In the corner my grandmother was still sitting in her rocking chair, her eyes, her hands, her body stone dead staring through a veil of white dust and in the centre stood her sewing machine still intact with a charred bobbin on top. Then under some rocks I saw my grandfather sleeping. He was dead of course and even though I knew it, I felt nothing, as if a switch in my head had extinguished the light of my life as well as his. There used to be eight hundred of us in that village, Nesto, and now…'

He tailed off and took another gulp of water. The glass trembled in his hand.

'But that's not all,' he continued. 'A few hours later soldiers came; about twenty of them led by a Lieutenant who ordered us out of hiding. We were herded into a refuge at the back of the church and left there all night without food or water. In the morning they came again and this time they took the women. My mother resisted but they took her anyway, to a barn where the soldiers raped her along with the others. They took her every night, and every morning she was thrust back into the refuge where she sat in a corner just staring into space. I tried to reach out to her, to comfort her, but I'd lost my mother even as she still lived. On the last day of that terrible week she was dragged away again but this time she did not return and now it was me who sat in the corner with my head between my knees. I didn't want to live either.

That afternoon a soldier drove a lorry into the yard, and in it were bodies piled one on top of the other with their arms and legs hanging over the side. I recognised some of them as our neighbours who'd been trying to get to our neighbouring village. The soldiers drove the lorry down to the willows next to a big house and ordered us to start digging. We made a deep ditch, even us children, and they tipped the bodies into it and we threw earth and rocks on top. I didn't cry even when I saw my mother's body added to the grave. I was right about those willows, Nesto. They *were* crying trees and they did the crying for me that day because I could not.'

Ernesto leaned forward and placed his hand on Jorge's arm. 'But why, Jorge? Why was your village such a target?'

'It was full of Republicans who'd fled from the city when Franco took over. I think my father must have sent them there. We'd taken them in and fed them and gathered an arsenal of arms stacked in the outbuildings behind the church. We children had been told not to enter but of course we did, and saw hundreds of rifles leaning up against the wall. We made our own play versions out of willow, wrapping several branches together to make them strong. We watched Paco teaching the young men how to shoot. By now he had quite a reputation as a marksman, and we copied everything he said, breathing and exhaling as he instructed, holding half the breath in so as not to throw off the shot. I soon found that if I held my breath too long, my heart would beat faster, and even my pulse could make me waver. 'Relax!' Paco would shout to his men, and we did too. They practised uphill, downhill, and across the valley. They practised into the wind, across the wind, and with tailwinds. Finally when Paco thought they had it right, he concentrated on the shot itself. 'Hold Your Aim,' he shouted and we mimicked his commanding voice, aiming our make-believe rifles into the trees. 'Squeeze the Trigger and Follow Through,' he shouted and we imagined we'd killed a rabbit or better still one of those terrible fascists who were threatening to kill us like rabid dogs. Everyone in the village admired Paco. He was brave and clever and a fantastic shot. Soon he was called out on all sorts of ventures. He was fighting in Malaga when those planes came over, so he didn't see what happened next and thank god he never did. My father, along with several other men, raced back to the village hoping to save us, but they were ambushed and put into the refuge too. I was so pleased to see him but over the next days, my father's men were executed one by one. The dreaded Lieutenant would arrive at the gate and point at someone, anyone, who would be dragged down to the mass grave. They took two or three people each day.'

'And your father?' Ernesto spoke quietly so as not to disturb the dead.

'His position in the government made him special so they took him into the bombed out church and tortured him for information, demanding he tell them where Paco was. I heard it all from the refuge but right up to the end my Papa never told, Nesto. He was a very brave man.' Jorge sat back exhausted. Steam was lifting off the pavements. They sat in silence surrounded by the rising mists. Ernesto waited. Had Jorge finished? Or was there more to come? There was. 'Those bastards took the lot, Nesto. After murdering my father, we were no use to them. They ransacked the barns for food, took the stored up rifles and set off for the railway line between Algeciras and Ronda, then on to their base in Malaga. There were just a few of us survivors; older women and children mostly. But we couldn't stay. There was nothing left so I joined the group setting off for Jimena, sleeping in churches and on the olive terraces until eventually I met up with Paco. We sat under a tree and he asked me about the family and it took hours before I could tell him that his mother and father and sister-in-law were dead and how they'd tortured his brother, my father, before executing him. How could they have been so cruel? Even so young, I could see that they had killed for enjoyment and that, I will never forget.'

'And the pact?' Ernesto asked.

'There and then under that tree, we put our hands together and vowed that one day we would get our revenge'

'And you waited twenty years?'

'Yes, my friend. It was our only chance and we took it'

Back in his room Ernesto lay gratefully on his bed. The hangover had passed and with Jorge's explanation laid bare, he finally felt at rest. He looked around at the bare white walls, and the plain old furniture. It was hardly luxury but it had become his refuge, his place of calm amidst the months of chaos. And now he had answers to ease his weary soul. 'Paco my friend,' he whispered into the room 'may you rest in peace.' He yawned; a fat, expansive yawn that filled him with satisfaction, and in this heightened state of calm and peace he began to wonder if perhaps he shouldn't become more involved with the world around him. Things felt different now. Jorge had exposed him to the courage and valour of ordinary people standing up to tyranny, knowing the repercussions, suffering the consequences, living their lives and living their deaths, and never before had he felt so weak and feebleminded. Could he ever be as brave as those villagers in Sauce del Valle? And he whispered in his heart that perhaps one day he could. Then he closed his eyes for the sleep he so desperately needed.

10. Funeral

An hour later he woke and knew for certain that the course of his life had to change. He'd tried half-heartedly to alter it before, but his wretched character had let him down, weakening his spirit, making him fearful. Now though he tried to be positive. Where to start? He walked over into the alcove of his room, opened his instrument case and pulled out the bundle of letters, examining them yet again for signs of disclosure. What was it about these paper missals that was so enticing? For weeks they had sat there in the green velvet interior and for weeks he had tried to ignore them, but now he touched them with his fingertips and brought them to his nose and inhaled their unique perfume. Was that rosemary? Or mountain thyme he could smell in the bundle? And then he realised that just like his fears, compacted and squeezed into the smallest part of his mind where they could never rise up and hurt him, so too these letters, restrained by rough string, were full of whatever mystery it was that Juan had wanted hidden, but what the letter-writer had surely wanted to reveal. Somehow he sensed that these letters were a gateway to another braver world so where better to start his new adventure into fearlessness than by reading them? But then there was his loyalty to the old man. Juan was a force of nature, a good man and Ernesto didn't want to let him down. *Take them quick and keep them safe* Juan had told him and that is what he had promised to do. So he pushed them back into his case and, once again, closed the lid.

He headed for the meeting room and found the weightlifter who, weeks ago, had told him those challenging, uncomfortable truths. This time the man seemed friendlier.

'My name is Manuel and these are my comrades,' he said waving a hand towards the two men Ernesto recognised from the square. To his surprise, Jorge was there too.

'I was hoping you'd come,' Jorge said. 'We're discussing Paco's funeral. Who will be there, who will speak.'

'You should say something,' Manuel suggested but Ernesto shook his head.

'You should,' Jorge urged. 'Paco admired you, said your friendship was absent of any demand for reciprocation. Who can ask for more?' But Ernesto wasn't convinced.

'Let me play my trombone,' he said. 'I can speak through that instead.'

'And I will play my guitar,' Manuel said.

Ernesto looked at the weightlifter's hands. How could those fat stubby fingers manipulate the frets without distorting the vibration? And how could those fingertips pluck the fine strings to produce the intricate trilling that this instrument demanded? Surely they were only fit for raising iron?

Another man brought them back to earth.

'Watch out for the Brigade.'

Ernesto was confused. 'The Brigade? I thought they were on your side. '

90

'No, my friend. We mean the BPS, Franco's secret police. Even now they use batons and cigarette burns and cut their victims with razor blades.' Ernesto shivered.

'They'll be at Paco's funeral. They have eyes everywhere.'

'Then perhaps I can stay with Dolores and watch out for them,' Ernesto said, mindful of his new commitment.

Next day, dressed soberly, Ernesto knocked at Dolores' door.

'I've come to pay my respects,' he said.

She seemed surprised to see him. 'What you doin' here? It's women's work, this mourning. Still never mind, come in.'

Paco's coffin lay across the kitchen table, barely reaching its edges and reminding Ernesto of the short stature of his one-time friend. Someone had sealed it.

'Buggers don't want us to see how he died,' she said settling down in the salon and offering him biscuits. Perhaps she was relieved her husband's rebellious spirit had finally been quashed or perhaps she was grateful for some company, because her voice seemed almost cheerful. But when she turned towards him, her eyes were reddened and her cheeks stained with grief. He wondered if Belle would be the same if it were him lying in that coffin waiting to be buried. Would she care as much as this widow? Dolores smothered the coffin with bunches of lavender to stave off the odour and they sat together hardly speaking until later that afternoon when a group of black-veiled women arrived. 'It wasn't normal,' one of them said; 'a man being here.' But they didn't seem to mind too much, so Ernesto lay awkwardly in an adjacent room trying to rest as the women began their vigil. First they sobbed in a staccato rhythm as if warming up their instruments in an orchestra. Then, when their voices were all tuned in, they began to wail in a macabre unison of organised sorrow. Later, the wailing grew stronger, the volume louder, the sadness heavier as Ernesto buried his head in a pillow remembering his friend. All night the black-clad women wailed in a volume that rose and fell as one woman took the lead and others fell back into the chorus, each one lamenting in strange voices as if summoning the devil itself. But as dawn arrived it seemed to Ernesto that their wailing had been transformed. Now it was more of a plea or an invitation to take on the inevitability of death; as if, in that modest kitchen, they were pulling on the very essence of life, hauling it in like fisherwomen drawing their catch from a cavernous ocean, exorcising the physical being of Paco and turning him into spirit. Ernesto thought about his music and the way he was drawn in, how performing was akin to perfection of the soul. And when the women had finished he felt cleansed and light and loving, as if life and death were the same thing. Later, Manuel and two distillery men arrived to collect Paco in his coffin but somehow Ernesto knew that the soul of his friend had already gone.

They heaved the heavy wooden casket onto broad shoulders and carried it out to the lift. Ernesto joined them, squeezing himself between the bulky warm flesh of the workmen and the smooth cold steel of the lift. As the door slid across to seal the compartment, the air became pungent with dried urine, stale sweat and the cloying odour of Paco's corpse. Ernesto put his hand over his nose so that he didn't choke and finally the door rattled open letting in the fragrance of the day. They left the soulless concrete building and carried their burden into a living, lively street, lined with mourners and curious neighbours watching the funeral of an old hero from times gone by. By now the day had warmed up and the perfume from Dolores' heated lavender lifted like incense into the sunlit air.

There were no women now, their mourning done. It was the men's turn, slow-marching through the streets in a solemn procession with Ernesto stooped under the coffin to keep himself level with the others. By the time they reached the cemetery, his back was sore. From his cramped position Ernesto studied a large crowd that had gathered at the gates. *Watch out for the BPS* someone had said but most of the crowd seemed genuine, except for two Civil Guards who stood on the pavement looking his way. One was whispering, the other was pointing. His stomach churned. It wasn't good to be so tall, so dark-skinned and different from the rest, especially at the funeral of a traitor. They reached the sepulchre. The coffin was lifted from his shoulders and he arched his back to release its tension. The two guards walked towards him. He felt the blood drain from his cheeks. What would they ask him? What would he say? But then a dog approached from between the sepulchres. It was a short stubby mongrel with tufts of scruffy black hair. Ernesto bent to stroke it and it wriggled with pleasure, and this gesture, so benign, so sweet, seemed to satisfy the two guards and they turned away, just a man stroking a dog. Again Ernesto caressed the mongrel, this time in gratitude and it shook and shimmied under his hand, then ran back between the rows of white marble into the cool shade. Ernesto waved it goodbye.

That afternoon he stepped onto the small stage in the meeting room, where only a few weeks ago he'd watched Paco perform. He brought the trombone to his lips and played his carefully chosen piece, *Trombones Triumphant* and everyone agreed it was suitable for their hero. Then Manuel came up to play his guitar, placing his left foot on a stool and lodging the curved body of the instrument between his thighs. Ernesto still doubted those short stubby fingers could produce good music on such a delicate instrument.

'How come a weightlifter can play guitar?' he asked Jorge.

'Manuel a weightlifter? You are mistaken, my friend. Manuel works at the distillery like all the rest, but he is famous for his strength, carrying two barrels full of sherry above his head, one in each hand.' Ernesto smiled at the misunderstanding and remembered his dream of the sailor with two barrels. Well at least he was right in his dreams if not in reality, he thought, as Manuel coughed for attention.

'As we all know, Paco was a terrible flamenco player.' Everyone laughed.

'It's true,' Jorge said. 'What happened at Sauce del Valle made him cynical and aggressive and he could no longer bear the quiet beauty of Sor or Falla. Instead he chose the music of suffering and turmoil; he chose flamenco out of anger not love.' Manuel interrupted.

'He should have stuck to his classical training, so this is what I will play for you now.' Ernesto studied Manuel's hands, still doubting their flexibility. But he was wrong. This brutish looking man ran his vast left hand up and down the board, carefully placing his finger ends between the frets while gently trilling with the swollen fingers of his right. Ernesto listened to the delicate rise and fall of Fernando Sor's studies reproduced so sweetly in the surprising hands of the man he had thought was a weightlifter. Ernesto closed his eyes realising how wrong he'd been about many things; about this man, about the neighbourhood, about Franco and about Paco too. Dear Paco who'd bashed out bulerias for the tourists and boasted of imaginary conquests. How wrong Ernesto had been in his assessment of his friend and how right Manuel's musical tribute was, in honour of such an intense and complex man.

Part Two

11. A Blonde

Everything had changed and nothing had changed. No more Paco shouting up from the pavement, no more bragging about his conquests, but life continued as it always did. The customary roll of Juan's shutters, the familiar clanking of the cyclist's wheels as they travelled across the cobbles, Ernesto adjusted to life without Paco with surprising ease. After the funeral, it was Jorge who started to call up from the pavement or knock on his door and they would cross the street to the bar. Now, two men, one old, one young, one tall, one short, sat at the same table watching passers-by and chatting just as Ernesto and Paco had done not so long ago.

'I've been given a scholarship to the University,' Jorge announced.

'What will you study?'

'Law, Nesto. Those poor souls, alive and dead, need justice for what's happened under this dreadful regime and I intend to provide it.' Ernesto nodded his approval. The University was close by and it would be nice to have the boy around. Besides, new ideas were rolling around his head and he needed someone intelligent and articulate like Jorge with whom to share them.

'I was wrong about your uncle,' he murmured.

'Don't worry, Nesto. No one knew Paco like I did.'

'Dolores perhaps?'

'Dolores didn't understand him either. God knows why she married him. She had no interest in his politics. They argued most of the time and in the end she betrayed him. Well that's what they say'

'She was scared Jorge. I saw it in her eyes.'

'She was a traitor more like. Trouble with you, Nesto, is you're too nice.' Ernesto shook his head.

'Not me. I'm not nice - perhaps a little stupid, thinking so highly of your General.' Jorge looked scornful.

'General Franco is playing us for fools, tempting the people with new roads and bridges, and it's true, the economy *is* improving but don't be taken in, Nesto. The Church and the Brigade are all at it, spying on us, searching out the would-be trade unionists and anyone still sympathetic to the Republic. And what kind of law is it that prevents more than three friends from meeting on a street corner? No Nesto, the law must change and I intend to change it.' Ernesto smiled at Jorge's ferocity. He'd never felt that passionate about anything except Belle and, of course, his music. 'And people are still disappearing,' Jorge continued. 'Surely you know that?' Ernesto nodded. He'd read it in *The Chronicle* and now in *The Monkey* too. 'You need to open your eyes, Nesto. See what's going on around you. Reckon you got Batista wrong too. They say he's made Cuba even more corrupt than when you were there.' An image of the old man from the Urania and his twin daughters drifted through his mind as Jorge got into his stride. 'I hear that there are plans for a proper revolution in Cuba,' Jorge said. 'A new society where everyone can prosper.'

'I hope so. I had a woman back there once. She was lovely.'

'So, would you go back?'

'Perhaps.' Ernesto said, not wanting to admit he was on the run. 'If the revolution comes, do you think the Mafia will leave?'

'Of course, Nesto. It's only a matter of time, you wait and see.'

Towards the end of October Ernesto had run out of money and had been forced to dip into his savings again. Even if the Mafia did leave Cuba and he was free to return, he still couldn't afford the fare, so something had to be done. Back in his room he pulled the table into the light, picked up a pen and paper and wrote.

Music Tuition. All ages. Trombone a speciality.

I'll be a terrible teacher, he thought, but nevertheless he placed the card in Juan's window and waited. A few days passed and doubts crept in. Perhaps no one was interested in learning to play the trombone or maybe because he was a foreigner they would be too suspicious to try. For distraction, Ernesto went to the meeting room.

'Thought I'd call in for some company,' he said to Manuel.

'If you want to be one of us, you must swear it.'

'I will, but not on a bible,' he said and they all laughed.

'Of course not, you idiot, there are no religious zealots round here.' They laughed again as Manuel brought over a bottle of rum.

'Here Cubano, swear your allegiance with a swig of your favourite.'

As the contents of the glass oozed down his throat, he felt the warmth of their company and joined them in singing the song of the Andalusian flag that Paco had sung and which was now repeated in the corner of a darkened room chosen deliberately for its clandestine acoustics so that no one outside could hear.

'They watch and listen to us all the time,' Manuel warned.

'Who? The Brigade?'

'Yes. People you wouldn't expect; ordinary people like you and me. Don't trust anyone, Ernesto. You never know where their allegiances lie.'

On the 31st of October Jorge and Ernesto went to Paco's grave, setting off at sunrise so no one would see them. For once, Ernesto had got up early and was already washed and shaven as Juan's shutters rolled up on the shop below. He was already fastening the belt on his trousers when the sound of that rickety bicycle floated up into his room. Ernesto pushed the leather tab through the brass buckle then paused, expecting the familiar clanking of bicycle wheels rolling away down the street. But no. The sound had stopped. This wasn't right. This wasn't the normal routine. He peered down and saw a woman placing her bicycle against the side of Juan's shop. A woman? Riding that bicycle? He shook his head. All this time he'd imagined a *man* riding along the street, moving through his dreams, awakening him to the routines of the day. But a woman? Surely not? Especially at this early hour. He leaned over to get a better look but the rising light made her face unclear. She was blonde and quite slim and, despite the October breeze, she was wearing a summery dress. What a contrast to the image in his mind of an older male wearing work clothes, with trouser clips round the base of his trousers, on his way to work at one of the distilleries. He looked at her carefully. What was she doing peering into Juan's shop like that? And writing in a notebook? Then she collected her bicycle, jumped on the saddle with quick athletic movements and cycled off down the street. Who was she? And what was she doing here?

At the cemetery Jorge was wearing a formal suit and carrying flowers which he placed against Paco's sepulchre. He was in full voice. Perhaps the formal surroundings had rendered him especially eloquent.

'Today, my friend is the Day of the Dead, but it is also the anniversary of the massacre at Sauce del Valle. So today we honour Paco and the rest of our family too.' Ernesto listened but didn't hear. He was still thinking about that woman? Who was she? And why did she break their normal routine?

In the first week of November he was sitting outside the bar with his back to the traffic, feet outstretched on the pavement as he always did. Jorge had already left and Ernesto was alone with his thoughts, wondering how he would pay next month's rent. Behind him a breeze caught the back of his neck making him shiver and with it came the faint murmur of an engine. Unlike the usual hollow sounding cars that passed along the street, this engine was powerful and soft and sounded expensive. Then he heard its tyres press quietly against the cobbles and its engine was purring like an exotic cat. He turned to look and approaching him was a Hispano Suiza K6. He gasped as it rolled into view. What an elegant car, with its deep-set running board curving gracefully from front to back and its two-tone bodywork shimmering in the pale sun. But why here? at such a disreputable end of the street? It came to a gentle halt outside Juan's kiosk. He heard the engine close down softly, like a woman slowly lowering her fan. Someone was getting out. It was her, the blonde woman, the cyclist. Ernesto got up, knowing in his heart that she was looking for him. In long strides he bound across the street taking in the way the bodywork of the K6 sparkled and the way the air shimmered from the heat still rising from its engine. Even before he reached the other side he'd already noticed that the driver wore a chauffeur's cap and that the rear of the car was blacked out making it impossible to know if someone was sitting inside. The woman stood on the pavement as Ernesto approached.

'Are you looking for me?' he asked.

'Are you the trombonist?'

'Yes. Do you want lessons?' He looked her up and down. She was pretty.

'No not me, it's for....for someone else.'

'Well who?' Ernesto asked, remembering the meeting room conversation. *Trust no one,* they'd said. The woman's eyes darted to the blacked-out window of the K6 and from behind the glass Ernesto thought he saw movement. Someone was in there. The woman composed herself.

'My boss wants trombone lessons for his son. I've been sent here to arrange them.' Her voice was steady and her gaze ice-cool. They agreed a time and date for the first lesson and the woman handed him a paper. Then she returned to the K6, and it moved slowly away down the street, leaving Ernesto filled with admiration and wonder. He'd encountered one of his favourite cars; he'd heard the powerful engine, seen the immaculate bodywork and smelt the aroma of luxury. He'd met a beautiful woman. She smelt nice too. And in his hand was a paper with the details of their transaction including the money he would earn that was generous enough to get him to Christmas and beyond. If Jorge was right and a revolution was to take place in Cuba, then soon he could be on his way home.

Lessons began the following week. Ernesto opened the door to a pale-faced child with deep brown eyes and an abundance of thick black hair. The boy held out his hand.

'Good morning, Sir. I am Francisco,' he said stepping inside and looking around the room. 'Are you poor?' he asked. Ernesto nodded. He could hardly deny the truth. He took the boy's coat - it felt expensive, and placed it on his unmade bed. Then he led him to the corner where his trombone case, was waiting.

'Inside here is my trombone. Do you have one also?'

'No, Sir. My father said I should use yours.'

'Well just for now, but this is a very special instrument and should be handled with respect.' He opened the lid and the boy peered in.

'It's old,' he said, unaware of the offence he was giving. Ernesto smiled.

'Better music then, with all that playing.' But the boy frowned as if he didn't understand. 'Experience son. The more you play the older it is, but the more you play the better you are.'

'I understand,' he said, but Ernesto could see that he didn't.

'Well then, shall we start?'

Ernesto took out the bell section with his left hand then removed the slide with his right. He placed the slide on the floor and slotted the bell on top.

'Now your turn.'

'That's too easy.'

'Well let's see.'

The boy took the two components and tried to fit them together. But when he'd finished, the parts were not quite aligned. Ernesto gave a gentle cough.

'Let me show you again,' he said swivelling the two parts and explaining the correct distance between them. 'Two fingers, here, like so.' This time the boy remained quiet. Finally, Ernesto twisted a screw to lock the two parts together.

'Can I play now?'

Ernesto shook his head. 'One thing at a time.'

He showed the boy how to hold the brace with his left hand and the slide with his right. 'Don't grab it, use your fingers and don't make a fist or you will tense up.' Then he undid the two pieces and placed them on the bed. 'Now let's see if you can put them back together.'

'But I've already done it once.'

'Well do it again!'

'What about the mouthpiece?

'Another day.'

The morning continued in this manner with Francisco assembling and disassembling until Ernesto was satisfied that the boy had gained respect for the instrument. By the time he'd learned how to put the trombone correctly back into its case, the horn of the K6 sounded below. It was time for Francisco to leave. Ernesto looked down from his window to where the chauffer had opened the rear door and was returning to his seat. Ernesto watched to make sure the boy entered the car and, as he did so, the arm of an adult appeared. He saw a tailored sleeve with a row of buttons along its edge and beneath that, the cuff of a pure white shirt. Then, as the arm leaned across to shut the door, there was a flash of gold from a cufflink glinting in the morning sun.

12. Limbo

November slipped into December, when spheres of green appeared on the orange trees along his street. For months they'd been camouflaged beneath dark foliage, but now they were ripening and soon they would swell and blush and turn a brilliant orange, demanding attention, saying 'look at me bursting through.' And each morning Ernesto lay in bed listening for the distant clatter of her bicycle, the wheels rolling unevenly over the cobbles, approaching his building, coming closer. He lay there letting the vibrations of her journey pass through him and when she reached his window, he jumped out of bed, opened it and there she was. 'And here am *I*,' he said to himself. How quickly his devotion had emerged and how quickly it had grown. Before, her bicycle had been no more than a soundtrack to his mornings, a rickety rise-and-fall routine that had faded with the preoccupations of the day. Now though, like those oranges suddenly appearing on the trees outside, her image had emerged as if from nowhere, demanding his attention and capturing his heart. Her wavy blonde hair, her broad shoulders, her slim waist, and the dress that flew up as she rode along the uneven street revealing her pale athletic legs, were all so irresistible that he watched her each morning and kept the image fresh by dreaming about her for the rest of the day.

He'd started making comparisons. Belle's sensuous darkness set against the woman's pale immaculate skin. Belle - no angel, versus this lady who seemed like a goddess. And more. Belle's desperate desire for approbation compared to this woman's self-confidence, riding to work when most women wouldn't be seen dead on a bicycle. He began to feel guilty. Oh, what treacherous judgements, and yet somehow the cyclist always won. 'I'm sorry, Belle,' he said, 'but what can I do?'

Jorge was unimpressed.

'What you need is a *real* woman. Someone you can touch and feel and enjoy. Not some fantasy female you idolise from afar.' Ernesto had to agree. He hadn't touched a woman's body for over a year now, not since Paco had introduced him to a working girl south of the city. It had been a disaster then and only emphasised his obsession now. Perhaps he wasn't capable of proper relationships with women anymore - even Belle, especially Belle. Perhaps keeping them at a distance meant keeping himself safe. Perhaps being an adoring outsider was all he could ever be. Of course this new woman had not spoken to him since their encounter on the pavement and, even then, it had been brief and cold. Yet she seemed to have a hold over him right from the start.

'On no account must you ask the boy about his family. Is that clear?' she'd said when they first met, and Ernesto had nodded obediently. But now that a few lessons had passed he'd become curious. The boy seemed melancholy. Why was that? And who was that well-dressed person he glimpsed after each lesson, closing the door of the K6? Was it the boy's father? Oh how he wanted to know more, but breaking her rule might lose him this job and the threat of losing his earnings was enough to hold him back.

The car was another matter. He was keen to find out about the K6, (a smaller, prettier version of the J12 owned by Franco). He longed to ask the chauffer if it was a pleasure to drive. What was

104

the turning circle? And was it costly to repair? After all, it was a Hispano Suiza, the most luxurious brand in Spain. Perhaps one day he would go down and approach the chauffer. He looked friendly enough. But maybe the blonde woman would be there too and she might disapprove of his forwardness. Besides he didn't know what to say to her now that he'd hesitated for so long. So he did nothing, trapped by fears that he might reverse the progress he had made with her, at least in is mind. And this wasn't the only problem. Since starting his lessons with Francisco he'd slipped back into fearfulness, returning to the state of indecision that had plagued him before. Without any challenge to his thinking, his commitment to bravery had slipped and gone.

'You still keepin them letters safe?' Juan asked one morning when collecting his newspaper.

'Yes of course,'

'Well here's another to add to the pile, but don't go readin' 'em mind. At least not yet.'

'Of course not,' Ernesto protested. 'You can count on me.'

Back in his room, Ernesto squeezed the eleventh letter into the bundle without examining it and shoved them back into his instrument case. Easier not to look, he thought. That way he could stay out of trouble. But Juan's words had disturbed him. What did Juan mean *at least not yet*? As if some time in the future he *should* read them? What was it that Juan didn't want him to read? Or maybe that now he *did*? Were his words some kind of challenge, something to rouse him from his state of apathy? He pulled the bundle back out and held it in one hand, flipping it over trying to divine some meaning. He pulled on the string and the knot opened with ease. The letters fell out onto the table and sat there in a pile as if announcing their arrival. But then he panicked. They are none of his business, he thought. 'Nothing to do with me' he said as he gathered them back up, retied the knot, returned them to their hiding place and clipped the case shut.

He was beginning to enjoy his classes with Francisco. At last the intricacies of trombone playing meant something to another human being and that made Ernesto content.

'When can I start playing?' the boy asked.

'You need to understand the instrument first,' he said and Francisco nodded as if he was beginning to accept Ernesto's pedantic ways. They had already progressed through 'feel the smoothness of the mouthpiece,' and 'use your little finger to hold back the slide,' and 'relax your wrist,' and 'just flick with your thumb to move the slide,' and today he was learning to extend it. But he was struggling. His arms were too short, his muscles too weak to maintain the extension. Instead he quivered at the extremes.

'You need an Alto. This one's too big.'

'So what's yours?'

'This is a King trombone, made for grown-ups.' The boy looked disappointed.

'My father won't buy me one.'

'Why not? He wants you to have lessons doesn't he?'

'He says I might lose interest and give up soon, so it's not worth it' Ernesto agreed. So far Francisco had only learned the technicalities of the instrument. Playing was another matter and he wondered if the boy had it in him. There was something truly humble about the trombone. It had a plaintive edge that came from its witness to tragedy and disillusion, elements that this privileged boy could never understand. But Ernesto did. He'd watched from the stage, seen the dance of life played out below him, the wink of a lothario, the clinch to hold her tight, the kiss, the tiffs, the drugs, the anger, and the betrayals. He'd seen it all and bit by bit, breath by breath, note by note, he'd withdrawn into his instrument, finding within its rise and fall a kind of holiness that had nothing to do with religion, but held a limitless ease that he could not find in reality. It was the same now. When he played he was completely present with no fears or fancies. No Cuba versus Andalucía. No Belle versus the blonde. No right versus wrong. Within his music he was free and there was nothing he would do to change that.

Francisco left and Ernesto slumped on his bed shaking his head, not to deny anything, but because it was a habit he'd got into whenever puzzlement loomed. He thought of Belle and then of the blonde woman. Why couldn't he choose between these two women, one of whom he didn't even know? He consulted the room but as usual it gave no reply. That night he dreamt of them both. He was floating above dark treetops playing Ravel's *Bolero* and wisps of clouds were quivering to the sound of violins. A mist was rising and his trombone was like oil, slipping and sliding in and out of the tree tops whilst down below, animals marched to the insistent beat of a snare drum. In the woods he saw nymphs, one blonde, and one brunette and dragons appeared, threatening their safety. The music became louder and the dream became thicker, the mist rose with more nymphs, more dragons, more animals, then violas, and violins, until a sudden change in the air pressure and that raucous glissando tearing at his soul, burning his lips, and the nymphs were banging on the sky in a discordant plea shouting 'Let us out! '

When he awoke he felt strangely satisfied. It was time to perform again. The dream had told him that. But where and with whom could he play? Jorge laughed when he asked him.

'You'll be lucky. If the censors find out they'll cancel before you even start.'

'But why?'

'Because your music is not from round here. Surely you understand that?'

'Like me you mean?'

'Ernesto, you have to understand, the authorities see your music as a threat to their traditional way of life.'

'Well let's try anyway.' So they went to the bodega to see if anyone was interested in playing with a foreigner. But when they moved into the back room they found Manuel on stage, not with his guitar but holding a microphone and addressing a large group of workers. They looked tired but attentive as Manuel spoke with such enforced gravitas that Ernesto cringed. He sounded obsessed, mad even, but the men were lapping it up.

'Men, the official syndicate is useless so we will start our own,' he said.

'I thought trade unions were banned.' Ernesto whispered to Jorge.

'Officially, yes. Only the Syndicate's legal. They decide the wages and working conditions which are then issued in decrees by the government.'

'So should they be doing this?' Ernesto asked looking over at the men eagerly signing up to Manuel's plan.

'It's the booze industry, Nesto, so they get away with it.'

Manuel returned to the microphone.

'Men, the first thing we should do is to strike - show them what's what, show them we mean business!'

'Striking's illegal too isn't it?' Ernesto whispered.

'Yes, my friend. Some even call it treason.' But this didn't seem to stop them. The men finished signing and sat huddled in corners making their case for collective bargaining and better working conditions and some even spoke of revolution. Ernesto kept his distance. It wasn't his battle.

On his way home he was surprised to see Juan pulling the shutters down on his shop.

'Closing early?'

'Here I've saved you these.' Juan said ignoring his question, then he handed Ernesto his papers before rushing off down the street.

Ernesto spread *The Monkey* on the table. He bought it daily now, as well as *The Chronicle*, in order to compare the two lines of thought; those of the government and those of the revolutionaries hiding in the shadows of the city. They were like roots spreading underground, searching through the darkness towards a common light, a communist light. Why hadn't he seen them before? He thought about the dark windowless meeting room where Manuel now held court with the workers, and those images of wives clutching photographs of missing husbands. Things he'd seen, but never really understood. He turned to the front page of *The Monkey*. It had improved its reporting style with less drama and gossip, more facts and figures to attract Ernesto's straightforward mind. *The Chronicle* had changed too, but for the worse. Now it was full of opinion and propaganda and a peevishness that made it look temperamental. The first article in *The Chronicle* confirmed his opinion.

CENSORS CLAMP DOWN ON ILLEGAL PUBLICATIONS

By Decree of the Government, from 1ˢᵗ January all publications not registered with the authorities will be banned. Would-be publishers have one month to submit an application to the authorities who will scrutinise each submission before granting authorisation. Meanwhile thanks to the efforts of our first lady Carmen Polo, our censors will continue their magnificent work in weeding out sedition, and support only those officially-endorsed publications currently available to our loyal populace.

Well that's *The Monkey* finished, Ernesto thought, remembering Franco's men ripping the batch of papers and throwing them into the gutter. Now that he was reading it daily, he wasn't surprised by their actions. It was full of barely hidden incitements to revolution and he doubted it had official approval from the censors. He turned to the back page and scanned the list of contributors, curious to know who they were. There were several extravagantly false names intended to conceal the writers' true identities. Why hadn't he noticed this before? There was someone called 'The Ghost of the Past' who, every week told tales of cruelty and injustice during the civil war. Another called 'The Pimpernel' claiming to be an aristocrat, perhaps in order to incite resentment by informing its readers on how the other half lived. Yet another was called 'Demented and Decanted' a connoisseur of brandies and sherries who, beneath the crazy rhetoric, made complaints about working conditions in the distilleries. At the bottom of the list was *The Monkey's Mouth,* the section he always read first and the one he sympathised with the most. It wrote idealistically about living a better, fairer life. He turned to it now.

BEHOLD OUR COMRADES ABROAD.

Comrayds, let's consider Cuba, our sister country rich in natral resources yet damagd by greed and repressun. Soon our compatriot country, so far away but so close to our harts will be transformd. Revolution is coming and it won't be long. What do you think of those brayve Cuban rebels training in the mountains of Sierra Maestra? Should we be brayve too? Do you dare consider it? Do you dare to dream?

How good it was to hear of his country referred to like this. More than half a century had passed since Cuba gained its independence from Spain but the two countries were still referred to as sisters and *The Monkey's Mouth* seemed to understand that. Ernesto recalled two decades ago a call to arms in his local Havana press asking for men to travel to Spain to help the Republicans fight in their Civil war and how he, an able-bodied, thirty something, had declined to go. It wasn't his fight so why should he get involved? He preferred the easy life; just him and his music. And yet here he was in that very same country, fraternising with rebels and being drawn into their fight whether he liked it or not.

13. Hispano Suiza K6

'Imagine you're standing on the shore.' Ernesto said. 'Can you hear the waves?' Francisco nodded. 'You must breathe like the tide. First it draws back, pulled by the forces of nature. Breathe in. Then it returns, unstoppable as it rushes across the sand. Breathe out.' The boy grinned. This was a good game. 'Get this right and you'll be playing your first notes by Christmas.' But Francisco choked as he breathed in and coughed as he breathed out.

'Not like that. Breathe and blow,' Ernesto demanded. 'Feel the rhythm, natural and calm.' The boy tried again. 'Breathe in.... more... that's it, then blow. That's better,' and Francisco was so pleased with his tutor's praise that he suggested   'Would you like to come down and look at our car?'

Ernesto raised his eyebrows. Yes please he thought, but would *she* be there? And would she disapprove? 'Don't worry,' Francisco said as if he knew what Ernesto was thinking. 'It's only our chauffeur Carlos today.'

They emerged into the street and immediately Francisco jumped into the driver's seat, clutching the steering wheel and peering through the windscreen as if driving through mist. Ernesto smiled at the boy's enthusiasm

'Great machine,' Ernesto said, taking in the pale yellow bodywork and the black wheel arches that swooped down to the running boards in such a gracious curve it reminded him of Belle.

'She's a beauty alright.' Carlos said as he opened the bonnet. Now at street level, Ernesto could see that the chauffeur was much younger than he'd imagined. Perhaps the peaked hat had granted him more maturity than he deserved. Carlos puffed his chest a little. 'It's a K6, Built in '37. Last of its kind you know.' And Ernesto *did* know. He knew all about the car and its beginnings, how it was a follow on from the J12 and that there were only a few made before they abandoned production.

'Yes, I believe they made aircraft engines after that.'

'You know your stuff,' Carlos said and opened the doors, one facing forwards, the other back, leaving plenty of space for Ernesto to see inside. The walnut dashboard sizzled in the sunlight and the air smelt of wax. 'Here, take a seat.' Ernesto positioned himself in the back and leaned against the leather upholstery, as smooth and well-worn as the seats of a twenty-year-old luxury motor car should be. He sniffed the interior and for a second thought he could smell perfume. Was it hers? He watched Francisco pretending to steer the car round a tricky corner, completely absorbed in his play and disinterested in adult conversation so Ernesto dared to ask the chauffeur a question.

'Why does your boss use this car? Why not a newer one for moving around the city?'

'Don Anselmo insists on this one.'

'Don Anselmo?' Ernesto repeated the name as casually as he could.

'Yes, the boy's father. He insists on it,'

'Ah, I see.'

Back in his room, Ernesto pieced together the fragments he'd just learned. Don Anselmo was the man who travelled in the rear seat of the K6. Don Anselmo was the boy's father and he owned one of the most beautiful cars in Spain. So he must be rich; that, or well connected. And what's more, the front door opened in the opposite direction to the rear. That's why Ernesto had such a clear view from his upstairs window, recalling the white-cuffed arm with a gleaming cufflink leaning forward to pull the door shut. And now something was nagging him, something about that image that wasn't quite right. The arm? The cuff? Yes. That was how he remembered it, the clothing was outdated; an old fashioned man in an old fashioned car.

On Christmas Eve, citizens descended from their apartments into the street. They travelled across the city by bus, by car, on foot, a mass movement of residents meeting up with cousins and aunts and brothers. In their steaming kitchens, women prepared plates of ham and cheese followed by roasted lamb and nougat and coffee. Ernesto was feeling down. If only he had a family with whom to enjoy such a treat. He met Jorge who was already sitting at their table outside the bar. A bottle of rum was half empty on the table in front of him as the smell of someone's Christmas meal wafted down from above.

'Smells good,' he said.

'If you like that sort of thing,' Jorge said, slurring his words.

'Don't you have family to eat with tonight?'

Jorge snorted. 'Pah! I prefer my own company.'

'What about Dolores? She's family.'

'Not interested.'

'But it's good to meet up once in a while.'

'What? To celebrate the arrival of some fictitious child?' Jorge raised the rum to his lips. 'No, Nesto, I'd rather be here with you.'

he grinned broadly. 'Here's to us lonely, angry, agnostic, socialist, bastards.' Ernesto raised his glass then looked up at the lights flickering in the windows of the flats above.

'What are they?'

'Oil lamps, Nesto. Look there, and there, and there. They burn all night to represent the arrival of little baby Jesus.' Ernesto laughed at Jorge's mocking tone.

'Seems dangerous to me, all those curtains draped close to the flames.' But Jorge wasn't listening.

'Then after supper they go to church for the Rooster Mass.'

'Rooster mass? Don't you mean Midnight mass?'

'Same thing,' Jorge answered. 'That or the Cockerel mass as others call it.'

'Why?'

'Who knows? Maybe 'cause it goes on for so bloody long, right up 'til the cock crows.' He stood up, knocking rum all over the table.

'Jorge please!'

'Your fault, Nesto; you shouldn't have introduced me to this deadly drink.' Then he raised his chin, pursed his lips and began to crow into the air. 'Cock-a-doodle doo!'

'Stop it, Jorge. I'm not in the mood.' But Jorge ignored him and crowed even louder.

'Cock-a-doodle-doooo! The things I do for you.'

Ernesto left him to it, crossing the street just in time to pick up his papers from Juan. But instead of closing the shop, Juan was watching television where images of the interior of San Felipe church gleamed from the screen.

'Pity it's not in colour, with all that gold,' Ernesto said as he watched an acolyte cleaning the incense burner and fixing it to a chain. Another was lighting candles, and yet another was setting up the altar. Ushers were preparing the offering plates and a priest was praying in a pew. 'Asking for inspiration for tonight's sermon I expect,' Ernesto offered.

'Hmmm! Mind control, that's all that is,' Juan said. 'And as for the congregation - hypocrites the lot of 'em. Some of them worshippers might be genuine but others won't be. And mark my words the Brigade will be there too, checking who's attending and more importantly, who's not. Neighbours too, keeping count and ready to denounce anyone they don't much like.' Then he leaned over and switched it off. 'That there San Felipe church used to be a mosque you know.'

'I didn't,' Ernesto replied as he collected his papers and went to his room.

Lying in bed, he hoped for a good night's sleep, but as he drifted off, church bells began to ring long and hard and intrusive. He covered his ears but they were insistent, calling in peals across the city saying *we are here, come and join us, come and join us, we are here* and the more he tried to block them out, the more they burrowed deep inside his head. The window! He'd forgotten to shut it, so he got out of bed and was closing it when the bells changed pace. Now it was a single insistent toll, steady like a slow-wagging finger, saying *don't just sit there, come to mass, come to mass.* He lay down again pulling the thin blanket up over his body and thinking of all those parents with reluctant teenagers, dressed in their best clothes, navigating the crowded pews, obliged to attend mass in the dead of night. The wagging finger continued *'you – must - come, you – must - come,'* and he remembered that dazzling interior he'd seen on Juan's television. He saw the acolytes at the altar. He heard the priest in the pew. His eyelids fluttered and then closed. The toll was softer now. He felt himself dropping into the dark. Belle came into view, dressed in gold like an angel, but she was frowning. Did she know? Had she found out he'd been unfaithful with the woman on the bicycle, at least in his mind? She wagged her finger slowly to show him that she had. Oh Belle. Don't reproach me for wanting someone here. I'm sorry, but I'm lonely and sad. Anyway what are *you* doing Belle? I suppose you're in the arms of another, so why not me as well? He slept for a few blissful minutes but was roused by the bells again. They had changed pace, lurching into a frenzy of multiple rings. *'We're closing the doors. We're closing the doors.'* On and on they called, demanding, *'Get to church, get to the church, we're closing the doors, we're closing the doors,'* and on every fifth chime they lost their rhythm as if one of the bell ringers couldn't keep up. Then suddenly they stopped. The doors *had* closed. There was silence. Nothing could be heard, not the choir nor the priest nor the worshippers' responses. All was sealed within. No one was allowed in and no one was allowed out. He closed his eyes, wondering if he would ever get back to sleep. But before his desired drop into darkness there was a loud bang at the door. He padded across to open it, muttering 'Not now for god's sake,' to the person on the other side. Jorge was leaning against the jamb of the door and for a second Ernesto thought Paco had returned from the dead.

'Done it, Nesto,' Jorge said.

'What have you done?'

'I have procured for you, your first and most splendid performance.'

'Couldn't this wait 'til tomorrow?'

'Manuel's found you some great musicians.'

'And?'

'Said they'd be honoured to play with the Cuban. That's you Nesto, you love to play don't you?' He came close up to Ernesto's face to check if he was right.

118

'You're drunk, Jorge. Let's talk tomorrow.' He tried to close the door but Jorge was already staggering in.

'These men play from the heart, Nesto.' He put his hand on his chest and hummed something unrecognisable.

'Jorge, please!' Ernesto could hardly keep his eyes open.

'From their hearts, Nesto. From their hearts,' He repeated, thumping his chest. 'What's more, these men are rebels like us. They refuse to toe the line.' Then he stopped talking and slithered down onto the floor in a disorderly heap. Ernesto fetched the pillow from his bed and pushed it under Jorge's head.

'Good night, my friend, we'll talk in the morning.' Then he threw himself onto the pillow-less bed and immediately fell asleep.

At dawn, a clarinet fluttered in like a bird and skittered up to the sky, hovering for a moment and squealing in a high pitch before floating back to earth. It was the first bars of *Rhapsody in Blue*, one of his favourites, and the whole orchestra was there in a violet sky. Next came his trombone in sombre echoes, like deep footprints on soft earth, and as he played, the bird fluttered again. Why am I dreaming this? But he didn't resist, instead, allowing the experience to roll over him as a mist began to rise. It felt warm and soft and he realised he was on stage and that a friendly audience was watching him play. Jorge was right. He loved to perform. A voice broke through

'Sorry about last night.' Jorge was standing by the bed offering him a cup of steaming coffee. 'But I got you that gig didn't I?' Then he slumped in the chair to recuperate.

'Who are these men, Jorge? And what instruments do they play? I need a bassist and a drummer at least.'

'Don't worry Nesto, Manuel says they're all good players, if a bit rebellious.'

'What do you mean?'

'Well the drummer's been denounced for singing the *Internationale* in his kitchen - some neighbour reported him I suppose - and another has just come out of prison for distributing pamphlets.'

'Can't a man sing in his own kitchen?'

'Seems not.'

'What kind of pamphlets?'

'No idea. Communist probably.'

'So when is the performance?'

'Set for the fifth of January, night before the celebration of *The Three Kings*.'

'Only twelve days! I need to meet these musicians as soon as possible.'

'All arranged, Nesto. Manuel will introduce you tomorrow.'

Ernesto picked the pillow off the floor and arranged it back on his bed. At last, a real venue, not busking in the street where nobody cared. Now his audience would be there by choice, seated and listening, or even better; on their feet and dancing. He would entertain them in the way he knew best, loud, and obsessed in the first half, then slow, and sexy in the second, just like he did in Havana.

14. Pedro

The flamenco district was the oldest in the city, where iron rings used to hitch donkeys, were still embedded in the walls, and cobbled streets were too narrow for motorised transport. The musicians' bar occupied a corner site where five lanes met. A sign swung overhead - Los Cinco Vientos – *the five winds*. Ernesto was expecting a small space much like other bars in the city but when Manuel pushed open the door and stepped over the raised wooden threshold, an enormous room opened up before him. There was a wonderful aroma too, of pulpo asado – grilled octopus - wafting out from a kitchen and the central space had a thick slabbed floor where several low chairs were positioned in a circle. Musicians were chatting at the bar. Manuel strolled over to join them leaving Ernesto to take it all in. A first floor balcony ran around all four sides filled with plants and flowers and as he looked up he felt a cool breeze against his cheek and realised that there was no roof, only the night sky, black, starlit, magical.

A big man ambled over. His eyes were set deep into his plump face and unkempt sideburns clustered on his cheeks.

'Ah! A King 2B. That's legendary. Can I hold it?' He took Ernesto's trombone and gently rolled it about in his hands before handing it back.

'I'm Pedro,' he said offering Ernesto his broad hand.

'And what do *you* play?' Ernesto asked.

'These,' Pedro answered holding his hands level with his shoulders and reeling off such a competent round of palm claps that everyone cheered.

'You could play bongos too,' Ernesto suggested. 'To add a Cuban touch.'

Pedro smirked. 'Ah the bongos! two drums, male and female, man and woman, bound together in a passionate night of rhythm and joy.' And once again the bar cheered.

'And you?' Ernesto asked a small, quiet man wearing a trilby.

'Name's Jose. I play anything you want as long as it's strung; double bass, guitar, piano even, and any genre, country, classic. You name it, I play it.' Ernesto nodded. He too loved all forms of music, New Orleans, modern jazz, the Big Band sound. All music inspired him and to him, all music was god. They arranged dates for their practice sessions then Manuel and Ernesto walked back into the city, Ernesto humming with the anticipated pleasure of his upcoming concert and Manuel asking questions.

'You miss performing, Cubano?'

'Very much and not just the music,' he answered, thinking of the laughter of people enjoying themselves. But then he remembered the cruelty of the Mafia and all those strangers who came over to his island, Americans mostly, with their relentless drug-taking and all that unofficial money slipping into willing pockets in the dark. *'It's surprising what you notice from up on stage,'* he used to say, until someone had told him to keep his mouth shut.

'So if you like performing so much, why'd you leave Cuba?' Manuel insisted.

Ernesto wasn't expecting this. After two years here, people had given up asking and he'd almost forgotten his practiced reply.

122

'I err… I needed a break from everything that's all, and …. He trailed off unable to recall his more convincing argument and at the same time unable to lie. Manuel snorted. It was obvious he wasn't convinced, and he seemed to be scowling too. But how could Ernesto explain? How could he convince his new acquaintance that he was trustworthy? He remembered what Manuel had said when they first met in the old bodega. *'You ain't from here and we don't know you.'* They continued walking, saying nothing, looking straight ahead. Had Manuel quickened his pace?

Back in his room, Ernesto examined his appearance in the mirror, hair tightly curled, nose too thin, and his frame so gaunt that garments hung off him like wet clothes on a washing line. Those musicians were much more appealing. Pedro with his fat cheeks and exuberant sideburns, and Jose, enigmatic and cool in his trilby hat. Both had a definition of character that he lacked.
'I have to change my image,' he announced to the room and the room seemed to agree. He opened his wardrobe then quickly shut it. There was nothing there that would do. So he went to the gentlemen's outfitters along the street. The shop sign had faded with the onslaught of a vicious sun and someone had placed a sheet of yellow plastic across the bottom of the window to protect the display. Even so the items looked jaded and the prices barely legible. He leant forward trying to work them out when he saw the shape of someone's head hovering above the screen that separated the window display from the interior. It bobbed up and down; moving along the width of the window then turning and moving back. Ernesto peered through the glass and now a face came into focus, staring at him over the waistcoats and cashmere cardigans and teetering as if on tiptoe. Ernesto pushed open the door and a loud bell signalled his entry. Before him stood a middle-aged man as wide as he was tall, with a frown across his forehead.

123

'What do you want, black man?' he snapped and Ernesto raised his eyebrows. Until now nobody in this neighbourhood had bothered too much about his differences, his height, his long face, and of course his colour.

'Just a cap,' he answered and the man led him to the back of the shop crammed with shelves, and beyond that a row of dressing rooms each with a curtain pulled across. Ernesto wondered irrationally if there were customers inside listening to their conversation.

'Most of my customers wear trilbies or fedoras,' the man said sneering and presented Ernesto with two flat caps to choose from. What dull colours compared with those in Havana.

'I'll take this one,' Ernesto said and as he paid he noticed that the man was picking his teeth quite ostensibly as if such uncouthness didn't matter in front of a black man. When he left the door was slammed gracelessly behind him.

For a week Ernesto didn't shave, allowing the tight, crisp growth to expand across his face until there was enough to sculpt out a small goatee beard that framed his long chin. He was satisfied.

'The cap suits you,' Jorge said when they met in the bar.

'Thanks.' Ernesto pulled it down over his forehead and brought the collar of his overcoat up to meet it. After five years in this country, he still found the winters uncomfortably cold.

'And look at that face-hair! So bohemian I hardly recognised you.'

'Thanks again,' he said, but Jorge frowned.

'It's not a compliment, Nesto. You want to be careful looking like that. You'll attract too much attention.'

'You think so?'

'I mean it. Take care.'

Even so, the image in his mirror made him happy. Here was the new Ernesto. Here was a confident man. So next morning he got up early and stood on the pavement waiting for the woman on the bicycle to ride by. He looked at his watch. She'll be here soon, he thought. In his hand was a ticket for the concert with no location shown, just a rendezvous point where everyone would be vetted. Manuel had said he didn't want every bastard knowing about the meeting room and all that went on inside it. But surely this woman was no threat. Surely she could do no harm. So here he was, legs firmly planted on the pavement, waiting for her to ride by. He was going to do this. He was going to be brave. As usual she slowed down over the cobbles.

'Morning,' he called out, and as she neared the kerb, Ernesto dropped the ticket into her basket. 'For you,' he shouted as she rode off leaving Ernesto beaming. He'd done it! He'd made contact.

Now the band had a pianist and a drummer, as well as Jose in his trilby and Pedro with his extraordinary palms. But perhaps they needed a woman to give the band focus. Ernesto sighed. If only Belle could be there to enchant everyone with her rendition of a Cuban bolero. But where would he find such a person here in Spain, where most women were so demure and shy? He began to wonder if she, the woman on the bicycle with none of the local timidity, might be a singer. He imagined her standing at the microphone with a diamond clip holding back her cascading blonde hair and dressed in a modest grey gown that highlighted the delicacy of her body, not curvy of course, but sophisticated and cool. What would she sing? Perhaps one of his favourites, like *Como Fue* by another Ernesto - Duarte Brito, with its talk of falling in love, and he sang it in his head as if they were performing a duet. At the end of 'their' song, Ernesto sighed, remembering Jorge's words 'You need a *real* woman,' and now Ernesto wondered if he almost had one. His mind leapt to the night of the performance. He would be standing on stage, ready to play as she walked in. He would wave and she would wave back. He would play the usual upbeat dance music that everyone loved, then a break to visit the bar. In the second half he would play *Como Fue* and he would look down at her and she would look up at him, and they would sing together and it would be glorious. He just had to convince the other musicians to include this song in their performance.

At rehearsal, Pedro and Jose had an argument.

'We must have a Tarantela.'

'Too old fashioned…'

'Then how about *Lucky Lucky Me*? Same rhythms but American,' Jose pitched in.

'Well if we're going to play American, how about *Why Do Fools Fall in Love*? And Ernesto wondered if Jose had seen inside his heart.

'And Perfidia for the older ones,' Pedro added, but Jose sneered.

'It's not just for the old folk. The new version's been in the top twenty all week,' Manuel coughed to interrupt the bickering.

'Don't forget this is Ernesto's concert,' he said

Ernesto seized the moment.

'So how about *Como Fue*? Pedro can adapt his flamenco rhythms to the beats of a Cuban bolero and I will sing.' Everyone agreed to this delightful mix of their two cultures and for a moment Ernesto drifted off, imagining himself gazing at her as he crooned of his sudden love into the microphone, and how he would respond when she gazed back. Manuel interrupted his daydream.

'Let's end the evening with something for the workers,' he suggested and Ernesto promised to find a protest song to suit their political inclinations.

The morning of the performance, Ernesto pulled at his broken wardrobe door and again looked inside at his small collection of clothes. He frowned. Most were too dark, too dull. He rushed back to the gentlemen's outfitters.

'What do you want this time?'

'That waistcoat in the window,' he said.

'It's probably faded by now.'

'Doesn't matter,' Ernesto said hoping for a discount. The man pulled it out and Ernesto saw that one side was as pale as sand and the other was the colour of golden corn.

'You can have it for half price.'

At a quarter-to-nine Ernesto stood on the stage with his goatee beard neatly trimmed, wearing his flat cap and tweed overcoat under which the audience could glimpse a smart yellow waistcoat.

'Hey, love the look!' Jose commented but Ernesto wasn't listening. He was watching Manuel open the big old doors. His heart was thumping. If the woman on the bicycle had found the rendezvous, she would have followed the others here. But where was she? The room was filling up with young couples, old widows and middle-aged ladies looking for distraction. A group of rough looking men came in too, and sat together at the back as Manuel closed the doors. Bang! But where was she? Then there was a loud rap on the woodwork. A latecomer was demanding entry. Ernesto held his breath. It must be her. Manuel pulled the door open and Carlos the chauffer walked in. What was he doing here? The doors shut again and everyone settled into their seats. Ernesto's shoulders dropped. She wasn't coming after all.

The concert went well and they finished with the protest song that Manuel had asked for. He came to the microphone.

'My friends, we close tonight with a song chosen by Ernesto.

It's about an honest man who works in the countryside. His land is green, and rich with palms and cane, but it is also red with the blood of his compatriots who fought and died in the great struggles of the early twentieth century. Ladies and gentlemen, we are honoured to play for you, the Cuban song *Guantanamera*. He bowed deeply before handing the microphone to Pedro. It was a strange combination - a Spaniard singing of Cuban oppression but how the man sang! Calling slowly into the air, his voice dipping and rising and crying for the lost souls of both nations. Within its lyrics and the soft undulations of the chorus, there was something for everyone. It spoke of oppression, injustice and sadness, but also of the seeds of life and the beauty of nature. Ernesto glanced over at Jorge who was sitting with his head in his hands, no doubt remembering his parents and the tragedy at Sauce del Valle. Then he looked at all the other faces in the hall, solemn and distant and he knew that the lyrics had affected each one of them in their own unique way. After the performance, Manuel shook Ernesto's hand.

'Good choice of song,' he said and the warmth in Manuel's comment seemed to suggest he was forgiven for being a stranger, forgiven for being him. 'Nesto, there are some people here who want to meet you,' he said, guiding him to the table of rough men he'd seen earlier. They shook his hand and congratulated him on his choice of song and Ernesto smiled and nodded, but he wasn't listening. Why hadn't she come, he wondered? He'd given her the ticket. Perhaps she gave it to Carlos instead. Anger surged inside him as he said his disturbed goodbyes.

Back in his room, questions came flooding in, each without answers, each one washed in resentment and hurt. What was she doing riding along his road every morning on a bicycle? Why didn't she travel in the K6? And why had she chosen *him* to tutor the boy? Surely she could have found someone else more suitable? And why had she told him not to pry. 'Don't ask questions. Respect the boy's privacy,' she'd said and he'd never defied that trust. But now he began to think about it. The boy was humble and respectful, not spoilt as Ernesto had imagined. And more than that, the boy seemed sad as if something was troubling him and this wasn't right either. So he decided there and then, sitting on his bed in his faded yellow waistcoat and his bitter disappointment that he would break her rule and ask the boy anything he cared to. Anything at all.

15. *Jurgen Voigt J-711*

The grin on Francisco's face was so wide, it had altered his appearance.

'Look what the Three Kings brought me,' he said, holding up a trombone case. 'It's an alto like you said.'

Ernesto opened it. On the inside was a small plaque with an inscription, *Handmade in Markneukirchen, Germany.* He took the instrument out and saw that it was made from a copper-toned brass. He corrected the boy.

'It's not just an alto, Francisco; this is a Jurgen Voigt J-711 and its one of the best you can buy.'

'That's what my father said. He told me to respect it and I told him I would.'

'So he thinks you will stick at it now?'

Francisco was breathless with excitement. 'When I first started, it was *me* who wasn't sure, but my father said to try a few lessons and now I think learning the trombone is the best thing ever. So I told him, and he bought me this!' Ernesto grabbed his opportunity,

'And your mother? What does she think?'

'She's dead.'

'Oh I'm sorry.'

'She died when I was born. I came out funny so it's my fault. At least that's what my father says.' His lip was quivering and Ernesto didn't know what to do. He started to rearrange the sheet music, listening to the boy's quiet sniffles. How stupid of him asking questions. How foolish to pry. And the father? How cruel to say it was the boy's fault she was dead. How could a father say this to his son? The boy was crying openly now. He should never have asked.

'It's not your fault,' he muttered to the weeping boy, and in an instant Francisco swung round and hugged him around the waist, his face pressed against Ernesto's chest, sobbing onto his shirt. Eventually he pulled away and wiped his face.

'My father says I shouldn't cry about her.' But he continued to sob quietly as if waiting for a response. Gently Ernesto put his hand on his pupil's head realising what he had just done. The cyclist had warned him not to ask questions but, because he was mad at her for not coming to his concert, he had done just that. And now he'd upset Francisco. How shameful was that?

Later, at the bar, Ernesto told Jorge and his reaction was unexpected.

'This could help our cause,' he said.

'What cause?'

'Getting close to the boy could help us find out what's going on.'

'Going on where?

'Look Ernesto, some of the men still don't trust you but *I* do, and I think it's about time I explained.'

'What d'you mean?' He had that lost feeling again, as if a secret agreement had been made in the community, of which he could never be a part.

'Look, you must have realised by now that Manuel is an agitator and a rebel. And old Juan? Haven't you worked it out yet? There

132

are things going on in this neighbourhood that you could be part of if you wanted. It's just that the locals aren't sure. They see you teaching the son of Franco's right-hand man and wonder what's going on.'

'Who, Don Anselmo?'

Yes. Anselmo. He's Franco's second-in-command in Andalucía and a member of the Brigade. Some say he had a hand in Paco's death.'

No, that can't be right! The man had just bought a trombone for his son, and was paying him for lessons! And even as Ernesto thought this, he realised how ridiculous his reasoning was. The man was cruel and uncaring, telling a boy not to cry over the death of his mother. Telling him it was his fault she had died. But as usual he passed no judgement. Better to wait and see.

'I'm not sure you're right,' he murmured.

'Go and speak to Manuel and Juan yourself, then you will understand.'

'Not yet. I have to think.'

Next day he woke to an unusually warm January air, as if spring had arrived early like a hibernating bear disturbed from its sleep, except that he was the bear, prodded awake by disturbing facts that wouldn't allow him to rest. At the bar he put a hefty drop of rum into his morning coffee while his head spun with Jorge's words. Don Anselmo was Franco's right-hand man. Manuel was an anarchist. And Juan? What did Jorge mean 'haven't you worked it out yet?' Well the answer was no. He hadn't worked anything out and he didn't know what to think about any of this new information. He'd only just come to terms with the fact that Paco had a wife! Everyone else knew it, but not him. And what about Franco? He used to think the General had saved the nation but after reading *The Monkey*, he realised this wasn't true? He finished his rum and coffee and crossed the road to the paper shop. Inside, Juan had already turned off the television and was preparing to close.

'Here you go,' he said, handing him his papers, and then pausing as if he wanted to chat. 'Still teaching that boy then?'

'Yes. His father's just bought him a trombone.'

'Good. That boy needs someone to care for him.' And as he left, Ernesto wondered how he knew.

A warm breeze had started up from the south. Ernesto lay on his bed. Here it comes again, the *levante* wind arriving like an unwanted guest, staying for days, raging in and out of the narrow streets like a trapped animal searching for a way out. People said it could send you mad if it stayed too long. Ernesto sighed, closed his eyes and surrendered to a rum-assisted sleep. What else could he do now that so many questions were weighing him down? There were no dreams. No masts, or nymphs or symphonies or sounds. He slept in an empty space, devoid of reason with the wind swirling around his building like a madman on the loose. When he awoke he reached for *The Monkey*. Somehow it had survived the new censorship law, probably because, as usual, it had more to say than the words printed on the page. There was a headline.

WISPERS IN OUR NEIGHBERHOOD.

Did you know our church of San Felipe was once a Mosk serving the Muslim comunity? Of course there's plenty of them catholics what will deny its origins in defens of their dogma, but there are those what searches for truth too. And they'll find it in the cellars of our modest little houses bilt against the church walls. Down there you'll see bricks from the old mudejar arches scattered around like fallen toomstones or reused to support the quorters of the living. Who knows what else lies beneath our feet, but one day arceologists, with

*their modest trowels, will unurth our secrets and discover things in
are neighbourhood aren't always what they seem.*

Ernesto reread the article and smiled in recognition. Many things
around here were not what they seemed. So the church used to be
a mosque. But didn't he know that already? Hadn't someone told
him that recently? Who was it? Then the words came back to him.
'Our church used to be a mosque you know.' That's what Juan had
told him on Christmas Eve and this is what Ernesto repeated now,
several times until he'd convinced himself that the old man who
ran the newspaper shop, was also the writer behind *The Monkey's
Mouth*. In fact he *was* the Monkey's Mouth. 'Haven't you worked it
out yet?' Jorge had asked him this morning. Well now he had. Juan
was a rebel just like Paco and also Manuel.

And what about Jorge? Perhaps trying to assassinate Franco
wasn't just a one-off revenge for his family. Maybe he was still
rebelling now. After all, he was studying to be a lawyer. *'The law
must change and I intend to change it,'* he'd declared and then he
remembered what else Jorge had said *'There are things going on in
this neighbourhood that you could be part of.'* His mind was drawn to
the meeting room and Manuel's comment *'If you want to be one of
us, you must swear it,'* and they'd laughed at him when he'd refused
to swear on a bible, as if it was some kind of convivial joke. Now
though, he realised there must be something else they all shared
apart from singing the forbidden song of the Andalusian flag or the
Internationale. Did they want to overthrow the government and
become a communist republic again? It would seem that they did,
especially Manuel and his syndicate. Ernesto frowned. He didn't
like it. It didn't feel right. It was too drastic, too extreme. What was
he getting himself mixed up with? Where was this leading? He
shook his head. What was the point of getting involved? He'd tried
to be brave; he'd tried not to sit on the fence. But Paco was dead
and his small efforts at courage had all been in vain. Besides, he'd
come here for a simple life and things were getting complicated

135

just like they had in Havana and he didn't want a repeat of that. No he decided. The side-lines were a much simpler place to be and that was that. He rolled over and tucked his head into his arms in order to fall asleep. But later, in the half-light between waking and dreams, he heard Pedro singing the lyrics of *Guantanamera* all over again, and this time it was the verse about dying either in the dark like a traitor or proudly with his face towards the sun. The words pulled him out of sleep making him feel shallow and ashamed.

He grabbed *The Chronicle* in the hope it was reporting something less controversial, something reliable and safe. But the International section was not.

COMMUNIST COUP IN HAVANA

Reports indicate that army personnel are defecting to the communists operating in the hills of Cuba. But, as we know to our cost, these experiments never work. We thank our blessed God that Spanish communism is dead my friends; broken on the shoulders of our rigorous law and order. Those Republican fools, who promised heaven, delivered nothing but hell. It didn't work here and it won't work in Cuba either. So let's rejoice, dear readers, that here in Spain our nation is stable and our citizens are content.

Ernesto held that last phrase in his mouth like a piece of putrefied fruit. 'Our citizens are content.' Well that wasn't true, was it? The men at the meeting room had made that clear. Whoever had written this either didn't understand, or was playing its readers for fools.

It was late and he was hungry, so reaching for his cap and overcoat he went across to the bar where he ordered bread and sardines cooked with lashings of olive oil. When they arrived he sprinkled salt over their crisply charred surface and with his fingers delicately holding each end, he brought them, one by one, to his mouth. With every delicious bite, the warm salty oil oozed

136

down his throat, or fell onto his chin and settled in his beard. But he didn't care. This was bliss. When they had all gone he dipped the remaining bread into the oil, wiping it around the plate to catch the last bits of flavour and pushed the whole oil-soaked chunk of bread into his mouth, cheeks bulging and unconcerned about manners because no one was watching. At least that's what he thought.

She strolled over wearing a dark fur coat with matching hat, and holding a small clutch bag in her gloved hand. Ernesto looked up, eyes wide with delight and face red with embarrassment as the last drip of oil rolled down his chin. Instinctively he wiped it away with the back of his hand and swallowed hard to get rid of the offending bread. She dragged out a chair and sat down in front of him, placing the clutch bag in her lap because the table was thick with oil.

'Thought I'd find you at this bar,' she said removing her gloves without a smile. She held out her hand in greeting, and he wiped his oily hand against his coat before shaking hers. She smirked, seemingly at his lack of etiquette. 'You seem different,' she said looking him up and down.

'It's the beard.'

'And the cap. It suits you,' she said, unclipping her coat and crossing her legs. Beneath the fur he saw a skin-tone dress that, for a moment, made her seem naked. Ernesto tried to focus.

'So why are you here?'

'My boss has a message.'

About what?'

'You asked questions when I told you not to,' she said. Ernesto blushed. There it was out in the open, as direct as it could be, and nothing would make it go away.

'I'm sorry I ignored your advice. I...'

'It wasn't advice. It was an instruction.'

'Yes I see that now,' he answered as she opened her bag and pulled out an envelope. His name was written on it.

'Here, take this.'

'What's inside?'

'How should I know? I'm his employee not his confidante.' And in the back of his mind he sighed with relief. Perhaps she wasn't Don Anselmo's mistress as he'd been starting to suspect. 'I'm Beatriz by the way,' she said, and this small offering, this small revelation to accompany her image, gave him a reason for hope.

'You didn't come,' he blurted out.

'You mean the concert? Not my thing. Don't like jazz or popular music and in any case I wouldn't be seen dead in a place full of drunks and lowlife.' She seemed to be enjoying herself.

'So you suggested Carlos go instead?'

'Yes,' she said getting up. 'He told me you were good.'

As she walked away the condescension in her voice hung in the air and Ernesto sat back, devastated at their first real interaction. What an uncouth idiot he'd been, letting oil run down his chin then wiping it away with his hand. Where were his manners? And how elegant she'd looked in her furs compared to him in his worn-out overcoat and dull-coloured hat. But Beatriz! She had told him her name as if she wanted them to be acquainted. And what a lovely name. It suited her. 'Beautiful Beatriz,' he murmured, then sighed. She was everything he wasn't; a composed woman of immense elegance and he an out-of-place musician with terrible clothes and terrible manners. And it seemed to him that she'd enjoyed their encounter a little too much, teasing him with her half open coat, and dropping him a compliment that he didn't deserve. Maybe she's like that with all men, knowing how far to go, to put them on the back foot and keep her at ease.

Next morning the envelope from Don Anselmo was resting unopened on the table. He'd let it sit there all night hoping that by some magic it would be gone by morning. But there it was, staring at him still. He prodded it to feel for money, a final payment, perhaps with a note, thanking him for his services but they were no longer required. This would be the end of his dreams. No more lessons with the delightful Francisco, no more purpose to his life, and no more saving for his trip back to Cuba. He picked it up and held it to the morning light. No money, just a single sheet of paper inside just like the letters Juan had given him. He sighed, knowing that things would be different after his questioning of the boy and he wasn't ready for life to change once again. He dropped the letter back on the table and hurried off to the bathroom, anything to distance himself from that envelope. Of course when he returned, it was still there. And when he finished his trombone exercises, it glowed even brighter in the morning sun, like the communion host taken after confession. In the end he couldn't bear it, but instead of giving in and opening the thing, he put on his coat and set off for the meeting room to talk to Manuel. Despite his resolution not to get involved, he was finally ready to ask questions.

16. Revelation

It was Carlos the chauffeur whom he found in the meeting room, leaning on one of the barrels that served as a table.

'I want to speak to Manuel.'

'He'll be out here shortly. We want to talk to you too.'

'What about?'

'You'll find out soon enough. Meantime you owe me a drink.'

'Why?'

'Haven't you read Don Anselmo's letter yet?

'Er no. But what's that got to do with you?'

It was *me* who persuaded him to give you a second chance.'

'A second chance?'

'Yes, Don Anselmo agreed for you to carry on with the classes.'

'That's wonderful,'

'But there are conditions.'

'What conditions? What does he want?'

'It's not Don Anselmo with conditions. It's *us.*'

'Us? Whose *us*?'

There was no time for a reply. Manuel had just emerged from the back room and shook hands with Carlos as if they were old friends.

'Take a seat, Cubano. It's time you knew.'

They spoke, slowly as if talking to a child. Carlos went first.

'We want you to work for us, Nesto.'

'But who's *us*? I don't understand.'

'We're a bit like the resistance in France, working behind the scenes, like they did in the war.'

'Doing what? I don't get it.'

'Patience!' Carlos laid a hand on his arm as Manuel lit a cigar and ordered rough sherry that arrived in a pint glass. He took a mighty swig then paused as if weighing up what to say.

'Thing is, Nesto, we're a big network, from right up North to down here in the South. You've never heard of us because we're clever. We never recruit until we're sure.

'And now we are,' Carlos interrupted. 'At the concert when you chose to play *Guantanamera*, the men were impressed, and the other day you comforted Francisco and then we knew.'

'No I didn't. I upset him.'

'Yes, but the boy told me you were kind, and that's what matters. Francisco trusts you.'

'So what's the name of this big organisation that I've never heard of?' Ernesto was finding it all hard to believe. Manuel lowered his voice.

'We're called the Maquis like the French, but down here we call ourselves the Monkeys.'

'The Monkeys? You mean like …'

'That's right, Nesto. Like the newspaper. Juan does the writing and we do the rest.' For a moment Ernesto was quiet, taking it in.

142

'Juan does the writing and we do the rest.' It was beginning to make sense.

'And what *is* the rest?'

'All sorts of things: searching for mass graves, collecting testimonies from victims, paying for people like Jorge to study law, and supporting widows like Dolores. Who do you think paid for Paco's funeral? Then there's surveillance. We do a lot of that too, don't we, Carlos?'

'But Carlos works for Don Anselmo.'

'Exactly!'

'You mean he's a spy?'

'Yes, Nesto, and that's what we want you to be too.'

'But I'd be useless,' he protested.

'We just want you to listen and report back.'

'Can't Carlos do that? He`s much better placed than me.'

'Every little helps. Besides Anselmo is the man who ordered Paco's death. Don't you want to get your own back?' Ernesto nodded. He was beginning to think that Manuel was right. 'And why do you think that woman of yours rides past Juan's shop every day?'

'She's not my woman,'

'Of course not. She's one of the Brigade, just like Anselmo. They know we're up to something but they don't know what, so she rides by everyday like clockwork, watching and listening, and they think we don't know.'

'But why would she do that?'

'She's trying to catch us out, discover our plans.'

Ernesto took a cautious sip of his drink. A gulp would be too indulgent. He was thinking of the concert invitation he'd given to Beatriz. Thank goodness she hadn't come otherwise she'd have found their secret place where all the dissidents hung out. This place in fact, this very place! Manuel interrupted as if he'd guessed his thoughts.

'Look, I know you invited that Beatriz woman to the concert. Carlos told me. But she didn't come, so no harm done eh?' Manuel was staring at him now, waiting for an answer and Ernesto felt giddy with fear, unable to meet the man's gaze. Beatriz could have exposed them to all kinds of danger and they all knew what he'd done. But instead of being angry Manuel was smiling. 'Come on, Nesto, 'he said. 'You know life will be a better with Franco gone and the Republicans back in power. You must do it for all our sakes.' Ernesto shook his head. What did he know about Spanish politics? And why should he get involved? It wasn't his fight. It was theirs. Manuel leaned over and patted him on the shoulder. His voice was gentle, almost kind. 'And what about Cuba? The rebels are assembling over there, just like we are over here. Join us and you could fight for your country if only by proxy, but that's a start!'

It was a strong argument. He liked the link with his homeland and the camaraderie this new arrangement promised. Manuel's eyes were gleaming now. 'Come on man, you know this is right.' Manuel moved in even closer. Droplets of sherry had accumulated at the corners his mouth and had turned to foam. He looked like an inmate from the local asylum. Perhaps Manuel was crazy. Perhaps this was all just a game. Well if he *was* insane, then all this plotting was fantasy too, in which case there would be no consequences if he agreed. What did he have to lose?

'I'll do it,' he said quickly before he could reconsider, and they bought him rum.

'So what *are* your plans?' he asked a little more relaxed now that he was one of them. Manuel leaned forward again. The gleam in his eyes had turned to fire.

'That's a secret, Nesto. But when it happens, you will know, and when it happens, it will be explosive.

By the time Ernesto reached his room, he was beginning to regret agreeing to their request, so to make himself feel better he lit the fire and pulled a blanket round his shoulders. He wasn't political and the thought of tricking Francisco made him sick. The father though, that was a different matter. The man had insisted Francisco take trombone lessons, and now Ernesto realised it was all a lie, using his son to get access to him because of the people he knew, and what hurt him even more was sending Beatriz to spy on him too. And had Don Anselmo sanctioned Paco's death? If so, what kind of man must he be? But maybe he hadn't done any such thing. According to Jorge, no one was sure. He looked at the letter, still unopened on the table. Could he guess a man's character by the words he chose to write on the page? He opened it.

January 20ᵗʰ 1958

Señor Ernesto,

It is with great disappointment that I discover you ignored instructions and made enquiries into our domestic situation. What happens in our family is no concern of yours. In addition, the manner in which you interrogated Francisco is not acceptable. The boy is upset.

However, as Carlos has indicated, there is a bond between you and my son and for that I am not ungrateful. Therefore I will allow the lessons to continue provided you refrain from making further enquiries into Francisco's family.

There is one other condition incumbent on this arrangement. You must write a letter of apology, stating regret at the repercussions you have created. My secretarial assistant Beatriz will collect it from you within the next few days.

Yours sincerely

Anselmo Jiménez

Ernesto frowned. What repercussions? And was the boy really as upset as his father suggested? The tone of the letter was arch and arrogant and he didn't like it. 'I won't apologise,' he said to the room. But the long silence that followed made him think again. Perhaps this was the answer; apologise, carry on with the lessons, and save his earnings for a return voyage on the Urania. By then maybe a Cuban revolution will have happened, the Mafia would have gone and he could leave here - escape. He sighed. How had he got himself into this mess? He'd come here for a simple life and how complex it all seemed now. A wind was raging outside, rattling the window panes and whistling its unsettling tunes. He reached for a pen before he changed his mind, hoping that a subservient tone would be enough to melt the father's austere heart.

21ˢᵗ January 1958

Dear Don Anselmo,

I regret most profoundly my enquiries into your family situation and any adverse repercussions on Francisco that might have occurred. Your son is a fine boy and it would be an honour to continue teaching him. With your generous gift of the Jurgen Voigt J-711, I am certain that he will make good progress.

Your faithful servant

Ernesto Costa.

Next day he stayed in his room, pushing old newspapers into a meagre fire in an effort to warm it before Beatriz arrived to collect his apology. And what would he say to her when she did? He wasn't used to women like her. Belle had been easy-going, taking the initiative, caressing his hair, kissing his cheeks, pushing him onto the bed. She was a panther always on the prowl, whereas Beatriz was as brittle as crystal and he was dazzled by her light. And now that he'd met her properly, he started to make excuses. It didn't matter that she'd rejected his concert. It didn't matter that she thought his associates were low-life or that she may be part of the Brigade. He was in her world now and despite her being a spy, he wanted to keep it that way. Then he remembered his new mission; *'listen and report back'* and his stomach dipped. Beatriz would see right through him, he was sure of that. How could he carry this off without being discovered? And what would Franco's henchmen do to him if he was?

She didn't come until the next morning. He was still in bed when he heard a scraping noise as she positioned the handlebars against the wall. Foolishly he'd imagined her arriving in an afternoon light that would bathe his room with a golden glow that softened its rough edges, and concealed the dust. But she was already downstairs, and he wasn't prepared. He leapt out of bed, threw on his clothes and smoothed down his hair. The door opened to his block. He heard her lightweight footsteps echo up the stairwell. He smelled his bedtime breath with the palm of his hand. Not good.

'Come in,' he said barely hearing his own voice. She strutted across to the window, her shoes clacking against the wooden floor, making an out-of-place feminine sound in his grubby masculine room. She sat at the table, crossing her legs slowly like she had in the bar. Was this some kind of sign?

'Have you got it?'

'Yes,' he said, handing her his letter of apology.

'Aren't you going to offer me a coffee?' she said.

'I've run out. We could go to the bar?'

'What, that awful place!'

'You're right, it's not a place for ladies. Perhaps somewhere else then?' he asked hopefully. But she was getting up. Her shoes were clacking again.

'Don't go,' he said quickly.

'Why ever not?' She was opening the door.

'We could talk for a while.' She was descending the stairs.

'About what?' she shouted back. The outer door banged shut and he shook his head in wonder at his daring. He had asked her out and she hadn't said yes, but she hadn't said no either. Perhaps he could ask more formally next time. He watched from his window as she collected her bicycle and rode down the street, and he remained there even after she'd disappeared from his sight. What a woman and here in his room! But then he remembered she was a spy, in which case maybe this visit was her opportunity to check him over. But now he was a spy too. Oh god what a mess! He examined himself in the mirror. Was there any difference in his appearance? An aura of espionage? A twitch of the mouth that betrayed a lie? But all he saw was a frightened man, forced into something he couldn't control, and he hated himself for it.

He went downstairs to collect his newspapers. What should he say now that he was a Monkey like Juan? Here was another secret to add to those letters. So should he nod in acknowledgement or give him a wink of collusion? Or would they carry on as normal? He considered not buying a newspaper ever again, but he'd miss the news and wouldn't know if the Cuban revolution had happened or not. No, he couldn't do that. He needed to keep up with the events over there, just as he needed to know what was going on here.

'I kept the back copies, reckoned you'd like to catch up,' Juan said with no sign of extra pretence. What a relief. At least with Juan he could carry on as normal. It was the same with Francisco. There were no signs of the grave repercussions mentioned in Don Anselmo's letter. Everything appeared routine when he came for his lesson and the boy seemed quite content, as they began revising what he'd already been taught.

'Do you remember what I said about the corners of your mouth?' Francisco nodded. 'Keep them tight as if you are smiling.' The boy gave him a grin as if he knew what was coming next. 'But keep

148

your lips soft as if you are kissing a girl.' Francisco blushed, then asked,

'Can we try the slide now?' Ernesto smiled. For some time now this question had been incubating in the boy's head.

'Of course. Extend your arm as far as you can. Good. Now breathe in four beats, blow out four.' Ernesto clapped out the timing and Francisco's eyes sparkled as the first note burst from the bell. 'Now bring the slide right in and blow again. There, well done.' The rest of the lesson went just as smoothly, with Francisco learning the first few positions on the slide. When he left, Ernesto heard him run down the stairwell, humming the notes he'd just played. Ernesto looked out of the window. Was she there? No, just Carlos who welcomed the boy into the K6 and waved up to Ernesto before driving off down the street as he always did. If this was meant to be his new world of undercover activity, it certainly didn't feel any different to before.

A few days later Beatriz agreed to meet him for a drink. Ernesto fiddled with his cap as she led him to an upmarket bar in the centre of town. Ernesto held out a chair. She sat gracefully. He sat opposite and offered a smile, trying to relax. But things felt different now. The spying had spoilt the chance of romance. The waiter brought drinks. Ernesto raised his glass.

'Cheers,' he said half-heartedly.

'Yes, here's to little Francisco and his trombone playing,' she said and her voice seemed more natural than his.

'To Francisco,' he agreed and they sipped at their drinks interspersed with long bouts of silence. He heard her breathing. It was heavy and punctuated by sighs that suggested she was bored. He lowered his head trying to think of something interesting to say but his tongue was dry and his jaw was tense. What else could he add to their conversation? He had to say something.

'Do you like modern jazz?' he asked.

'Can't stand it. I prefer a proper tune. '

'Do you go to the theatre?'

'Sometimes,' she said. Another silence.

'Or cars? Do you like cars?'He said hopefully.

'Not really. The K6 is nice I suppose.'

He shifted in his seat and stared at the perfectly white tablecloth spread out between them like a perilous ocean. Silence again, then she asked him,

'Do you like the sea?'

Ernesto hesitated, thinking of Belle thousands of nautical miles away.

'No. Not really.'

'I do,' she said, head up, defiant. 'I swim every day.'

He hesitated, struggling to find a response. But she was getting up now, extending her hand to say goodbye. He watched her go and then realised. He could have told her about the Malecón, the coast road that ran along the outskirts in Havana and how all the world seemed to congregate there at weekends to watch the sunset over the ocean. Damn it, he thought, mad at himself for closing down their conversation, then he slumped back in the chair. How assured she was, and how insecure was he.

Next day Carlos came to pick up the boy.

'What did you say to Beatriz? She said she wasn't coming today.'

'Nothing,' he answered and realised that was true. He'd said nothing that interested her and that small truth stung.

February came and oranges were ready to harvest. A month later a multitude of sturdy cotton plants began to grow in the marshes, and light showers fell but soon disappeared. By May a white floral dust gathered on window sills, as olive trees conceded their blossom to the breeze. In July more dust appeared, red from the hot Sahara wind and deep shadows formed as the sun rose higher in the now-blue sky. People retreated into the homes and pulled down the shutters from the intruding sun, and by August the heat hung in the streets like robbers searching for jewels.

Manuel called him to the meeting hall.

'Well?' he said. 'What have you got?'

Ernesto shook his head. 'Nothing I'm afraid.'

'It's been six months, Nesto, you must have something.'

Ernesto shook his head. 'Sorry, but Beatriz has stopped coming.' He didn't want to admit that he'd messed up their first real date.

'Not good enough, Nesto. Every bit of information is useful, no matter how small and insignificant you might think.'

Ernesto was frantic to explain. 'I see her riding by but I don't get a chance to speak and I'm forbidden from asking Francisco questions, so what can I do?'

'And Don Anselmo?'

'He stays in the car so I've never even met him.'

'Hmm, that's not the point. You're one of us now. We expect you to make a contribution.' Manuel swigged back his brandy and went for another. 'Well there's one thing you *can* do,' he said fetching a calendar from the bar. 'It's the Vendemia next month and we should have another concert for our comrades. That last one really brought us together.'

'Vendemia?'

'Harvest time, Nesto. When we celebrate the grape.' There was a slight slur in Manuel's voice. 'I've already booked this place and planned the rehearsals.' He waved an arm around the room and his action seemed to throw him off balance. 'But no one gets through these doors unless we trust 'em.'

A few days later, Beatriz turned up at Ernesto's door. Her hair was damp as if she had just been for a swim.

'Aren't you going to ask me in?'

Once again her heels clacked across the wooden floor, making disconcerting echoes of the time before. He watched her saunter over to the window but there was no crossing of the legs this time, no seduction, just straight talk.

'I hear you're having another concert,' she said lightly. Ernesto sat on the edge of his bed and studied her face. How did she know? 'I overheard someone talking about it,' she said, as if she knew what he was thinking. 'I should like to hear you play this time.' Her voice was bright, light, and innocent in its tone. Ernesto bristled. She mustn't come. The place would be crawling with dissidents. It would be a disaster. He had to dissuade her.

'You wouldn't like it there,' he said, trying not to sound desperate.

'Why not?'

'It'll be rough.'

'I'm coming to listen to *you*, not watch a crowd of misfits enjoying themselves.'

'No you mustn't.'

'Mustn't? Why on earth not?'

'Because I'm terrible,' he said without thinking.

'Rubbish. Carlos told me you're good, remember? Maybe you don't want me to come?

'It's not that. It's just that it's a bit ...' He paused searching for the right words. 'Unrefined for a lady,' he said looking at the floor.

'Then I'll add a bit of glamour to the place,' she said and

laughed. It was true. She was even more glamorous than before. Had she done something to her hair? Even damp as it was, she looked stunning, as though she should be chauffeur-driven in a Cadillac or a Chevrolet Bel Air, instead of that old bicycle she rode each morning.

17. Don Anselmo

Ernesto rushed along the street. What was he going to say? How would he explain? He found Manuel in the meeting room.

'What the hell do you mean she's coming to the concert?'

'I'm sorry but she insisted.'

'Didn't you try to dissuade her?'

'I told her she wouldn't like it.'

'Idiot! Tell a woman that and she'll like it even more.'

'So I said I was terrible, and she got suspicious.'

'No wonder!'

'Look, I told you I'd be no good spying,' Ernesto protested. 'and there's no way I can stop her now.'

But Manuel was thinking ahead.

'Never mind, Nesto. We'll use it to our advantage. She and the rest of Franco's cronies have been watching us for far too long, but we can halt their suspicions once and for all by making the concert a family show.'

'But how will you do that?'

'Dolores can get all the women together. Tell them to dress

respectable, and make sure their husbands behave themselves, that they don't drink too much and start singing. Bad enough the song of the Andalusian flag, but the *Internationale* would give the game away completely.'

'Well Beatriz has been riding by for years and hasn't discovered us yet.'

'True, but that doesn't let you off the hook, Cubano. If she sees through our charade, the whole group could be in jeopardy.'

When he collected his papers, Ernesto didn't stop to chat. He didn't want to worry Juan with his latest foolishness. He should have come up with a better excuse, made sure Beatriz didn't come. Instead, his slow thinking had made things worse. So with a nod, he left and traipsed upstairs to his room. Here, with his flattened palms, he spread the two publications out on the table, grateful for the veneer of order which these smoothing routines provided. Today *The Monkey* and *The Chronicle* were reporting the same event. The Monkey's Mouth – or rather *Juan* writing as the Monkey's Mouth - was ecstatic.

DAVID'S VICTRY OVER GOLIATH

In a <u>battle</u> lastin' 11 to 21 July, Castro's guerrillas capturd 240 men while losing only three of theres. 'La Ofensiva',as they called it, took place in the montains where they will stay til such time as our heroes Fidel and Raul Castro, together with their comrade-in-arms Che Guevara, march on Havana and overturns them corrupt band o' crooks they calls the govanment of Cuba.'

Ernesto read it again. Where did Juan get this information? The Cuban press had been censored for months, so it could only have come from one source, the Urania that docked in Cadiz every month. He thought of the old sailor with his twin daughters, and wondered what had been their fate.

The Chronicle report was more defensive.

SAD DAY FOR CUBA

A group of upstart rebels have captured government soldiers. But there is still much support for our friend and colleague Fulencio Batista and negotiations with the Americans are planned for early September. Then, with US aid, the Cuban Government will quash this amateur insurgency once and for all.

Ernesto allowed himself a little optimism. Of course, if *The Chronicle* was right there would be no change but if *The Monkey* was right then Batista and his cronies would be overturned, the Mafia would leave the island and he could return. He decided to study the papers carefully for signs of revolution, musing that such an event might not be good for his country, but it would certainly be good for him.

Or would it? All this time he'd been dreaming, imagining, hoping for a chance to return to his homeland but what about Belle? Did she still love him? And did he still love *her*? For two years he'd carried her memory, as smooth and glossy as a natural pearl. But recently it had been replaced by the sharp-cut crystal that was Beatriz. How could he love two women at the same time? Or did he? Perhaps Beatriz was nothing but a passing phase because he was lonely. And what about Belle? What had she been up to in the years since he'd been gone? Perhaps she'd gone off with someone else. Perhaps even someone from the Mafia. He shook his head. Belle would never do that, would she? There was so much to think about. So much he didn't know.

For his next performance Ernesto wanted a dash of Cuban colour and the gentlemen's outfitter was having a sale. He found the man sorting the rails at the back of the shop.

'You again?'

Ernesto shook his head, annoyed at how this man seemed to confound him.

'Do you have trousers?' he asked almost in a whimper.

'Of course I have trousers,' the man waved a hand half-heartedly towards a rack of clothing as drab as his hats. Ernesto studied the greys and blues, and the assortment of indistinguishable styles.

'Do you have anything more colourful?'

'What d'you want colour for?'

Ernesto selected the trousers he wanted and sighed. Why couldn't the man be civil?

The door opened. A customer entered. Ernesto heard the shopkeeper say, 'how delightful to see you,' as he bowed his head almost to the floor.

'I need a blazer for the festival, something discreet,' the customer said trailing his hand indifferently over a rail of jackets as if any one of them would do. Ernesto noticed he was already wearing a similar jacket with several buttons on the sleeve that ran down to a brilliant white cuff. Ah! The outstretched arm that leans over and closes the door of the K6. The gold cufflinks that glint in the sun. Don Anselmo; the man whom he'd offended by asking questions about his family, the man who paid his wages. Ernesto took cover amongst the rails and studied the broad shoulders, the oiled hair and the immobile features on Don Anselmo's big round face. He looked so stern. But how freckled was the hand, and how wrinkled was the wrist. Then it dawned on him. Francisco's father was fifty or so, not young like a father should be.

He knew he was staring so he turned away but Don Anselmo had noticed.

'Ernesto, is that you?' he said already extending his hand. Ernesto shook it as firmly as he could, mostly to stop himself from trembling. It felt stronger than his would ever be.

'Err yes, Don Anselmo.'

'So we finally meet,' he said with no hint of the cruelty that may have sent Paco to his death.

'Pleased to meet you, sir.'

'Likewise. You've made quite an impression on my boy.'

The shopkeeper interrupted. 'You know this man?'

'Yes of course. He teaches my son.'

'Well if you come this way Don Anselmo, I will show you our latest blazers,' he said, steering the man across the room. Ernesto winced, feeling snubbed, not by Don Anselmo as expected, but by the rude little man who owned the shop, so he left without making his purchase.

At the end of Francisco's next lesson, Ernesto accompanied him downstairs to the K6 where Beatriz was sitting inside. Her hair was damp and clinging to her head but she made no attempt to adjust it. Francisco jumped in and was about to close the door when Ernesto leaned in with an excuse to make contact.

'I met your boss the other day.'

'Yes I know, in the gentlemen's outfitters I understand,' she said. 'I assume you were buying an outfit for that concert you don't want me to come to.' She said it so coolly he started to panic. Was she still suspicious? Could she see straight through him? Carlos spoke up and it was obvious he'd received instructions from Manuel.

'I will accompany Senorita Beatriz to the concert,' he said in a matter of fact tone. 'I will make sure she enjoys herself and has everything she needs.'

'Good idea,' Ernesto replied, grateful for the intervention. But even as he said it he was already thinking. What if she enjoys Carlos' company more than his? After all he was handsome and much younger than him. But perhaps that was a good thing. Events were taking place in Cuba. There was a light at the end of the tunnel and he didn't want it extinguished by developments here. He needed to escape and get back home. Yes, that's it he thought as he climbed back up the stairs. I need to get back home. But would Belle still have him? Would she still want him after all he had done?

That night another watching dream came tumbling in. He was high above a stage, standing on the lighting tower. Below, Belle emerged through a gap in a curtain that yielded to her movements as if she were air. She moved around the stage like the breeze, wafting this way and that and never once did she look up. He tried to attract her attention but she curled and spiralled like smoke in the darkness and each time he reached out she floated away. He deserved this rejection of course, him with his longing for another woman. How could she love him after that? He tried to keep her image in his thinking, but dreams have other plans. A spotlight ran through the audience and all he could see were accusing faces, Manuel, Carlos, Juan and Don Anselmo. Each moved smoothly across his mind as if swimming through oil. 'You are watching us but we are watching you,' they seemed to say. Then Paco appeared. Had they sent his old friend to pull him down too?

At four o'clock he woke sweating, his thoughts prickly with unfinished sleep. Perhaps going back home was a bad idea. If Manuel found out he was leaving he might try to stop him, because he knew too much about the Monkeys and their ringleader to let him go. And leaving would not be easy to conceal, especially if he was on the run. So what was he to do? It seemed there was unfinished business here and unfinished business there too, and whatever he did required a level of courage he didn't possess. He thought of Paco and how brave he'd been, seizing the moment in trying to shoot the General. What an extraordinary thing to do! Yet Paco had been in the right place at the right time, taking advantage of that fleeting moment when Franco had come to town, an instant that could have changed history, a moment to confront one's true self. Could he ever be like Paco, seizing that opportunity? And when that moment came, wherever, whenever and whatever that might be, would he even recognise its importance? And then would he be bold enough to act? 'Yes' he said to both questions. 'I would!' But vows, made before dawn, are easily forgotten in the morning, so, just like the elusive, silken image of Belle; the rash promise he'd made in the sweat-soaked dreams of the night before, quickly fell away.

When Francisco came he was tearful.

'I don't want to play today,' he said, throwing himself on Ernesto's bed.

'What's up, little man?'

'My father is cross with me.'

'Surely not. What did you do?'

'I asked him about my mother again. I know I shouldn't but I did.'

Ernesto froze, remembering Don Anselmo's letter, his stern round face and that fierce handshake. How should he respond now that he was forbidden to ask? He took a step towards Francisco who was looking lost, head down quivering with emotion. Oh how Ernesto wanted to help him but then he remembered the letter. *What happens in our family is no concern of yours.* What was he to do? He settled for something inoffensive.

'I understand,' he said without conviction.

'No you don't,' Francisco snapped. 'Nobody does. They never talk about my mother. Everyone tells me not to ask. But I *want* to know. I want to know all about her, even how she died. I know it was my fault but I just want to know how.' He threw himself across the bed and buried his head in the counterpane, presumably to hide his tears. Ernesto wanted to embrace him, tell him he wasn't responsible for their mother's death, and hold him tight until his sobbing had subsided. At least he should let the boy talk about his mother in order to ease his pain? But he knew it was impossible. He would lose his job if he allowed that to happen and Beatriz would never speak to him again. Instead he put the boy's trombone on the table, went to the kitchen and made him a cup of hot chocolate.

'Here,' he said, placing the steaming cup on the table. Francisco took it in his trembling hands and bent towards it, allowing the steam to mingle with his tears. For several minutes Francisco didn't look up and Ernesto didn't look down. Instead he waited for the clipped rise and fall of the boy's sobbing to ease, whilst their unspoken conversation sat heavy in the room, Francisco silently asking for his tutor's help and Ernesto terrified to give it. He shook his head. What should he do? *No concern of yours,* the letter had said, and Don Anselmo was right. Why should he stick his nose into other people's business? But the boy was starved of love and affection, the boy was sad. Then, drawn from the back of his mind, Ernesto remembered the questions he'd asked himself just before dawn. Firstly would he recognise a moment of truth when it arrived? And secondly, would he be brave enough to act? And his answers to both had been yes. Ernesto looked down at Francisco. Surely this was his moment, his stand-alone opportunity to do something right? But there would be repercussions. If he asked questions it would trigger more excitement from the boy. At last someone was listening. At last someone was on his side. And then what? With Ernesto's apparent endorsement, Francisco was bound to pursue more questions with his father, and this intrusion could cost him his job. And if that happened he could no longer pay for his escape, and he could no longer spy for the Monkeys. Perhaps Don Anselmo would get suspicious too. He seemed so defensive about his son that anything could happen. But then he looked towards Francisco quietly sipping his drink. The boy needed answers, the boy needed *him*. Nothing mattered more than that. Courage was required, and suddenly it felt mighty. He sighed, surrendering to the full consequences of the words he was about to speak. They came softly from his mouth like slowly melting butter, as if expressing them louder and faster, might turn rancid his resolve.

'Tell me. What *do* you know about her?'

Francisco looked up sharply; his eyes shining with a mixture of leftover tears and newfound excitement. He sat upright, put down his cup and wiped his eyes, eager to tell.

'I know she was pretty. There's a painting in the hall.'

'Well that's a start.'

'It's a portrait and in the background there's a church.'

'You mean a real place?'

He nodded eagerly. 'With an inscription.'

'What does it say?'

'It's the date when it was built – 1923 I think.'

'So not an ancient place then?'

'No. It looks clean and almost new.'

'I see,' Ernesto said although he didn't know how this could help. He was still feeling nervous, so he whispered again. 'Francisco, please don't tell you father what I've asked you. This is our secret.' The boy nodded, already reaching for his trombone case.

'I'm ready to play now.'

The moon was up, bright light pouring through the window. A cloak of sleep had robbed him of reason and his unconscious mind was incubating the half-sown seeds of the day before. It was

163

four o'clock when it came to him. 'I've heard that date before,' he declared. '*There was a bakery, a bar and a church.*' Those were the words Jorge had used to describe his village and the date on the church, 1923. If this wasn't the same building then either Francisco was mistaken or it was a coincidence beyond comprehension. He sat up with a grin as wide as his face and his words burst out.

'The painting in Francisco's hall - its Sauce del Valle!' And the laugh that issued from his lips sounded like that of a madman. 'I'm right, I know I am,' he told the room and the room seemed to acquiesce.

He hadn't seen Jorge for days. Now though, he went straight to his hall of residence and banged on his door. 'Let me in. It's important.' Inside was dark except for a small lamp whose light fell on a desk full of loose papers. 'God it's stuffy in here,' he said, eager to tell Jorge his theory. But Jorge was excited too.

'I've been up all night going over these.'

'What are they?' Ernesto leant over and saw a pile of handwritten papers.

'They're lists of people executed without trial. But these documents are unofficial. If anyone in authority finds them, we're done.'

'Where did you get them?'

'There's a splinter group of us Monkeys hiding up in the mountains. They're compiling an archive, first-hand accounts, that sort of thing.'

'I see,' Ernesto said, but couldn't quite picture it.'

'You've no idea, Nesto. After their victory the fascists had no mercy, no desire for reconciliation - all those rebels just taken out and shot.' Jorge threw himself into a chair. He looked exhausted. Ernesto sat on the bed to give himself time to think. Poor Jorge immersed in these atrocities as if sinking in quicksand. Perhaps now wasn't the time to divulge what Francisco had just told him. But Jorge asked, 'Why are you here? And what's so urgent that you came to see me in my digs?' Ernesto produced a bottle of rum from his pocket and placed it on the table. 'Let's have a drink first, and then I'll tell you something you won't believe. '

18. Fraud

Ernesto returned to the shop.

'I've come back for those trousers,' he said.

The shopkeeper yanked them from the rail and stuffed them in a bag 'You're that trombone player then?' he said

'Yes I play trombone.'

'So are you playing next week at the Grape festival?'

'Yes, but how did you know?'

'Thought so,' he said, ignoring Ernesto's question.

Performance day arrived and Manuel was looking serious as he got the band together on stage before opening the doors.

'It won't be easy dealing with our special visitor. Smile, be courteous, swear as much as you like. But for god's sake, don't say, "in the name of the Republic" Ernesto winced. It was his fault that Beatriz was coming and they all knew it. 'And we'll have to cut *Guantanamera*, it's far too mutinous.' Ernesto could see that Manuel was worried. For years he'd managed to keep this place a secret, away from prying eyes, and now *she* was coming. The enemy was entering his den and there was a chance Beatriz would see through the charade of a family show and recognise some of the audience for the subversives they were.

From a chink in the bodega door, Ernesto watched people gathering in the narrow street, fanning furiously to agitate the air, where the heat lingered as heavy as his guilt. Inside, Ernesto retreated to the stage. Manuel checked his watch again. Someone opened the doors and the smell of heat and sweat surged in creating a cocktail of odours that made Ernesto feel sick. Dolores was first, dressed in black and accompanied by five other women dressed the same.

'Why so many widows? Ernesto whispered.

Pedro looked at him in disbelief. 'Do you know nothing about our history, Cubano?' Ernesto cringed. His question had been foolish. Dolores positioned herself at the door, checking that everyone had followed her instructions. But there was no need. Best dresses, polished shoes, fans fluttering, older women wearing their hair bouffant style and younger ones with ponytails or French buns. Young men had flicked and twisted their hair into extravagant quiffs and older ones had smoothed theirs down with oil. Everyone had made an effort. A group of men strolled in without women. Ernesto recognised them, remembering how they'd been introduced to him at the last concert, but he'd taken no notice, being distracted, thinking of *her*.

'Who are they?' Ernesto asked.

'They work at the distillery,' Pedro explained. 'First to sign up to Manuel's syndicate. They have a bit of a reputation.'

'For what?'

'Oh you know, got an opinion about everything.' Ernesto watched as Manuel patted each man on the back, congratulating them for their appearance, as they headed for the bar. The hall filled, but two reserved seats at the front remained empty. Ernesto scanned the room. Where was she? Manuel walked on stage.

168

'Welcome and might I say how smart you all look tonight?' Someone cheered and Ernesto felt a sting of shame, knowing how much effort they'd made to conceal his folly. But where was Beatriz? Maybe, like before, she wouldn't come. Perhaps all this subterfuge was unnecessary. He looked over their heads. Had she chosen to sit at the back? But instead he saw the shopkeeper from the gentlemen's outfitters sitting with his arms folded across his chest. What was he doing here? Then, to his relief, Carlos walked in with Beatriz on his arm, leading her through the narrow aisle to their seats on the front row where she slipped off her coat, revealing the same skin-coloured dress she'd worn when they'd met in the bar. Still no curves, Ernesto observed, but it made no difference. She was glorious and this time she was here. 'Ah, Senorita Beatriz,' Manuel said loudly so that everyone would know who she was. Unnecessary, Ernesto thought. How could there be any doubt? 'Welcome to our little gathering.' He bowed and Ernesto wondered if this little charade was as much castigation directed towards him, as it was a welcome for this blonde stranger. The crowd murmured their hellos and when Beatriz turned around to look behind her, everyone was smiling.

Ernesto came to the front of the stage and adjusted the microphone. She was just below him now, looking beautiful with her bright red lipstick and elegant clothes. She gave him a tiny smile, just enough to make him thrill. They took a bow. The show went perfectly, performing the same songs as in their winter show and one extra piece that Ernesto had chosen especially for her. Pedro came forward to announce it. Immediately his cheeks grew wide and his sideburns twitched as he grinned and whispered into the microphone.

'This is for all you frustrated lover-boys waiting for your woman to consent,' he said. Then he paused for effect, leaning across to the crowd and winking. 'It's called *Perhaps, Perhaps, Perhaps.*' The women tittered. The men grunted. He began to sing. Ernesto kept his eyes on Beatriz, but she had her head down, sitting quite still. Didn't she realise he'd chosen this song especially for her? Was she not listening to the words? Oh how he wanted her to understand the message he was sending. That he adored her and when would she accept the love he was so keen to give? When would she say yes? Oh Beatriz, please look up. But still she didn't move. Pedro crooned like Nat King Cole, and the audience sang too. *'Perhaps, Perhaps, Perhaps.'* But not her. Sing Beatriz, please! Finally she raised her head and Ernesto's stomach lurched. Beatriz was looking up at him, but she wasn't smiling. He sang loudly to encourage her. Why wasn't she joining in? She knows I want her to and he couldn't bear it because now her lips were pressed firmly together and her arms were folded tight against her chest. She dropped her head making it clear she wasn't going to participate. She wasn't going to be part of his plan. How could she be so cruel? How could she hurt his feelings like this? Then he gasped. There was something on the crown of Beatriz's head, a division in her blonde hair, a shadowy line running from front to back. He leaned in closer and frowned because he was looking at the dark roots of her natural hair. He felt his jaw drop in realisation that Beatriz wasn't a blonde. She was a brunette just like any other Spanish female. Pedro sang but Ernesto couldn't hear him. The woman he thought was a golden-haired goddess was a lie, a falsehood, a stealer of dreams. He grimaced, angry with himself for not seeing through her illusion and took a step away from the microphone. The woman wasn't special. She was just as ordinary as anyone else.

In the interval Ernesto ordered a large glass of rum. He didn't want to talk to her now. Why should he? She'd rejected his feelings and shown herself up as a fraud. Besides, Carlos had bought her a Cinzano and their heads were so close they almost touched. The room was dark. He searched along the rows of seats to find a friendly face. There were husbands and wives talking quietly, widows fluttering fans, men smoking cigarettes but where was the shopkeeper? His seat was empty. The man had vanished. There was a noise behind him as the group of distillery men came out of the toilet laughing. It was obvious they were drunk because in the second half they heckled the songs they disliked and joined in with those they favoured. Manuel played a solo on his guitar and the men praised his virtuosity with exaggerated applause. The concert finished and everyone agreed that it had been a success and left a little happier than when they'd arrived. Except for Ernesto, who'd noticed how Beatriz was clinging onto Carlos as they strolled out through the tall doors. He followed them into the street and watched as they drove away in the K6 leaving him wondering if perhaps the young chauffer and Don Anselmo's assistant had become closer than they should.

The arrests began next evening. First the five distillery men, then after finishing his late shift, Manuel was taken off the street and marched to the police station too. Everyone held their breath. Who had denounced them? It must have been someone from the concert. Ernesto cancelled his lesson with Francisco. He had to think. Was it Beatriz? Was this her doing? Or could it have been Dolores? After all, they say she denounced Paco. But surely it wasn't her? Not after helping to get all those women to the concert. More like she was trying to make amends. So was it the shopkeeper? But he'd only stayed for a while and there was nothing untoward for him to observe. Everyone had been on their best behaviour. No one had spoken out of turn, or sung the *Internationale*. The more Ernesto thought about it, the more he decided it had to be her. It had to be Beatriz with her bleach-blonde trickery; after all she was Don Anselmo's spy. The words buzzed in his head like a dying fly. Even if she was the one who had denounced them, they would all blame *him*. After all it was *he* who had brought her into their safe and private location. His fault. Him.

It was late but he hurried to Jorge's student residence and found him in his darkened room still studying his documents.

'It's my fault,' Ernesto said sinking into a chair. 'I made Beatriz suspicious and now she's seen through our charade and told the authorities.'

'Never mind that now. Look what I've just been given.' He showed Ernesto another file. Inside, the pages were yellowed with age and written by the same unpractised hand as the ones he'd seen before. Jorge was grinning with expectation.

'What is it?'

'It's a list of people killed during the war.'

'I can't read that now,' Ernesto said, still distracted.

'Look, Nesto. Look at the location!' Running along the top of the page Ernesto read; Location - Sauce del Valle - date 31st of October 1936. 'See? It's the day the planes came.'

They stayed up most of the night. The light was dim, the writing almost illegible but eventually they found what they were looking for. First the entry for the death of Jorge's grandfather; Alfonso Garcia, age 53, carbon maker, then his grandmother, Amparo Roman, age 54, seamstress, followed by Jorge's mother Julia Martinez, age 28, basket maker. Then there was silence whilst Jorge traced his hand down to the last name on the list - the last man standing – his father. He dropped his head and handed the page to Ernesto.

'You read it, Nesto. I can't. '

Ernesto took the paper from Jorge's quivering hand. Then, in as calm a voice as he could muster, he read the entry.

Alfredo Garcia, age 34, Regional administrator.'

When he looked over, Jorge was crying.

19. A baby's rattle.

Francisco seemed cheerful.

'It's my eleventh birthday and father says I can have a party.'

'That's good,' Ernesto said. If only he could tell Francisco about the possible connection between his mother's portrait and the church in Sauce del Valle. What a wonderful birthday present that would be. But he couldn't stain the boy's innocence with such horrific deeds from the past. Besides, those documents came from some hideout in the mountains. Telling Francisco would expose the trusted rebels who passed these documents to Jorge and then they would all be dead. He looked over affectionately at the boy raising the mouthpiece to his lips. One day, he told himself, one day everything will become clear.

Towards the end of the lesson Ernesto gazed out of the window, knowing that Carlos would be coming to collect the boy. Despite his disappointment at the concert, his fascination with Beatriz had not diminished. Yes, he hated her now, but he adored her too. Beatriz had fooled him but wasn't that part of her mystery? Wasn't being different part of her charm? He shook his head in confusion. As usual he wasn't sure what to think, except that he'd hated seeing Carlos and Beatriz together like that. He went downstairs with Francisco. Carlos was leaning against the bonnet of the K6 looking pleased about something. Ernesto daren't ask him what. He assumed it was about Beatriz, so he made a different enquiry instead.

'Have you heard anything about the men?'

'Not yet. But someone must have denounced them.'

'Perhaps it was Beatriz,' Ernesto said hoping to steer the conversation his way.

'Not so sure about that.'

'What do you mean?'

'Well she didn't seem interested in politics.'

'No?'

'She talked about herself mostly, things I hadn't a clue about.'

'What do you mean'?

'Well for a start she was married.'

'Married?'

'Yes, but widowed now. Her husband was killed in the war.' Ernesto hadn't imagined her in bed with a man. His dreams of her were more unworldly, as if she were some angel sent from heaven. He kept calm.

'Which side did her husband fight on?'

'The *other* side of course, in Don Anselmo's battalion in Morocco where Franco got all his medals. You see, they're all in this together.'

'So she's known Don Anselmo a long time?'

'Before she got the job as his assistant.'

'It's true then, she *is* a spy, so it *must* be her that denounced Manuel.'

'Not necessarily, Nesto. She seemed a bit of a lost soul to me.' Ernesto could see that Carlos was smitten.

174

'She's too old for you Carlos. Get yourself a younger woman,' he countered before he could stop himself.

'She's not interested in me or anyone else as far as I can see.'

Ernesto went back upstairs, relieved that Carlos was not a rival for his romantic aspirations. But still in love with her dead husband! Surely, for him this was worse?

By evening all the arrested men had been charged and everyone was asking the same question. Who had denounced them?

'People are saying it was you,' Juan said when Ernesto bought his newspapers

'It wasn't me. I would never tell on my friends.'

Juan nodded. 'I know you wouldn't. It's most likely that Beatriz woman. I swear it was her who sent those men round to wreck my shop last year.' Ernesto didn't want it to be her, but he didn't want to be accused either.

Next morning Ernesto was awoken by Jorge banging on his door.

'Get up man. Let's go to the bar. We've got work to do.'

Coffee steamed between them as Jorge whispered his plan.

'I've decided to go to Sauce del Valle to see for myself where my father died.'

'Good idea,' Ernesto agreed and his mind was racing. Perhaps he could go too, and see the church Francisco had mentioned.

'Come with me, Nesto,' Jorge said and Ernesto grinned.

'Of course,' he said. This time there would be no hesitation. This time he would not let Jorge down. 'And we can search for the church in the portrait too?'

'Exactly. A double investigation. You and me on an adventure.'

'And perhaps Carlos too?'

'Well he's the one with the car, so why not?'

It wasn't quite dawn when they left the city. Carlos steered the car south, before turning east into the countryside, flicking the wipers to keep off a deluge of morning rain. They passed old settlements, where grazing horses appeared like watery visions through the rain-run windows, and open landscapes were strewn with the sodden stubble of harvested wheat. Every now and then Ernesto noticed gated driveways leading to grand houses set back from the road, reminding him of the Dominguez estate. He wondered again how Paco had really met his death and if Manuel had been taken there too. Then abruptly, the sun rose over the fields and shone directly into Carlos' eyes.

'Let's stop and have breakfast,' he suggested and turned off the road onto a single track with no road signs and no indication of any settlements.

'Where are we going?' Ernesto asked.

'Not much further,' Carlos replied.

Eventually they arrived at a hollow surrounded by stark scrubland, making it look like a crater on the moon. Set low within this landscape was a modest single storey building with nothing to indicate the name of the tavern, nor proprietor's name written above the door. It was an anonymous building in the middle of nowhere.

'How did you find this place?' Ernesto asked, thinking no one would find it from the road.

'Came across it in my travels,' Carlos said lightly but Ernesto sensed the lie, and when the owner came over like an old friend and put his arm on Carlos' shoulder, Ernesto knew he was right.

'You seem to know the terrain round here,' Jorge mumbled

through a mouthful of sandwich.

'Don Anselmo lets me use the K6 whenever I want,' Carlos replied evading further explanation, and as the two men continued to make small talk, Ernesto pondered his next move.

He interrupted. 'Carlos, do you ever go inside Don Anselmo's house?'

'No. I wait in the car.'

'So you've never seen inside?'

'Never. Why?'

'So you've never seen a portrait in there?'

'No. I told you.'

Ernesto gave up. Carlos and Jorge weren't interested in his portrait. They were getting to know each other and this gave him time to sit back and observe his companions. Whom could he rely on most? The loyal, athletic Carlos, always ready for action, or the slightly older, intellectual, Jorge, already wearing glasses from reading all those law books in his dimly-lit room? Either way he felt a bloom of love for both of them, and raised his cup in the air.

'Here's to us.'

'Here's to you, Cubano.'

'It's good to be with friends,' he said.

Back on the road, the flatness of wheat plains gave way to rising hills densely planted with cork trees and separated by rich green fields each containing a single bull. The rain had stopped, and the sun was burning off the puddles forcing an opaque mist to rise around them. It reminded Ernesto of early mornings on the cane fields in Cuba. Not that he was a country man. The city was where his heart lay, yet here he was, riding through a rural mist with his new friends, as if it were a dream, and he smiled with the pleasure of it all. Carlos threw the car into second gear and it rose easily to the brow of a hill where they stopped to take in the view. The landscape stretched far into the distance, making the cork trees lose their luscious green tones and merge into the blue-grey mist as if floating on air. Ernesto smiled again. There was a wonder to this place that he was beginning to enjoy.

'Look,' Jorge said, pointing south. 'There's the Atlantic Ocean and further out is Africa.' Ernesto fixed on the thin, grey mass in the distance where the land seemed so thin and insubstantial, stretched out like a single note drawn on the bow of a violin. Yet a whole continent lay within that narrow arc, filled with mountains, deserts, savannahs, cities, and ancient settlements. He sighed, thinking of Cuba; so distant, so far, yet so near in his heart. Carlos pulled at the gears and they set off again, dragging Ernesto out from his daydream.

Jorge fell asleep in the back and Ernesto whispered to Carlos, 'You know why we're making this journey don't you?'

'Something to do with Jorge's past, but he won't tell me what.'

'Jorge is looking for his family's grave but I'm looking for something too - a church in the village. And when I find it, I'll need your help.'

The K6 moved on across a smooth open plain full of wondrous light that bounced off the ocean below. Then they turned inland where the light lost its grandeur as they made their descent into a valley. Jorge stirred, perhaps sensing the gear change in the engine, the downward slope, the roll back home. He sat up, searching for familiar landmarks. This was his territory.

'Not long,' Jorge said, and Ernesto noticed that his voice was laced with emotion. Was it excitement at going back home? Or fear at reaching a place that had destroyed his childhood? Soon they were at a junction.

'Which way?' Carlos asked.

'My parents are buried somewhere down there,' Jorge said pointing right, towards a large old house and a row of willows. 'Or we can go left to the village.'

'No, my friend. First we visit your family.' Carlos turned the K6 onto an old track. Weeds had flourished on both sides, and large stones, washed out from the fields, were resting in the mud, making progress slow.

'Do you know where?' Ernesto asked.

'After twenty years it's hard to remember.'

'So you've not been here since?'

'Neither Paco nor I could face it.'

They stopped. Jorge got out, stretching his legs and looking about to get his bearings. 'Down there in that field,' he said, pointing to the willows.

They walked towards the row of trees, the ground feeling softer at each stride. The two younger men jumped over a ditch into the field, but Ernesto stayed at the edge, out of his depth in this rural setting. Instead he watched them carefully navigate the mud and scan the field to identify anything unusual. Jorge approached the willow trees where low-hanging branches trailed in a slow-running stream. Close by was a long narrow channel in the soil that, at first sight, looked like any natural undulation. But within its long shape, stinging nettles grew in abundance; a sure sign that something organic had been present below. Then, as if to remove any doubts, Carlos shouted,

'Look! There, on the edge! 'At the far end of the channel was a small wooden cross pressed into the ground.

Jorge fell to his knees 'This is it,' he said.

Ernesto stepped over the ditch to join them, gently pressing his foot to the soil, imagining the bodies that lay beneath him, with all remnants of hope buried alongside them. The greenery was clustered in the dip and he realised that for twenty years this earth had been nurturing a colony of nettles that had grown and flourished, then died and replenished, year on year, time after time, like the turbulent memories of an unquiet widow. Ernesto helped Jorge to his feet. He was covered in mud.

'Let's see if we can find somewhere to clean you up,' he said. They walked up through raggedy pines to a house they'd seen earlier. It was positioned in the centre of a wide gravelled drive and the front door had been warped by the sun.

'There's no bell or knocker,' Ernesto said, unsure what to do next.

'No need,' Carlos said kicking it open with his boot. They stepped into a courtyard where brambles grew out of every wall and where, between the stone slabs, weeds had formed into a chequered lawn with tufts as high as their knees. The place had been abandoned years ago. They pulled up water from a central well and rinsed their boots in the scullery sink. Carlos was excited. 'Come on, let's explore,' he said, leaping up the staircase causing a cloud of dust. All the rooms had been stripped of furniture, fireplaces ripped from the walls.

'Looters,' Jorge said, looking at the damage.

Carlos agreed. 'Bloody fascists,' he said spitting on the floor.

But Jorge shook his head. 'No Carlos, more likely envious Republicans that ravaged this place before getting caught.'

'No it couldn't have been us. We didn't do that sort of thing,' Carlos said, and Ernesto could see he was annoyed at the challenge to his way of thinking.

How would you know? You were only a baby when all this happened.' Jorge retorted. 'Look, we may have been on the side of the angels but there were devils amongst us too.' He slapped Carlos on the back as if to show him no ill-will but Carlos shook his head and it seemed to Ernesto that he was too blind or naïve to see that war had heroes and villains on both sides. Then he laughed to himself because, perhaps just for once, his inability to take sides was the right approach. Perhaps this time, sitting on the fence made sense. But in his heart he knew that this was only partially true. Looting was one thing but the outright cruelty of the fascists; their pleasure in inflicting suffering was another, and he was beginning to realise that here in his chosen country of exile, cruelty was rife. They moved from room to room where plaster cornices too high for grasping hands were still gloriously intact, and thick brocade curtains still bloomed at the windows. He reached out to touch one but it fell apart in his hands giving off a cloud of old dust. Jorge patted Ernesto on the back. 'Some things cannot endure Nesto, no matter how much you want them to.' Ernesto nodded, recognising in Jorge's voice, the six-year-old boy whose life had been shattered so close to where they now stood. They went up the final flight of stairs to the servants' rooms in the attic, where spaces were cramped and small windows let in little light.

'Those poor servants, how were they supposed to keep warm up here?' Carlos said with a catch in his throat.

Somewhere along the corridor Jorge called out, 'Look what I've found.' He shook a small tin box and the contents rattled. 'I found it inside a cupboard on a top shelf, as if the owner didn't want anyone to find it.' He put it in his pocket.

Carlos was impatient. 'It's getting late. We have to get back so I have time to wash the car before Don Anselmo sees the state it's in. Let's go to the village.'

There was no village. According to the map, it should have been located two kilometres uphill, but there were no roads – only overgrown tracks, and no houses, just rotting timber beams lodged between the weeds and masonry lying in the tufted grass, like fractured tombstones representing the dead. Jorge sighed. His once thriving settlement had, like half-forgotten memories, blended into the landscape and merged with the soil.

'It's all so different. I can't get my bearings,' he said, eyes wild, ransacking his childhood mind for a map of his past.

Carlos had wandered off, but now he was calling. 'Here! Come and see.' They followed him into a small clearing. In the centre stood a large roofless building, its cruciform foundations unmistakeable.

'It's a church,' Carlos announced, pleased with himself. 'Look here's the nave and there's the transept.'

'It's *the* church,' Jorge said, his eyes flashing with recognition. 'This is where they kept my mother and me, and then my father.' Once again Jorge sank to his knees and the others made no attempt to comfort him. What could they do in the face of such brutal memories? Ernesto strode to the front where the façade of the church was almost intact, and with each stride he felt increasingly certain of what he was going to find. He turned the corner and squinted into the sun. There it was - just below the ruins of the bell tower - an inscription that told no lie. *'Constructed by the men of this village 1923,'* the same words Jorge had used about his village and the same date Francisco had described on his mother's portrait that hung in Don Anselmo's hall.

On the way back, Ernesto would not let it rest.

'Carlos, you have to get into Francisco's house.'

'I know. You've already told me that.'

'I have to be sure you'll do it.'

'I said I would, didn't I?'

'You need to see that portrait, make sure the boy was right.'

'Alright I get it. But how can I get into the house in the first place?'

'I don't know, but you'll work it out.'

On their return they headed for the bar. There was news. The distillery men had been released.

'How come?' Carlos asked the barman.

'Well first they were charged with unlawful assembly.'

'What's that?

'It's when groups of three or more people meet. According to the government this automatically means they're planning a mutiny'. The barman laughed at his own sarcasm and continued. 'But their lawyers argued that the meeting room was a private establishment, and the judge must have agreed 'cos he let them off.'

'So it wasn't unlawful after all,' Ernesto said.

Jorge nodded. 'Exactly. It's only illegal out on the street.'

'But someone didn't know that and went to the police?'

'Seems that way, whoever he was.'

'*He*?' Ernesto queried.

'Yes. The report says they were in the men's toilets when they met.'

'So it couldn't have been Dolores, not in the gent's,' Jorge said.

'Nor Beatriz either,' Ernesto added with relief.

The tin box sat on the table between them. 'Aren't you going to open it?' Carlos said turning the tin this way and that, and rattling it for effect.

Jorge shook his head. 'Not yet. I'm not ready,'

Ernesto frowned. Was there a reason for this hesitation? Was confronting the artefacts of the past so difficult, even after all these years? Poor Jorge. Facing the truth was an uncomfortable business as he well knew. Carlos started drumming his fingers.

'Come on, man! There could be all sorts in there,' he said but Jorge kept silent and seemed to be scrutinising the table. Carlos sighed. 'I've had enough of this,' he declared grabbing the tin box and forcing it open. A handful of small items spilled onto the table; a baby's rattle, a cigarette packet, a pipe and hairpins and a brooch of the most ordinary kind, not luxurious items that a lady of the house might wear. 'Is that it?' he said, flicking through them. 'Not much is it?'

But Jorge could only just manage to speak. 'You're too young to understand,' he said, holding the baby's rattle gently in his hands and touching the teeth marks clustered on its edge.

Carlos frowned and the lines across his forehead signalled incomprehension. 'What are you on about? I don't get it.'

'They're mementoes, Carlos. Things left behind by people who....'

'Who what?' He still looked bewildered.

'People who were executed, my friend.' Then he repeated it slowly so that Carlos would understand. 'Things left behind by those poor souls who were taken down to that field then shot.'

20. A spy?

Beatriz's bicycle clattered over the cobbles. Ernesto ran to the window. 'Still here my love,' he called out as if she could hear him from below. How thrilled he was to watch her ride down the street, how glorious to observe the way she held her head so high as if she could conquer the world. And how happy he felt in his journey from adoration to anger, then cautious indifference then back to honouring her loveliness. She may have been cool at his concert, but now he understood her rejection. 'Still in love with her dead husband,' Carlos had said. So she definitely wasn't Don Anselmo's mistress as he'd supposed she could be, and she hadn't gone off with Carlos as he'd thought she might, and she hadn't denounced the five men in the gents' toilet as he'd suspected she had. After all his fears and condemnations, his hopes were up. Perhaps he still had a chance to prise her from her dead husband's arms and convince her of his love.

A rush of wind came up the stairwell making Ernesto shiver. He pulled a blanket over his knees and closed his eyes, bored now that Beatriz had passed by. He pictured Jorge in his digs similarly hunched against the cold, going through those old documents or rifling through the contents of an old tin and Carlos sitting in the K6 plotting how to get access to Don Anselmo's house, and

Manuel alone in some cell wondering when they would come for him, when he would die. Guilt crept into Ernesto's bones. He pulled the blanket around his shoulders, but his culpability lingered, gnawing at him like a carcass being picking at by a lion. It was his fault that Beatriz had come to the concert. It was his fault that the shopkeeper had come too, piqued with curiosity about his foreign client. So if that wretched man was the informant then it was his fault that Manuel had been arrested. He got dressed and went across to the bar.

'Give me a whole bottle,' he demanded.

'You sure?' the barman cautioned.

'Of course I'm sure.' He pushed the bottle deep into his pocket.

'Any news about Manuel?' he asked.

'Nothing.' Ernesto said. 'Maybe I should go to the police station and ask.'

'Good idea, but are all your papers in order?'

'Yes. A friend at the Spanish embassy authorised them for me when I told him I wanted to leave Havana. He seemed pleased I was emigrating to his country, and wrote me a decent letter of reference, although I didn't tell him why I wanted to come.'

'So why *did* you come, Cubano?'

'Long story. Another time perhaps. I think I'll go to the station now.'

'Take care then, you never know.'

The station was located opposite San Felipe church, housed in an elegant building that, in another era, could have been the private residence of a high-ranking lawyer or perhaps a government official. He climbed the steps to a raised entrance and pushed at the heavy, ornate wooden door that finally yielded to his efforts. Inside, the floor was an expanse of white marble, scuffed by the

186

passage of policemen's boots and curving down into the hall was a wrought iron staircase grimy with neglect. A policeman sat behind a booth made of cheap pine, its crude yellow varnish glaringly out of place against the gold and white plasterwork of the ceiling. Ernesto took a deep breath and approached.

'I've come to enquire about Manuel Barrosa. Is he here?'

'Who are you?'

'Just a friend. We play music together.'

'Show me your papers.' Ernesto pulled them from his pocket. The policeman flicked through his visa, his Cuban passport and Spanish residence card. He peered at the photograph and checked it against Ernesto's face

'You've grown a beard.'

'Yes. The ladies like it,' he said with a deliberate smirk and the policeman smirked back. It was going well. The man opened the letter written by the embassy and signed by the Spanish consul. He read it aloud and his voice bounced around the vast echoing hall making every word sound important.

I hereby certify that Senor Ernesto Costa, natural of Havana, is a Cuban citizen well known for his excellent contribution to Cuban cultural society. I have no hesitation in recommending him as a person of good, steady character and willingness to comply.

The policemen stamped his visa with the date and handed it back with those last words ringing in Ernesto's ears. *Willingness to comply.* In the past he'd liked that phrase, reading it many times over to satisfy himself of his respectability. Now though, read out in a foreign accent, resonating in this cavernous hallway, it made him sound small and dull and weak, as if he was of no harm to anyone and no challenge to the status quo. He scanned the words again and wondered, is this who I am? Someone so willing to comply that I stand for nothing?

Two constables appeared, one young, one older, who took him through to the back. He was told to sit on a bench in the cloister where he could see several rooms going off. He looked for access to dungeons and listened for the clanking of locks but there were no such signs or sounds, just a series of small rooms around a central courtyard. One door was open and inside, the walls were covered in floral wallpaper, faded at regular intervals where bookshelves used to stand. Was this once a library where the family came to read? Was this their place for discussion and debate? Perhaps they weren't government officials after all. Perhaps they had been intellectuals who opposed the regime. If so, what had happened to them? Where did they go? At the rear of the building someone screamed. Just once, like a single shot from a gun. Christ, what was that? he thought, imagining a woman struck so hard that she'd been silenced. Not Manuel then. It was too high pitched for that. He heard a cough behind him.

'Ernesto Costa?' A small, uniformed man was standing over him, looking like Franco himself with the same moustache and the same combed-back hair. 'I am the Chief Superintendent. What exactly do you want?' Ernesto studied the man. His stature was small and if Ernesto were to stand he would have towered over him. But this didn't make him feel any better. The man was scowling as if whatever Ernesto said would be unacceptable. He stuttered.

'Err… Just here to see my friend, if I can.'

'Well you can't. Political prisoners are not allowed visitors. According to your papers, you are from Cuba.'

'Yes sir.'

'And?'

Ernesto didn't understand the question. 'It's very nice here,' he offered.

The man bristled with annoyance. 'I mean what do you do? Are you working? Are you contributing to our society? Do you pay your taxes? We don't want strangers wandering our streets, living off our charity, getting up to no good.'

'I am a musician and a teacher, sir.'

'Hmmm, so whom do you teach?'

'The son of Don Anselmo. Do you know him?'

'You mean young Francisco?' Ernesto nodded and the superintendent stared into the air then abruptly turned his back, clipped his heels as if on parade and went into his office. There was muffled talk on a telephone and the younger policeman reappeared.

'You're free to go, but don't bother coming back. We don't allow visitors.'

'At least tell me he's alright?' Ernesto said in a more desperate tone than he'd intended. The young policeman looked at him cautiously.

'I'll accompany you to the exit, sir,' he said ushering Ernesto away from the earshot of the superintendent. When they stood outside he whispered, 'he's due in court at twelve tomorrow if that helps.'

Ernesto ran towards home, heart racing at the powerful manner of the superintendent. He turned the corner to the safety of his own street and at the gentlemen's outfitters he stopped to catch his breath. In the window, the same faded colours and the same jaded styles stared back in moribund silence, and as he gazed in, the shopkeeper's face appeared in the window like a disconnected spectre in his own window display. Ernesto shrank back. There was something nasty about that man, something deeply offensive caught up in that big round face. Then he realised he was right.

Who else could have denounced the men in the toilet but another man? And who was the only male stranger in their midst? The man who ran this shop.

When he collected his newspapers, Juan wanted to chat.

'That boy still doing ok?'

'Yes. Why do you ask?'

'Well, like I said, he needs someone to look after him, and you seems to be makin a fine job of it.'

Ernesto remembered how the boy had sobbed into his chest.

'But why do you want to know,' he asked, curious at Juan's interest.

'He's got no mother, that's all' Juan muttered, turning his back to rearrange the newspapers into neater piles and making it clear that their conversation had finished.

Back in his room Ernesto took a mighty swig from the ill-advised bottle and as it ran down his throat like liquid gold he opened *The Chronicle* at the international section.

WITHDRAWAL OF US MILITARY MISSION

The United States government has removed all military support to Batista, therefore opening the door of opportunity to the rebels in the hills. Asked if this now meant that America supported the rebels a spokesman for the US government said "we believe it is typical of Latin youth to be radical and we are confident that when they take over the country they will mature into a full blown democracy."

Ernesto was relieved. He didn't want to return to the chaos of revolution. He preferred the quiet life and the innocent Cuba he'd known before the Mafia spoilt it. So if there was to be change, then please let it be gentle. But *The Monkey* headline was different.

190

UNITED STAYTS GONE. Thay've left Cuba for good and rebels are marching from the Maestro montains towards the capital; a march that will destroy the brootal dictatorship of Fulgencio Batista and creayt a full blown communist state. It wont be long my frends. It wont be long.

Ernesto re-read both articles. Which version was true? Would there be revolution or not? According to *The Chronicle* there would be a natural progression into democracy but if *The Monkey's* version was true, a bloody battle could go on for months. So which one was right? He couldn't decide. He didn't know. He took another swig of rum and closed his eyes wishing it would all go away. Change was his enemy. Change was disturbing and he wanted it to stop. But the doubts kept coming and the rum was making his head swim. He pictured those tiny humming birds that thronged the eucalyptus trees back home. Is that all this was - the harmless flit of a tiny bird in search of pollen, a hum of revolution and nothing else? Or was it the noisy rebellion of a swarm of bees seeking a new home? He'd seen a swarm once, so intense, moving in unison this way and that, clustering urgently and ready to sting whoever challenged their queen, whoever challenged their big idea. And communism *was* a big idea. Was this what the revolution would be like, drastic with casualties? He sighed, unsure what would happen and what he would do about it when it did. Would he stay here in Spain? Or would he go back home?

A loud bang on his door dislodged his thinking. Carlos and Jorge were standing there gasping for breath.

'They've got Dolores,' Carlos said bursting in, 'and if she tells, then it's the end for all of us.' Ernesto shook his head to loosen the rum.

'What do you mean, *all of us*?'

Jorge took over. 'Just that, Nesto. The big prize is Manuel of course, leader of the Maquis in Andalusia, but they'll go after all his associates like you and me and Carlos.'

'Me? Why me?'

'Because you are here, because you are a foreigner and especially because you are Cuban.'

'Why? I don't understand.'

'Isn't your country in the middle of a revolution? Aren't they about to fall to the communists? The very thing Franco's lot detest, the very thing, twenty years ago, they overthrew? Stands to reason they will go after you and think you're a spy.'

'Me a spy?' He took another swig. True, he'd signed up to the Monkeys but so far he hadn't done anything.

Carlos took over, rubbing it in. 'Or at the very least an agitator from a foreign country, come to stir up unrest here, especially since you're friends with Manuel.'

Ernesto frowned. What a fool he'd been. 'I went to the police station today to ask about him,' he said quietly.

'There you go then!' Carlos was almost triumphant. 'And did you see or hear anything when you were there?'

'I heard a scream. It must have been Dolores.'

'Then she's bound to talk,' Carlos said, banging his fist on the table. But Jorge wasn't so sure.

'Depends. She might have denounced her husband but that was out of spite. Besides she made up for all that at the concert.'

Ernesto agreed. 'She followed Manuel's instructions perfectly.'

'Anything else happen at the station? Carlos asked.

'A young policeman told me they're taking Manuel to court tomorrow.'

'What time?'

'Twelve o'clock.'

Carlos tapped his shoes on the bare floorboards. 'We need to do something *now*, before it's too late.'

The sound echoed around the room making it difficult for Ernesto to think.

'But what?' he asked.

'Leave it to me. I'll think of something,' Carlos said.

They sat together for the rest of the evening whilst Ernesto slowly emptied the contents of his bottle, raising his head from time to time to protest,

'I'm not a spy, I'm not.'

Before they left Carlos turned to Ernesto. 'I almost forgot. There's no need to wheedle my way into Don Anselmo's house. I've been invited to Francisco's birthday party, and so have you.'

21. Escape

His head was pounding, stomach lurching. The room was moving. Ernesto felt sick. He hadn't eaten for hours, so he went to the kitchen for food and met Carlos coming up the stairs.

'Come on, you've got to see this.'

'Wait,' he said, stuffing bread in his mouth.

'I told you I'd do something. So come on.' They hurried down the street, Carlos striding and Ernesto stumbling behind. They turned the corner into Main Street where the bells of San Felipe were chiming twelve and large groups of people were marching towards the police station. They joined in with the crowd, striding along in unison with the chiming of the bells. Despite his alcohol-induced headache, there was an orchestrated rhythm to it that pleased Ernesto's musical mind and made him relax. He pushed the final piece of bread in his mouth and Carlos pulled him forward. 'Any minute now,' he whispered as the crowd slowed. The bells stopped. The crowd came to a halt. The square outside the police station was full. As usual Ernesto's height allowed him to see above their heads. The station doors opened. The young policemen he'd seen yesterday stepped out onto the raised entrance and the older one joined him carrying a truncheon. The crowd gasped. Manuel appeared, bigger and heavier than his two jailers. He had a black eye and his hair clung to his forehead as if he'd been doused with water. He was scanning the faces as if searching someone out. People cheered and called 'Manuel, Manuel' as the policemen pulled him down the steps and into the crowd. Ernesto could still see the top of Manuel's head bobbing, wet and dark, through the crowd. But the people were moving too, shoving and calling, surrounding Manuel and his jailers. The older one raised his baton but the younger one held back. Now the crowd were waving their hands above their heads, reminding Ernesto of the white handkerchiefs in the square the day Franco had come to town, everyone standing on tiptoes to see their man. Except this was a different man, a different kind of hero. Someone shouted, 'Manuel Barrosa forever,' before slipping away into the crowd as others raised rebellious fists and Manuel lifted his arms in reply, revealing huge handcuffed hands above his head. Everyone cheered. It was then that Ernesto saw it; a hand in the crowd, holding a pistol. There was a shot into the air. Everyone screamed. The crowd surged forward. There was a scuffle. The older policeman was down. Ernesto searched for Manuel but he'd disappeared. Carlos was grinning. 'Come on,' he said. 'Keep your head down. Don't attract attention.' It took forever to push through the crowd until eventually they were free. 'Walk nice and slow,' Carlos said. But the moment they were out of danger, they ran, bowling past vast distillery doors and tiny local shops, along shaded back streets and into sunny squares. Their footsteps echoed on the cobbles. Ernesto's head was pounding, the booze still circulating in his veins. He couldn't keep up. He leant against a wall. 'Don't stop now,' Carlos shouted, but *he* had slowed down too. They'd arrived in the flamenco district where men in modest doorways sat on low-slung chairs, and the delicious smell of pulpo asado wafted from their kitchens into the street. Ernesto looked around and saw the familiar sign Los Cinco Vientos swinging above his head. An old man pointed to an alleyway. 'Down here,'

Carlos said swerving into the gap and Ernesto followed. It was dark. A disembodied voice spoke through the gloom.

'Upstairs!'

Carlos bounded up a narrow staircase. Ernesto followed, groping his way through the dim light. Out of breath he reached the top where Carlos was already bending over the bulk of a man crouching in the eaves of a tiny attic space. Carlos started unlocking Manuel's handcuffs and they were both grinning like mad men. 'I knew it would work,' Carlos said. 'Now let's get out of here.'

That evening everything had to look normal, everything routine. Carlos returned from wherever he'd taken Manuel and spent the rest of the day cleaning the car. Ernesto and Jorge sat at their usual table on the pavement and ordered their customary drinks. Casually they spoke about the October rains that were about to fall and Jorge described his new professor at the University whilst Ernesto spoke about the boy and his lessons. Eventually, when the bar was noisier, he leaned forward, checking that no one could hear.

'Where have they taken him?'

'I don't know, Jorge said. 'And the fewer people who know the better.'

'It'll be out of town, that's for sure.' There was a pause. Then they looked at each other in recognition, declaring simultaneously, 'The house at Sauce del Valle.' They sat back pleased with themselves for having worked it out.

'Did you find anything else in that tin?'

'Just this.'

Jorge handed him a battered packet of cigarette papers and pulled the top one out with unexpected reverence. Ernesto took the flimsy sheet from him, remembering how Paco used to roll his black tobacco and send plumes of pungent smoke into their communal space. He sighed, holding the delicate paper between his finger and thumb and reading the words written with such a blunt pencil they were almost indecipherable. *My dearest wife, as I die I think of you.* Ernesto's heart fluttered like the paper itself. Here was a stranger's last note to his love, scrawled in the hope that she would read it after his death. He offered it back to Jorge, feeling in that insubstantial paper, the terrifying weight of the past. But Jorge raised his hand.

'No, you keep it. It'll be safer with you.' So Ernesto placed it carefully back in the package and put it in his pocket. They sat in silence until Jorge spoke.

'They'll interview both of us you know.'

'Will they?'

'Bound to, us being friends of Manuel, but we don't know anything, do we?'

'No,' Ernesto answered, worried that he knew far too much, and would be unable to contain it. 'Have you heard anything about Dolores?'

'They let her out. Didn't talk apparently.'

'Perhaps she didn't know anything. She struck me as a simple woman.' But Jorge shook his head.

'No, Nesto, you're wrong. Of course she knew stuff, but she kept her mouth shut, even when they hurt her. So in my eyes she's a hero. It was a shrewd move, Manuel paying for Paco's funeral. It made Dolores see sense. She's learnt her lesson. She's one of us now.' Ernesto winced. How would *he* react to torture? Probably whimper, perhaps even cry, and in his heart he knew he would eventually fold. When they parted Ernesto headed across the road to his room but stopped half way across because outside his block, arms folded across his chest, was the older policeman.

'Come with me, Cubano,' he said grabbing his arm and marching him down the street towards the police station. As they passed the gentlemen's outfitters Ernesto saw the shopkeeper staring over the window display, no doubt gloating at his predicament. Was there something in his hand?

They put him in a room on the far side of the courtyard, perhaps the same room where Dolores had screamed. The walls in this room were papered with faded images of exotic birds and green foliage but, just like in the library where he had been before; there were dark rectangular patches where paintings must once have hung. He imagined the salon full of women sitting, chatting or sewing together by the fireside and he shivered at how the décor, so succulent and rich, had yielded to time and neglect and how its genteel purpose had been forsaken in favour of violence and spite. The superintendent came in and laid his truncheon carefully – significantly, on the table between them.

'Where is he then?' he said without preamble. Under the table, Ernesto squeezed his hands together to prevent them from trembling.

'Who?'

The superintendent leaned forward and scoffed. His moustache twitched like a villain in a melodrama.

'Don't mess with me, Cuban. You know who. *Your* friend, *our* escaped prisoner, Manuel Barrosa that's who.'

'I am afraid I don't know, sir.'

'You were seen in the crowd, so you must know.' Ernesto pressed his fingernails into his palms until they hurt.

'Well, I mean I knew something had happened, of course, but I've no idea where he might be. We just play music together.' The superintendent looked annoyed but then the phone rang and he called the younger policeman in.

'Keep an eye on him while I take this call.'

The young policeman leant against the wall and fixed his gaze on the floor. Ernesto copied him, realising that any glance between them might betray the tip-off given to him last time he was here, or expose the fact that that he was surely the one who had given the key to Carlos to open Manuel's handcuffs. How brave this young policeman must be to operate subversively in this environment. These things were treachery. These things could lead to execution. And when the superintendent returned, Ernesto noticed that, like him, the young policeman was trembling. 'No need to look so nervous, Cuban. Seems you've got friends in high places. You can go but if you hear anything about Barrosa's location you must tell us, otherwise we'll know you're up to no good.' Then he snatched up his truncheon and walked out. Ernesto left too, shoving his hands in his pockets so no one could detect his fear. Inside he felt the cigarette packet with its delicate paper message, written by a captured rebel to his soon-to-be-widowed wife. He sighed in relief that they hadn't searched him, for they would have asked him where he got it and he knew in his heart that he would have told them of the very house where their escaped prisoner was now in hiding.

At midnight Jorge came staggering into his room. Ernesto helped him onto the bed.

'Christ what happened?'

Jorge lifted his shirt to reveal his skin marked with red circles where a truncheon had been shoved into his abdomen. 'I told them I'd been studying in my room when Manuel escaped, but they interrogated me anyway, wanting to know *who* Manuel was, as well as where.'

'So they don't know he's the leader of the Maquis?'

'I don't think they realise,' Jorge said, curling up as best he could and closing his eyes. Ernesto threw a blanket over him, and settled himself in his upright chair trying to encourage sleep. But Ernesto's brain was overactive. *You've got friends in high places,* the superintendent had said and that could only mean one person; Francisco's father. But how did Don Anselmo know he was at the station? Then an image came to him as clear as if he were seeing it now. The shopkeeper of the gentlemen's outfitters watching him being escorted to the station, the man had been holding a telephone. Yes that's it. The wretched man must have called to inform Don Anselmo of his arrest. Ernesto frowned. Secrets everywhere. This city was full of them. How was he meant to keep up? But why had Don Anselmo rescued him? Not once but twice? Surely if he suspected his son's trombone teacher was a rebel he could have had him arrested, put in a very dark cell and thrown away the key. It just didn't make sense. He remembered their encounter at the outfitters too. How graceful Don Anselmo had been, and how friendly he was now, inviting him to Francisco's birthday party. Why would a man of such high standing befriend a stranger like him? Especially one who associated with his political adversaries? None of it made sense. Perhaps tomorrow at Francisco's party, I'll find out, he thought. But then he checked himself. Did he really want to be in the company of Don Anselmo? The man who might have ordered Paco's death? But then again, here was an opportunity to study that painting in the hall, to check that the façade of the church truly was the same as the one they had visited and to confirm the date on it for certain. Then he would be able to reveal some important information to his beloved Francisco.

Next morning Carlos collected Ernesto in the K6. They headed west along wide avenues planted with plane trees casting fulsome shadows over smooth black tarmac that suggested they were in the smarter part of town. A man stepped out into the road wearing the unmistakeable green cape and black shiny cap of the civil guard. Behind him was a road block with two more guards armed with rifles. The hunt for Manuel was getting serious. The guard raised his hand. Carlos slowed almost to a halt but as they neared, the man must have recognised Don Anselmo's car, because he waved them on. Saved yet again, Ernesto thought.

Now each house was set apart by tall walls and wrought iron gates that revealed picturesque gardens with sumptuous flowerbeds and elegant palms. Carlos was jerking nervously at the wheel. Ernesto tried to calm him.

'You did well yesterday, getting that crowd together.'

'I know who to trust, that's all.'

'But how did you get them to act so bravely?'

'They've had enough, Nesto. We're in the second half of the twentieth century and other countries are flourishing while Spain's stuck in the dark ages. We need to move on. Something's got to change and that's the argument I used to get those people together. As you say, they were brave, every one of them.' Carlos was right. So far Ernesto had observed a paralysis that prevented people from speaking out, let alone taking action. He sympathised. Wasn't he like that? Scared to have an opinion, scared to take a stand? But now thanks to the Monkeys there was a charge in the air. Something was stirring like a provocative genie, moving through the city, arousing feelings of hope, and he was beginning to feel it too.

They reached the suburb where Francisco lived.

'I think its best that *you* study the painting rather than me,' Ernesto said. He didn't want to be seen showing an interest in Don Anselmo's family, not after that letter. Carlos turned into a side road and sighed heavily. Ernesto read his mind.

'Don't worry, Carlos, I'm sure Don Anselmo doesn't suspect you of arranging Manuel's breakout.'

202

'I hope not. He's been fine all day, even insisting that I come and pick you up.'

'I don't know why he's being so pleasant to me.'

'Maybe it's a trap.'

22. The Party

They pulled into a driveway where a stone fountain threw up ripples of watery light. Ernesto's stomach dipped. The house was even grander than he was expecting with ornate marble columns framing a wide front door. It felt so overpowering that he wondered how on earth they would get a chance to study the portrait without raising suspicion. Carlos swung the K6 into the back yard where a second fountain was dribbling intermittently into a cracked stone bowl. Ernesto frowned. How grand was the front façade and how humble it was behind. An unsmiling housekeeper appeared and took them into a small salon panelled with dark wood. It smelt musty as if it hadn't been aired properly and the room was so dark and cheerless that it took Ernesto a moment before he realised that their host was sitting there in a high-backed chair reading a newspaper. Don Anselmo put the paper down - *The Chronicle* - Ernesto noticed, stood up and moved towards them with an outstretched hand.

'Good day to you both. Thank you for coming,' he said smiling.

Francisco appeared at the door offering his hand in the same elaborate manner as his father. 'Good day,' he said and Ernesto shook his hand, impressed at the boy's grown-up ways.

Don Anselmo sat back in the chair. 'Francisco wants to show you around, so why don't you take a tour and I will see you later.' Then he picked up *The Chronicle* and resumed reading. They had been dismissed. Ernesto stifled a sigh of relief. They would get a chance to study the portrait after all.

Everywhere were signs of disinterest and neglect. On the first floor, marble statues stood silently on guard in dusty corridors, where the housekeeper had obviously not swept. They entered a salon where medals sat decommissioned under glass and a music room with a grand piano, lid closed, music un-played. Then into an orangery where brown-tinged plants sat starved of water, barely alive. There was another room full of trophies tarnished for want of polish, and under domes of glass, rigid gamebirds were poised for impossible flight. The heads of wild boar jutted from plaques on the wall, their shiny glass eyes belying their sudden death. On the top floor they walked through empty bedrooms draped with brocade, and glimpsed dressing rooms with elaborate bathrooms; one for him and one for her. Except there was no *her*.

'My father had the house built just after the war,' Francisco said, arching his shoulders in the same bombastic manner as his father's. 'They finished it in 1940.' Ernesto nodded. The style was unmistakeably old fashioned with shiny brown tiles on the floor, dark wainscoting on the walls, heavy mahogany furniture in the salons, and tired looking wardrobes in the bedrooms. Even the brightly painted ceramic lamps had turned beige with layers of dust and he wondered if the housekeeper had been instructed not to touch them. Ernesto longed for the colours of Havana with its fancy stucco facades painted the hues of the ocean, or the blush of morning glory and the vivid orange of the cannas that grew in his back yard. Here though, every wall, every floor, and every piece of furniture showed the old-fashioned, conventional taste of its owner and every speck of dust and grime seemed to suggest a residence irreversibly cancelled by time. And beneath these impressions, all

Ernesto could think of was that portrait of a young woman waiting for them in the hall. He already knew that she would be as bright as life itself whereas this house spoke only of death and decay.

Finally they descended the staircase.

'This is the main hall,' Francisco announced and there she was, in a gold frame hung over an unlit hearth, a beauty in a bright blue dress, holding a bouquet of yellow roses. Ernesto beamed. His instincts were right. She may have been dead for years but she was the only lifelike feature in this moribund house. Francisco was standing close to the frame, lovingly studying his mother's face. Had he kept their secret? Had he chosen not to tell his father that Ernesto knew who this beauty was? By his composure and gentle smile it seemed that he had. Ernesto sighed with relief. Well done Francisco he thought and silently thanked his pupil for the loyalty that his silence implied.

Carlos was jittery. He approached the painting.

'What a beautiful girl,' he said moving his head from side to side, searching for the evidence he'd been instructed to find. It wasn't easy. The artist had smudged the church into the landscape, giving the background a soft contrast to the crispness of the woman's face. Don Anselmo joined them.

'Ah, I see you're admiring our painting,' he said quietly and Ernesto thought he heard a catch in the man's throat. Carlos moved closer.

'I love the brushwork, sir, especially how the artist has blended the background into the church facade.' Then Carlos turned away so that only Ernesto could see his face. He winked and the gleam in his eye confirmed the date.

They moved into a dining room. More dark panelling but here sunlight streamed in through a single window. Beatriz was standing next to it, almost translucent. Her hair was wet as if she'd just been for a swim and she was dressed in a soft woollen dress that clung to her body making her look even more desirable than before. Ernesto could smell her perfume from across the room and was mesmerised. Noticing his lingering interest, she took a drag on her cigarette like a femme fatale in a detective film. Was she teasing him again? Don Anselmo followed them in.

'Sit, sit,' he said.

They obeyed, positioning themselves cautiously on the edge of their seats while the housekeeper brought in plates of dry-looking sandwiches. Ernesto glanced over at Carlos who was fiddling with his tie. Don Anselmo picked at his sandwiches and Beatriz drank tepid tea. Carlos looked at his watch as if he'd done his bit and wanted to leave and Ernesto glanced across to Francisco, innocently sipping juice then wiping his mouth with a napkin. He thought about the church in the painting and how he'd stood next to the original in Sauce del Valle. Somehow there was a connection between this boy of eleven, and what happened in that village twenty odd years ago. But what? Finally Don Anselmo broke the silence.

'Your man Manuel Barrosa got away then.'

Carlos coughed. A piece of sandwich had lodged in his mouth. Ernesto froze. What did Don Anselmo just say? And how should he react?

Beatriz saved him. 'I rather liked Manuel. He played like a maestro at the concert.'

Carlos managed to swallow. Ernesto recovered too. He was angry. Don Anselmo was playing with them and it wasn't right, especially here at Francisco's party. He took a deep breath and spoke up.

'Manuel is a good man, always thinking of his fellow man,'

'Ah, you communists are all alike,' Don Anselmo said laughing.

Francisco must have sensed the mood and tried to change it.

'Ernesto, did you have a good journey here?' Words wouldn't leave Ernesto's mouth. What was Don Anselmo playing at? 'And do you think it will rain tomorrow?' Poor Francisco, he was desperate. And when no one answered he tried again. 'Will you have another concert? Can I come too?'

Don Anselmo coughed loudly to indicate Francisco should stop talking. Poor boy, living in this dreary house, gagged by his own father. He seemed terrified. The housekeeper carried in a birthday cake with eleven candles and when they had all been extinguished, she cut the cake with a silver knife - it seemed to take a lifetime - and placed portions onto plates edged in gold. There was silence again. The cake was oversweet. They could hear each other eating. The clock in the corner was ticking louder than it should and Don Anselmo's recent words hung in the air like a putrid smell that no one cared to mention. Carlos looked agitated. His eyes said 'get me out of here,' but Francisco began opening his presents, a replica of the Santa Maria sailing ship from Carlos and a leather music case from Ernesto.

'Thank you,' he said with what seemed like genuine delight, but no amount of childlike joy was going to improve the atmosphere now. When they were finally ready to leave, Don Anselmo said,

'Wait outside, Carlos. I have something to say to Francisco's tutor in private.' Ernesto felt his legs give a little as he was ushered into Don Anselmo's private study. Here come the accusations, he thought. Here comes the trap.

The room was an affront to his senses. Every wall was covered in religious paintings and above the curve of the chimney breast was a portrait of a younger General Franco, dressed in full military uniform with an array of medals across his chest. In the middle of the room, set diagonally as if to disorientate unwelcome visitors, was Don Anselmo's heavy wooden desk. On it was a brass letter opener, a miniature Spanish flag and a small statue of the Virgin Mary. Don Anselmo, still smiling, sat down and motioned to the chair opposite his. Ernesto obeyed and now the portrait of Franco was directly above Don Anselmo's head, as if supervising what was coming next.

Don Anselmo leaned back in his chair, no longer smiling, mouth turned down, courtesy gone. 'You owe me a favour,' he said. Ernesto didn't argue. He was expecting this, but still he couldn't handle the truth.

'Do I sir?'

'You know you do, but let's not discuss that now. I need your assistance.'

'Assistance?'

'Yes. There are things I need to know and you're the man to help me.'

Ernesto frowned. 'I don't know what you mean.'

'I think you do.' He reached into the top drawer of his desk, pulled out a single sheet of paper and read from it, speaking firmly as if giving military instructions.

'Paco Garcia, ex-sniper, enemy of the people, agitator, drunk. Dolores Cruz, wife of said drunk. Barman at that dreadful bar you frequent. Used to be a rebel, maybe still is. Cousins Pedro and Jose, Gypsy musicians, criminal records as long as your arm. Old Juan the newspaper seller and that silly publication, *The Monkey*, Manuel Barrosa, union man, agitator, dangerous.' Don Anselmo narrowed his eyes. 'Señor Costa, you know all these people, don't you?'

'Yes but…'

'However you're not like them, are you? You're a musician, a tutor. Not an activist. I can see that.' As if by design his tone seemed to soften. 'Besides you're a foreigner so it's not your fight, is it?'

Ernesto didn't know how to answer. 'Yes it is' would incriminate him, 'No it isn't' would betray the friendships he treasured. Don Anselmo wasn't waiting for an answer. 'And whatever evil these men hold in their hearts, you don't have to be like them, do you?'

'Err, no.'

'So it is of no consequence to you to watch what's going on in your neighbourhood and report back to me, is it?' Ernesto couldn't answer. Words wouldn't come. But it didn't matter. Don Anselmo was still talking. 'So if you see anything treacherous, hear anyone criticising our government I want to know.' There was a long pause. Don Anselmo's chair creaked as he manoeuvred into a new position that felt even more threatening than the last. Ernesto's mind was racing. He wants me to spy. He wants me to inform on my friends. *This* is the reason I've been invited here. *This* is the trap. Don Anselmo seemed to know what he was thinking. 'I can make things very difficult for you if you don't,' he snapped. 'If you're not careful we'll start thinking that *you* are a rebel just like them, and you wouldn't want that would you?'

Tears gathered in Ernesto's eyes. He held them back. The man was waiting for an answer, a confirmation of his compliance. *Willingness to comply* that's what his letter of reference had said. That's what people thought of him, someone who could blow with the wind; someone who was easily persuaded. The chair creaked.

And don't forget I pay your wages, so think if it as part of our contract. Your services rendered.' Ernesto nodded. The man's money was his only means of escape. How else was he going to get back home? What else could he do?

'So we are in agreement then?'

Ernesto held his breath. Don Anselmo sat back. The chair creaked again.

'Alright,' Ernesto said.

Then wished he hadn't. But it was too late. Don Anselmo was standing, Ernesto too. This was the end of their negotiation. Time to go. Carlos and Francisco were waiting in the hall.

'Car's out front,' Carlos said impatiently. Ernesto turned to say goodbye and saw that Don Anselmo was smiling again and holding out his hand in the same friendly manner as before.

Ernesto stared out at the passing landscape, his head crammed with conflicting thoughts. So this was why he'd escaped arrest and torture, because Don Anselmo had arranged it. And this was why he'd been summoned to his home. Not for Francisco's birthday celebration but to persuade Ernesto to spy on his friends. Oh god what had he done?

Carlos broke into his thinking.

'You're very quiet,'

'Yes.'

'Well? What was all that about in his study?'

'I can't tell you.'

'Yes you can.'

'I can't'

'Is it about Manuel? Or me?'

'No its not, that's all I can say.'

'Well I don't think Manuel will be happy, you keeping secrets from us,' Carlos said and Ernesto tried to change the subject.

'Are you going to see Manuel soon?'

'Of course. Our man needs food and an update on what's happening.' Carlos sounded angry. He was sure to tell Manuel about this. Ernesto felt sick but he had to keep calm.

'Well tell him I am still one of the Monkeys and probably in a better position to report back than I was before.'

'Let's hope so, otherwise we might think you're changing sides, then you'd be in real trouble.' Carlos swung the car into Ernesto's street and dropped him off without saying goodbye.

Ernesto opened the door to his building and stopped on the halfway landing, hovering between the dangers of the outside world below and the internal safety of his room above. Dust was floating in the air, the particles illuminated by the skylight above his head. They circled the space as he tried to clear his mind. How did he get himself into these situations? First in Havana, caught between the Mafia and Arsenio, and now here, tricked by Don Anselmo and pressurised by the Monkeys. What was it about it him that attracted such extremes? And why was he always in the middle, never on one side or the other? What had he done to deserve this continual entrapment? He sighed, knowing he'd made a mistake. His agreement with Don Anselmo had come rushing out before he could compose himself. He wasn't ready. It wasn't his fault. He'd done nothing wrong.

But maybe it *was* his fault. Maybe his inability to say no was the problem. Maybe he should have refused to cooperate with Don Anselmo and taken the consequences. He shook his head in distaste. There was a name for this behaviour and he could hardly bear to form the word in his mind. He felt his jaw tighten. Cowardice was like a disease for which there was no cure.

Ernesto raced up the remaining stairs as if outrunning the truth. He opened his apartment and threw himself onto the bed with Don Anselmo's list repeating itself in his head; Paco, Dolores, the barman, Pedro, Jose, Juan and Manuel. How did the man know all these names? Someone must be informing him. Then he remembered the man at the gentlemen's outfitters, how he'd been at the concert, how he watched through his window and how he'd been talking on the telephone when he'd been arrested. The shopkeeper was the neighbourhood informant, watching them from his faded little window display. A colourless, drab observer of their comings and goings, someone with no passion of his own, a parasite living on the borrowed exploits of the street. And now Ernesto was one of them too, tied to the Monkeys and owned by Don Anselmo, caught between two extremes with no real commitment to either. He was the average of the two extremes, neither one thing nor the other; as beige as the clothes in that shop.

That night a dream came seeping in, accompanied by strings, woodwind and a choir. Belle was listening as she often did, to a recording of Maria Callas singing *La Habanera* from Bizet's *Carmen*. His mind hovered over the lyrics. That was my Belle, he thought, too wild to tame, too strong to be subdued. Not like him, conceding to everything, giving up and giving in. Now she was looking him hard in the face. 'You need to be strong, Mulatto,' she seemed to be saying. 'Because soon your character will be put to the test.'

Part Three

23. The Letters

Ernesto was woken by a faint tap on his door.

'This is a surprise,' Ernesto said, inviting Juan in.

'I came early so no one would see,' Juan said, sitting tight up against the table with his fingers clenched. Ernesto fetched coffee, sensing the importance of the old man's visit. He wanted to tell Juan about his new arrangement with Don Anselmo, how the man had forced him to spy on his friends, but he dared not share this treachery, so when Juan started with some small talk, Ernesto was eager to play along.

'How's Jorge?' Juan said.

'Don't know. I'm seeing him later.'

'Bastards, picking on a student.'

'Didn't go after you though?' Ernesto said with a question in his voice.

'Not worth the bother no more, although that Beatriz keeps coming by to check if I'm up to me old mischief.'

'And are you?'

'Am I what?'

'Up to your old mischief?'

Juan grinned. 'Me? Course not.'

Ernesto frowned. That wasn't true. Despite his poor diction, the man sitting in front of him was the editor and lead writer of *The Monkey*, a publication that only just passed scrutiny by the censors. Somehow through the dense, badly-spelt prose, his message was getting through. Surely this was a skill no ordinary man possessed? He decided to play devil's advocate.

'Great articles by the Monkey's Mouth,' he said. 'Whoever writes them must be a genius.'

Juan grinned again.

'I'll pass your compliments on to the author,' he said without a flutter of recognition.

Now, with coffee on the table, Juan's tone became more serious.

'I've decided to let you in,' he said.

'Let me in where? I don't understand.'

'Those letters? You still got them?'

'Of course.' Ernesto went to his trombone case and pulled out the bundle. He hadn't inspected them for some time.

'Juan grasped them and held them in front of Ernesto's face. 'These is the most precious things I've ever held, my friend.' Then he pulled another letter from his pocket and placed it on top of the pile.

Ernesto frowned. 'Really? Are they that important?'

'Yes, but I won't try to convince you. Read them. Read them all and you can figure it out fa ya'self.' Then he got up and left.

Ernesto listened to the dull thump of Juan's slippers trudging down the stairwell and to the outside door banging shut. He stared at the pile of envelopes in front of him, and the new one sitting on top. He remembered when Juan had told him not to read them. *At*

216

least not yet, he'd said, and today he was telling him to do that very thing. So why now? But inside he felt a thrill. For months these things had sat in his trombone case taking up space, occupying a corner of his mind like a squatter he couldn't evict, and now he had a chance to satisfy his curiosity.

He took a deep breath and with restless fingers undid the knot and spread the envelopes out onto his tiny table where they overlapped each other as if competing for attention. He noticed how the string felt rough like the sort used to support tomatoes on their stakes, or attach the branches of grapevines to their frames. Ernesto scanned all twelve and realised that the date stamp showed one for each consecutive year. He set them out in date order and opened letter number one.

October 1947

Papa, you abandoned your daughter and now I am abandoning my son. Do you think me cruel? Well, only as cruel as you for leaving me.

I cannot look after this child so you must do it for me. I have named him Javier after his father and despite what you might think, we are in love and you will not split us apart. Together we are fighting to bring down the cruel regime you helped to create and I will not put our son in danger by keeping our baby here.

They say you took arms against your own flesh and blood. Is that true Papa? If so, your heart must have turned to ice. Perhaps this child will melt it again. Perhaps he will save you Papa, because I cannot.

Goodbye from your once proud daughter Emilia,

P.S. And goodbye to Javier. I will write again next year.

At first Ernesto smiled. What an unusual and pretty name - Emilia. But then he frowned. This wasn't what he was expecting - no military secrets or political intrigue - just some domestic dispute between a daughter and her father. Why in heavens name was Juan hiding this? The second envelope was stamped October 1948. He opened it with just a little impatience. Surely there was more to this? He read it aloud to the room,

October 1948

Father, the photograph is not for you. It is for Javier on his first birthday so that he can know his mother's face. Make sure he gets it. It's all I have to give. We are still here. I will not tell you where, because we are working against you, documenting the evil deeds done in your name. You and your cronies have told the country to be quiet, to shut up, and forget. But they won't, Father, not in the least. Bit by bit, people are coming to us with their recollections and we are writing them down. We are young ears listening to old horrors and one day everything we have heard will be revealed to the world. Did you think I was too young to understand? Did you think my grandfather would shield me from it all? Well you are wrong. He brought me up as a true socialist. He brought me up to think critically as any good citizen should. He's gone now, deported years ago, and at his age I doubt he's survived the conditions in that camp. But I am here and Javier's father too. You still have family if you care to look. And to Javier – goodbye my son, we will talk again next year. Emilia.

Ernesto searched the envelope but there was no photograph. Then he noticed that there were bumps of extra glue applied along the seal as if someone had opened it already then sealed it again. He checked the first one and that was the same, then he flicked through the rest, and saw that the next two had been tampered with also. Who could have done this and why? Ernesto panicked. *The most precious things I've ever held,* Juan had said but they didn't look precious to him. They looked like trouble and he was in enough of that already. So he packed the letters together in a messy pile and shoved them back into his case.

When Francisco came for his lesson, he seemed pleased.

'Did you like my house? He asked.

'Yes.'

'And the food?

'Of course.'

Ernesto watched with pride as Francisco finished his lesson, cleaned his instrument and placed it, disassembled, into his new case. Ever since he'd allowed Francisco to talk about his dead mother, the boy seemed so much more at ease with himself.When he was ready to go, Francisco lingered at the door.

'My father told me a secret.'

'Well if it's a secret you must keep it to yourself.' The last thing Ernesto wanted was even more things to conceal.

'But I want to tell it.'

'No Francisco, you must not.'

'I suppose you will read about it soon.' Ernesto sighed. The boy was teasing, wanting him to ask so that he could tell. But Ernesto didn't respond. He had more serious things to think about. So they said goodbye without further mention of the boy's little charade.

Next day, Ernesto walked slowly towards Jorge's residence desperate for some camaraderie and wondering if he should share the burden of those letters that Juan had made him hide. And what about this new arrangement with Don Anselmo? Here was an even worse secret, so great that he imagined a badge of shame with the word 'Informant' emblazoned on his lapel, elaborately stitched by some dedicated embroiderer, determined to expose him with her skilful artisan hand. How did he get himself into this mess? He sighed, desperate to tell Jorge everything, but should he trust Paco's nephew and let it all out?

Jorge looked exhausted but the cut on his face had almost healed.

'You been up all night?' Ernesto asked,

'More or less.'

Ernesto made them strong coffee then searched for a place to sit amongst the pile of documents strewn across the room. He was about to speak, to blurt out the secrets that weighed so heavily on his mind, but Jorge interrupted him.

'Look, I found this,' he said.

'What?'

'It was in the same archive you and I looked at before, dated 31st of October 1936 but this document shows the survivors, not the dead.' Jorge pulled a sheet from the file and Ernesto peered over his shoulder.

'Is this reliable? The writing looks so immature.'

'Seems pretty accurate to me. Look, here,' he said, reading out loud, *Jorge Garcia, 6.* That's me, Nesto, *son of Alfredo Garcia (tortured then executed) and mother Julia Martinez (shot)* so whoever wrote this has it right. Ernesto leaned in to look, more out of politeness than interest.

'That's good Jorge, but I have something to tell you…'

Jorge wasn't listening. He was still talking; still reading from the list.

Gonzalo Jimenez, age fifty three and his granddaughter Emilia…

Ernesto gasped and leaned in further. What was this? He grabbed the document from Jorge's hand and read the complete entry. *Gonzalo Jimenez, age fifty three and his granddaughter Emilia Jimenez, age eight.* Ernesto read the name again. *Emilia Jimenez.* He shook his head. That unusual and pretty name again. Instinct told him that reading about two Emilias in one day was too important to ignore. Nothing was that much of a coincidence.

220

Quickly he copied the details onto a scrap of paper, deciding to think it through later, and then asked, 'So you were six and this girl Emilia was eight and you both lived in the same village?'

'Seems that way but I don't remember her. This list covers the whole valley.

Ernesto glanced at the rest of the documents.

'Why didn't the police find these when they arrested you?'

'I took them to Dolores and she hid them.'

'Good thinking.'

'I'd be dead now, if not.'

'So how are you getting hold of them, Jorge?'

'Easy. Juan gets them for me.'

'Juan?'

'Yes, good old Juan. They're brought to him from somewhere in the mountains, I pick them up and when I've finished I return them, and Juan arranges the pick up.' Ernesto nodded then smiled. Despite the old boy's denials, Juan's was still up to his old mischief not only as a writer, but also as a runner of documents that, if discovered, would have him shot.

'So are there lots of rebels in this chain of distribution?' he asked.

'I guess so, although it would be too dangerous to know the whole picture. Besides, some have been caught by now and have disappeared in police custody or they've been put into internment camps.'

'Camps? Where?' Ernesto asked, remembering Emilia's second letter.

'All over Spain and in France, sent up there during the war. The last one closed in '49.'

On the way home Ernesto took a short cut through narrow alleys where tall buildings with overhanging balconies meant the sun hardly reached. He looked up at the red flash of geraniums, the only natural survivors in this darkened strip of life, and it seemed to Ernesto that these bright little flowers were a symbol of promise and hope, searching out the light when everything else was so grim. And although he didn't understand much, things seemed to be coming to light; places, people, dates, emerging like ghosts. He looked down. Dried-out leaves from the nearby mulberry trees had floated in the air, dropping lightly on the pavement where they gathered in the hollows. But soon children would be coming out of school to kick them free, enjoying the crunching sound as they buckled under childish feet. Then later, gushing rains would wash away their brittle remains, leaving the pavements smooth and clean, and soon he would resolve the mystery of the letters he was yet to read.

A good night's sleep gave him clarity. Instead of ignoring those letters he decided to read them carefully because in his heart he knew they were important even if he didn't understand why. After taking his morning coffee he returned to his room with today's newspapers as usual, but he no longer desired to read them. Emilia's letters were the priority now. He folded the papers away and fetched a glass, opened a bottle of rum and set the messy bundle in front of him on the table, arranging them back into date order, and picked up letter number three. Like the reader of a compelling serial in a magazine, Ernesto was consumed with Emilia's story.

October 1949

Dear Father,

Another year. Javier must be walking now. And talking too. He's sure to take after his own father, admired as a great orator. I am more of a writer than a speaker, and when all this is over I intend to honour the victims of this terrible regime by publishing all that I know for the entire world to see.

Is my boy happy? I think of him constantly and try to imagine his face. Does he look like me? Does he look at my photo? Does he call me 'Mama'?

You'd be surprised how much I know, Father. There are people who whisper in the dark and their murmurs reach me and tell me you are raising him well, just as I hoped you would. We may be on opposite sides, but I am grateful for that.

Please wish my son a happy second birthday.

Emilia

There wasn't much to go on. Her lover was an orator, she was a writer, and news had reached her that Javier was safe. He re-read the notes he'd made from Jorge's file. If this was the same Emilia as in those documents then he might be able to piece together her story. He began to scribble some calculations in the margin; Gonzalo Jimenez, age fifty-three, so the grandfather would be about seventy-four now and at some point he'd been sent to an internment camp. So Emilia was probably right to think he hadn't survived. But *she* had. 'Granddaughter Emilia Jimenez, age eight.' She'd be about thirty now, and her son Javier would be eleven. He calculated again - she was eighteen when she gave birth. That made sense of her petulant tone. She was really just a child who had chosen to give her son away to keep him safe. He sat back pleased with himself. Everything was a little clearer than it had been even a few minutes ago. He packed the letters together, returned them to his case and picked up *The Chronicle*.

El CAUDILLO TO VISIT CADIZ

Following last year's successful visit to the region, our illustrious leader General Francisco Franco will visit us once more. Here to inspect the new industrial installations in the area, he will complete his tour by attending mass at our magnificent Cathedral in the city of Cádiz.

Hmm, he thought, yet another propaganda visit to keep the people in their place, and then he smiled at his new political observations. How far he had travelled in his thinking since joining the Monkeys and how much clearer was his world view now!

Carlos came by. He seemed friendlier, as if he'd decided to trust him.

'Have you seen the news? Franco's coming.'

'Yes. So?'

'Don't you see? This is our second chance'

'Second chance for what?'

'To do what Paco and Jorge couldn't manage before.'

'What? Take another shot at the general?'

'Better than that.'

'What do you mean?'

'Well, its Cádiz isn't it. One way into the city and the same way out. The road across the salt flats is perfect for a highjack.'

'Don't be stupid, they'll see you for miles.'

'Well a bomb then, something to detonate at a distance.'

Ernesto couldn't stop himself. 'Are you mad?' Carlos raised his eyebrows.

'No, we are not mad, Nesto. Manuel is planning it all as we speak.'

'But it's mass murder. You could be killing lots of people.' Carlos didn't answer. He stared at him as if he were the enemy, then departed, leaving Ernesto wondering yet again if the Monkeys were a serious rebel force, or a bunch of fanatics, with no real plan except revenge. With no conclusion he went to the shelf, slid the trombone aside and yet again pulled out the package of letters. These days Emilia's story was the only thing making sense.

Letter Four

October 1950

Father how could you be so evil? How could you send your soldiers into that valley full of women, children and frail old men who would do you no harm? I told everyone that they were wrong - that you wouldn't have done it, not with me - your daughter and your parents there too. But they insisted it was true and said they'd get proof. And they found it in a file smuggled from the barracks in San Roque, Franco's signature and yours right beside it - Anselmo Jimenez - Your signature father seen with my own eyes. Shame on you for following that man. She died in that raid you know, your own sweet Mama. On that day 31ˢᵗ October 1936 I lost the woman who raised me and it broke your father's heart. From now on my letters will be for Javier. Not for you. I will no longer address you in my letters. You are dead to me father. Dead.

Is it any surprise that I work for the Maquis now? Listening and writing about everything that has been done under the name of your beloved leader. And beware, because we are not just chroniclers. We are also your judge and jury. And what's more we have a strong network stretching across the country and beyond. We will not be bowed father. We will prevail.

Happy third birthday, son.

Your loving mother, Emilia

24. Family Tree

Ernesto's stomach was churning. He took a huge swig of rum, terrified to register what he was thinking. He stared at the notes he'd made from Jorge's documents, holding them up in his right hand and Emilia's last letter in his left. *Anselmo Jimenez - your signature father, seen with my own eyes.* He frowned. Anselmo – Don Anselmo? Two more names alike. Was this another coincidence? And then he remembered Don Anselmo's letter of complaint to him last year. The man had signed it Anselmo Jimenez – the same name he was reading now in Emilia's letter. So were they one and the same man? Surely this can't be true, he said to the room but the question burst out anyway. Could Don Anselmo be Emilia's father? And what's more, Emilia Jimenez had a child called Javier whom she had left in the care of her father. The boy would be ten or eleven now. And Don Anselmo had a son called Francisco and he was eleven too. Could Francisco and Javier be the same boy? He shook his head unable to make the facts work, trying to dislodge the truth. 'It can't be,' he said, but logic had already crept in and taken residence. The freckled hand, the moribund house, the old fashioned car - it all made sense. Don Anselmo wasn't Francisco's father, he was his *grandfather*. No, he said, this can't be.

But he already knew he was right. And the young woman in the portrait - the one with the blue dress and the yellow flowers? This was Emilia, the boy's mother. But according to Francisco she was dead. He rifled through the bundle of letters searching for the last envelope, the one Juan had recently delivered. Yes here was the date stamp October 1958, written this year and confirming that Francisco's mother was writing to him even now. He gasped. Of all the revelations laid before him this was the one that gave him the most joy. How wonderful to release the boy from believing he'd caused his mother's death. And even more; to tell Francisco that she was alive and well and thinking of him as any mother would. And as if to confirm things further, he noticed something about the address on the first four envelopes. All this time he'd ignored them because it was too smudged to read properly, but now he could just make out the C of Casa and the Fue of 'Fuentes' – the house of the fountains. He remembered the two fountains at Francisco's house, one at the front - bright and light, and the one at the back - dismal and cold. He rushed downstairs to Juan's shop, pushed the door firmly shut and turned the sign from open to closed.

'Those letters were for Don Anselmo, and the mother's alive,' he blurted out. 'I mean, Francisco is Javier and his mother is still alive and apparently working for the Monkeys.'

He beamed and Juan did too.

'Well done. I knew you'd get there sooner or later.'

'But why did Don Anselmo tell the boy that horrible lie?'

'Well there was a grain of truth in there. It was Don Anselmo's *wife* who died giving birth to Emilia and they say he never recovered. Turned him sour they reckons.'

'And this Emilia. Where is she now?'

'Can't tell you I'm afraid. It's secret. In fact you 'n me are the only ones what knows about this, 'cept Don Anselmo of course, and I'm keeping me powder dry on that one.'

'What d'you mean?'

'There'll be a time when they comes in handy don't you think?' Ernesto nodded. These letters were dynamite and he was full of questions.

'Where did you get them, Juan? At least tell me that.

'Well Dolores gev me the first un and the rest well it's too risky to tell.'

'And why did you bring them to me? And why ask me to read them now?'

'Originally I gev 'em you jus for safe keeping, you bein a stranger. But then you started giving Francisco lessons and I couldn't believe me luck, seeing him arrive every week, able to keep an eye on him. He seems so happy.'

'So?'

'The boy respects you. Anyone can see that.'

'But what's that got to do with these letters?'

'Well now he's eleven I reckons he needs to know the truth.'

'What do you mean?' Ernesto asked, but he was already dreading what was coming.

'Reckon you're the man to tell 'im,' he said.

Ernesto shook his head. 'No. Not me, Juan.'

'Not now, do it when the time's right. Makes sense, you being like a father to the boy.' Ernesto frowned but he could see what Juan meant. Nothing would give him greater pleasure than to reunite mother and child. But not now, he thought, not yet. He shook his head but Juan seemed determined. 'You read the rest of them letters and then you'll understand.'

That night Ernesto dragged himself into bed and lay there waiting for sleep to plunge him into thankful oblivion. But it didn't. Four letters, packed with roundabout meanings, were circling inside his head. *Arms against your own flesh and blood.* That sounded terrible. Tears fell down Ernesto's cheek remembering the raid that Jorge had described; first the planes, then the bombs, and the soldiers who came later to round up the villagers. He remembered some had escaped, so Emilia must have been one of them and her grandfather too. But did Don Anselmo really know that his parents and daughter were in that valley when he sent his soldiers in? Surely not! Because if he did, then what kind of man must he be?

And *He brought me up to think.* So she was raised by her grandfather, just as Francisco was being raised by his. But why does Don Anselmo call the boy Francisco? It seemed so cruel, to rob him not only of his history, but his name too. Then Emilia asked *does he look at my photo? Does he call me Mama?* Poor girl, not realising that Francisco believes she is dead. How could he explain all this to Francisco? And why did it have to be him to shake the boy's foundations? Why should *he* be the one to tell him that the young woman who had watched over him for years from the portrait in the hall, was still alive and cared about him more than he could imagine? And how could he explain why she'd abandoned him at birth? Would he understand it was for his safety? And what about the change to his name? How could he explain all that without hurting him? Perhaps the boy would be angry and challenge his father – no – grandfather. This could send Don Anselmo into a frenzy of accusations. And then what? The man was sure to follow up on the threat he'd made in his study. *I can make things very difficult for you* he'd said. And this meant the Monkeys too. They were in danger by this revelation and so was he. What a heavy burden Juan had charged him with. And more than that, Emilia had written *we have a strong network stretching across the country and beyond.* She must have been very angry to disclose that. Had Don Anselmo read this part? If so why wasn't he rooting them out? And if by chance he hadn't, how could Ernesto share these letters with Francisco without them reaching Don Anselmo's eyes? Because if they did, then the whole Monkey network would be in jeopardy. He sighed and shook his head. It was impossible. If he spoke up, all sorts of consequences would be triggered, and if he confided in someone like Jorge, Carlos or Manuel, they might misunderstand, might think he was hiding the letters *for* Don Anselmo and that he was on the man's side, when in fact, every letter was bringing him closer to a different conclusion. Yet despite his worries he closed his eyes in order to summon sleep and when it finally came there were no watching dreams, no blood soaked loafers, no visitations from Belle or Beatriz plaguing him as they usually did. Instead he slept deeply; as if his brain had reached the limit of its understanding and had simply shut down to give him some peace.

Next day he walked across town to the graceless flats where Dolores lived. He moved quickly, anxious not to be stopped in case someone searched him and found the first four letters in his pocket. He sat at her kitchen table as Dolores wiped the greasy oilskin with a cloth.

'What do you want?'

'You gave some letters to Juan. I want to know where you got them.' The colour drained from her face as she sat down, studying his eyes, as if searching for a reason to trust him. Eventually she began.

'You won't know nothing about them years straight after the war.'

'Probably not.'

'I had to work. Paco was up north and I needed money. But there weren't no unions and not much work neither. There was those what worked for the government and the rest of us scrambling around for what we could get.' Ernesto realised this was going to take some time. He leaned forward.

'Tell me everything, Dolores. I want to know.'

'So every day us women met at the statue of our old leader - that Azaña Diaz bloke - in the square. It's gone now, ripped out, but back then it was the only place we was allowed to meet in large groups, waiting for them rich ladies to arrive. One was a fat woman in a posh car, used to come early to get the best girls. Cash in hand, get in the back, shut your mouth and she took us to some mansion in the north of the city. Just built it was, with huge pillars round the door an' a sign saying Casa de las Fuentes. Turned out that fat old girl was only the housekeeper, so no more posher than me. The real owner was a gent. Never saw him in the house – it was so big - but one day I hears a baby crying upstairs and he was shouting like you don't know what. The fat woman told me to keep my head down and clean his study and that was when I found it.'

'What did you find, Dolores?'

'A letter of course. Stuffed in the grate, covered in ash.'

'You mean this one,' Ernesto said pulling the first of Emilia's envelopes from his pocket. She squinted at it trying to remember.

'Yes that's it,' she said smiling in recognition. 'And after all them years!' But then she frowned. 'How comes you got it?

'Never mind. Did you read it?'

'You be lucky. Can't read, can I? But I figured it was important – what with that baby crying and 'im shouting - so I puts it in my apron pocket just in case. Next day I was waiting by the statue with the others, but the housekeeper never came. Heard she'd been sacked. Never went back to that house neither. They didn't want me.

'What did you do with the letter?

'Took it to Juan didn't I? What with him a journalist in the war. When he read it he was mighty shocked I can tell you.

'And the others? There were four letters opened in total.'

No idea. 'Didn't know there was more.'

He returned across town pondering what he had learned. Apart from the first one, Emilia's letters hadn't come from Dolores so if she didn't give them to Juan, then who did? His mind leapt to the journey that he, Jorge and Carlos had made to Sauce del Valle and the tavern in the hollow where they'd stopped to eat breakfast. According to Jorge, his documents came from somewhere in the mountains. So perhaps they were dropped off at the tavern then collected by Carlos, passed to Juan and then on to Jorge. If his instincts were right, then how easy it would be for Emilia's letter to be slipped into the pile of other documents and neither Jorge nor Carlos would suspect a thing.

Jorge was waiting at his door looking agitated. His hair was dishevelled as if he had pushed his hand through it too many times, wrestling with a dilemma.

'I've been told to talk to you.'

'Who by?'

Jorge didn't answer until they were safely inside. 'The Monkeys of course. They want to know if you're on their side, if you are *in* or *out*. They think you're getting soft.' Ernesto laughed.

'I've always been soft, didn't you notice?' he said, taking off his coat.

'You're not soft, Nesto, just kind. But you are going to have to toughen up. I did, so you can too.'

'But they're talking about killing innocent people. Is that what you want?' He threw his coat on the bed.

'No, of course not. Don't you think I've struggled with this myself?'

'So you know it's wrong then?'

'Yes, but this is war, Nesto.'

'Why, Jorge? Tell me why it's war.'

Jorge ran a hand through his hair. 'For me, it's simple. I want revenge.'

Ernesto shook his head. 'Revenge is a dead end, my friend. Where is the reasoning? Where is the ideology for a better world? You of all people should be aware of that.' But Jorge was distracted, looking over at Ernesto's bed where all four letters had spilled from the pocket of his coat.

'What are these?' he said picking them up.

Ernesto felt the heat rise in his cheeks 'Nothing. They're private.'

'Hmm. You're up to something, Nesto, I can tell.'

Ernesto stared at the envelopes clutched in Jorge's hand. Could he trust him? He so desperately wanted to. His shoulders dropped. What else could he do?

'Alright, read them then you'll see,' he said sitting down and watching anxiously as Jorge read them. He took his time until, at the end he nodded as if he understood. 'So what do you think?'

'Well everything she says rings true, the attack at Sauce de Valle, the dates, the boy.' How clever of Jorge to work it all out so quickly. But now Jorge was mumbling.'Nesto, who gave you these?'

'I can't tell you I'm afraid.'

But Jorge wasn't listening. He was yanking at his briefcase, holding a file, moving under the light. 'Christ I don't believe it! Look at this.' He pulled out one of his documents. 'I was on my way to give these back to Juan, but look!' Jorge spread it out onto the table.

234

'Not more papers, Jorge, please!' Ernesto complained.

'No, you idiot, look at this.' Jorge laid Emilia's letter up against his other documents. 'Look at the way that *j* has the same curve on the downside - look! And see how smudged the handwriting is as if she is left-handed.' Ernesto sat up and peered over his shoulder, first at Emilia's letters and then at Jorge's documents. He was right. The scrawl of handwriting was definitely the same.

'But this is only one. It must be a coincidence.'

'Look, for weeks I've been staring at these things. Don't you think I would know? I'm telling you, the girl who wrote these letters also wrote these documents. All of them, I swear.' Jorge pulled out another file and they checked that too. 'It's her, I'm telling you.' For a moment they sat in silence taking it in. Then Ernesto broke open the envelope to the fifth letter.

'Let's read this together, it might give us more proof.'

October 1951

My dear Javier, they have advised me not to write to you anymore in case it jeopardises our chain of communication. But your Mama has found a way to ensure my letters reach you and no one else, so I will continue with your birthday greetings and perhaps one day, some kind person will reveal them to you and help you understand.

It's your fourth birthday and I miss you so much. Sometimes I think it was a mistake leaving you with my father. But then I remember that you are safe and I am not. Your parents are busy, Javier. We may live in a small hamlet in the mountains, but we are big, Javier; very big. Our community of Maquis goes from north to south and east to west, from Bilbao to Cádiz, from Salamanca to Valencia. Your father travels everywhere to get our message heard whilst I stay at home listening and writing. I started when I was nine, when all about me were crying of hunger and grief and I was the only person who could read and write. Can you imagine that, Javier? Me with a pen and paper and all those old people queuing up to tell their stories to a child? And I am happy my dear Javier, happy to work for our socialist cause. Some people call us Anarchists, some call us Marxists and others shout 'traitor' because they are scared. But the only name that bothers me is the one Franco calls us when he says we are not Citizens of Spain but Citizens of Nowhere. This hurts me so much and I don't expect you to understand, but one day you will. One day I will be free to take you in my arms and explain all this to you myself.

But don't let me frighten you with my melancholy. Will you have a party? Save me some cake, little one.

Your loving mother Emilia.

There was silence whilst both men considered their discovery. Not only had the girl been bombed from her home, then raised by her grandfather, and become an exile in her own country, but she was the very chronicler that Jorge had been relying on for his research, recording testimonies to the brutalities of this dreadful regime. Ernesto slumped back in the chair. How could he explain all this to Francisco? First his change of name, then the truth that his mother was still alive, and that she was a rebel labelled a traitor in the country where he was born. Poor Francisco, it would be too much for his eleven-year-old mind to comprehend. Even so, he had to tell him. But not yet, he thought, remembering the Urania – his route back home – his escape. Not yet.

Jorge was smiling. 'She's clever calling us the Maquis and not The Monkeys. That way no one can link us to the newspaper.' Then he grinned. 'Of course! Juan gave you these letters didn't he?

Ernesto sat upright again. 'Trust you to work that out,' he said, 'I asked him to tell me where Emilia was but he refused.'

'You can't ask him that, Nesto. Juan is sworn to secrecy. Anyway it would put in jeopardy all those brave souls who collect and deliver our correspondence, those who watch and listen and tell us the

236

truth. They are the links in the chain of our communications and hundreds of them have already disappeared. We mustn't expose them to more tyranny. In any case, Juan would never tell - not even us.' Ernesto slumped down again but Jorge was still smiling.

'Don't look so miserable, Nesto. Can't you see? This is great news.'

'How come?'

'If Don Anselmo is Emilia's father, then he's in real trouble.'

'Why? I don't understand.'

'Ask yourself, does he really want people knowing his daughter's a Monkey - or rather a Maquis – doing so much damage, conspiring against the regime? If *she* is a traitor then he is too. No one will believe otherwise.'

'Do you really think so?'

'I do, Nesto, and you should too.'

'But the man is dangerous and very clever. He sets people against one another. He's...' Ernesto didn't dare explain about his arrangement as an informant for Don Anselmo and the fascists, not even to his friend.

Jorge was laughing. 'Don't be scared of the father. He lives in the shadow of his follies.' Ernesto frowned. He hadn't thought of Don Anselmo like that. He was a man of power, a strong man to be feared. But now he could see another reason why Don Anselmo had protected him at the police station, why he'd turned him into an informer. He wanted to find out if anyone had discovered his family secret. Juan had been right to say he was 'keeping his powder dry.' Ernesto smiled as he realised that Jorge was right too. Don Anselmo was a frightened man. Those letters were indeed dynamite. Jorge interrupted his thoughts.

'So? Will you answer the question I came for? Are you in or out, Nesto? You've got to decide once and for all.'

Ernesto stared at the floor, unable to nod or to shake his head, as usual paralysed by indecision. But Jorge didn't wait for an answer. 'Look, it's now or never. Carlos says you must come to the meeting room to make an oath of allegiance, or else.'

'Alright. But not now, Jorge. Tomorrow, after my class with Francisco.'

25. The Long Read

Out of respect, Ernesto decided not to read more letters. It felt too intrusive to poor Emilia, missing her son. Instead he tucked them back inside his trombone case, and went to the bar for an early rum and his morning coffee. The day was clear with no sign of the expected November gloom. Instead a weak winter sun peeped through the clouds, making the day feel brighter than his mood. So many slivers of information, so many unfinished questions. He ordered a second rum to soften the edges of his thinking, then crossed the road to collect his newspapers. Yet again Juan wanted to talk.

'Haven't seen the boy recently. Is he alright?'

'Perfectly. He'll be here later.'

'Glad to hear he's doing so well.' Ernesto nodded, then, as he tucked the papers under his arm, another thought hit him, another conspiracy unravelling before him.

'It's you isn't it!'

'Me?' Juan asked.

'You're the one sending messages to his mother.'

'Messages? I don't know what you mean.'

'Of course you do because you are informing her of his well-being!'

'Me?'

'Yes, why else do you keep asking me about him?'

'Don't be ridiculous,' Juan protested, but Ernesto could see he was right. He laughed.

'It's alright, old man, your secret's safe with me.' And he left, humming to himself at his sudden insight, surprised at how quickly his mood had improved.

He spread the two newspapers on the table as he always did. The Chronicle was reporting on Cuba again as if it was obsessed with the future outcome of the country's troubles. There were so many links between Spain and his old country and here he discovered yet another.

GOOD BYE AND GOOD RIDDANCE

Hundreds of Spanish youths have left our country to fight with communist rebels in Cuba. These blinkered souls whose parents were defeated so thoroughly during our own three years of anguish, are set on disturbing the peace yet again, this time in our former colony. And all for an outdated philosophy that brings nothing but anarchy and harm. So hurrah we say, good riddance, and may these foolish youths never return to our shores.

Then this in *The Monkey*.

RECIPROCITY

Hundreds of our yung are travelin cross the oshun to help them Castro brothers fight for liberty, just as, years ago meny Cubans traveled here to support ares. They came here then, and were goin there now. So in the name of frendship cross the waves, hurah we say, Bon voyage and may they come back safely to our shores.

240

Ernesto was relieved. Cuba was going to have a revolution. The Mafia would be thrown out and he could go home. Perhaps then, he would testify against Arsenio's son, after all he felt stronger now, not as scared as he used to. And just before he left he would tell Francisco about his mother and Francisco would finally be at peace. Ernesto kicked off his shoes and threw himself onto the bed. The early rum had made him desperate for sleep. He closed his eyes, determined not to think of the oath of allegiance he was being asked to make to the Monkeys later that day. For once his conscious mind felt almost at rest.

Sadly, his unconscious was not.

He was in the clouds. The land was flat, the wind was wild. The sea rose up and the Valkyries came riding in. Belle was up front, Beatriz behind, bursting the restraints of their armour. Blood was everywhere. Who will they choose to survive and who will they leave to die? Ernesto was desperate. There was evil in his thinking but it was necessary. He blew and blew. The horns did too. Wagner was screaming, violins cascading. A cymbal crashed. There was a knock on the door. Ernesto woke up and looked at his watch. It was midday and Francisco was there for his lesson.

'Come in,' he said searching for his shoes and not finding them.

The boy walked straight in saying 'Can I tell you my secret now?' and looking flushed with happiness.

'No you can't. Look, I won't be a minute.' He rushed down the corridor to the toilet - too many coffees, too much stress. He relieved himself quickly and washed his hands then regarded his image in the mirror. 'What a mess!' He threw water over his face and brushed down his rampant curls. The boy's sudden arrival had made him flustered. He hadn't set up the music stand or selected the pieces to play. It took a few minutes to get straight and when he arrived back to his room, Francisco was standing in the middle of the floor with his feet wide apart and both arms raised. His face was no longer flushed, but pale, his expression no longer bright, but bleak. In his right hand he held Ernesto's trombone.

'I got this out to help you get ready,' he said, 'but then I found these.' In his left hand he held Emilia's letters. Ernesto's heart jumped. Oh god, no! 'These belong to my father,' Francisco continued coolly, turning an envelope towards Ernesto so that he could see the address. 'So why have *you* got them?' There was anger in his voice as if he'd been betrayed. Ernesto folded. He sat on the bed. What could he say? Should he lie to the boy? Take the letters from him and make light of it? But Francisco was standing immobile in the centre of the room, holding both the trombone and the package of letters high above his head like a warrior making a declaration of war. He wasn't going to let them go. 'Why do you have letters here addressed to my father? and who is Emilia?' He'd obviously looked inside. Ernesto felt as small as the insects that scuttle across his floor at night. What was he going to say? How could he explain? And why now before he had time to prepare? Yet here they were, with no forewarning; man and boy staring at each other across the room in a perilous silence. Something had to give.

'Sit down, Francisco,' he said, buying time. The boy plonked himself at the table by the window, his expression even fiercer than before. Ernesto let out a huge sigh. He couldn't lie to the boy. It was now or never. He had no choice. 'The envelopes you are holding come from your mother. She is alive and well and lives somewhere here in the mountains.' He allowed the words to float across the space between them, all the time watching Francisco's face for a flutter of reaction. The boy sat perfectly still, his face unmoved. Had he understood? 'Your mother,' Ernesto repeated. 'She is not dead. She lives. Your mother is alive.'

'No, my mother is dead. Papa told me.'

'No Francisco. Your mother is alive and she misses you very much.'

242

'I don't believe you.'

'It's true, read the letters and then you will understand.' Francisco released the first letter from his grip and started to read. *'I have named him Javier after his father.'*

'But I am Francisco.'

'You were Javier once.'

'And my father's name is Anselmo.'

Ernesto didn't know what to say, didn't know how to explain.

'Read the letters, Francisco. Please.' He felt sick.

'And who is this person Emilia, and why is she addressing my father like this?'

'Francisco, she's your mother, surely you can see?' Francisco shook his head. Tears were welling in his eyes.

Ernesto sighed. 'Read them please, and you will see.' Francisco looked angry or was it confusion? Poor boy. He pulled another letter from the pack. *'You still have family if you care to look.'* Then the third: *'Does he look at my photo? Does he call me Mama?'* 'What photo? What does she mean?' His tone was defensive but Ernesto could see it was sinking in. Francisco grabbed at the fourth and scanned the letter to the end, reading aloud. *'Happy third birthday my son. Your loving mother, Emilia.'*

There was a moment when the clouds seemed to stop moving. Ernesto watched Francisco check the date - 14th October 1950, sent the day before his birthday. Then the clouds moved again as recognition passed over the boy's face. Ernesto went forward to comfort him, but Francisco leapt from the chair, his face screwed up, his features distorted in anguish. It was all too much.

'You're lying! None of this is true!' He raised the remaining letters above his head and released them to the air. They tumbled to the floor haphazardly this way and that, like broken kites plunging to a shattering end. Some landed on the bed, others skidded underneath it. Francisco stared at where they'd fallen.

'I should pick them up, but I won't,' he said and he ran across the room, yanked the door open and flew down the stairs into the street. A gush of wind roared through the building. Ernesto shouted into the stairwell.

'Wait, Francisco! Come back!' Ernesto found his shoes and ran barefoot down the stairs. As he struggled to put them on, he watched Francisco running fast covering his face against the driving rain. Ernesto followed but it was too late. Francisco had passed the gentlemen's outfitters and was almost at the fountain. 'Francisco!' But the boy had already turned the corner.

Carlos emerged from the K6.

'What just happened?'

'I've upset the boy. Help me find him, please!'

Carlos drove slowly up the street, wipers flashing while Ernesto went back upstairs and opened the window, letting in the rain as he peered out praying to see the K6 turn the corner into his street. He gathered up the letters, stained now with rain and tears. 'Christ what have I done?' he said to the room. But there was no reply. It felt as empty as his heart.

An hour later, still no car, but there was a sharp knock on his door. The shop keeper from the gentlemen's outfitter stood there, his face as thunderous as the storm outside. Behind him Francisco stood drenched. The man stepped forward and leaned into Ernesto's face.

'Saw the boy from my window, running like hell to get away from you. Found him in the square at the back of my shop, sobbing his heart out, he was.' Ernesto went to speak but the man was determined to have his say. 'The boy didn't want to go home. Insisted I bring him back here for some reason. But I've called Don Anselmo and Carlos will be here to collect him this evening.' As the man left, he scanned Ernesto's modest room and sneered as if he might be infected by its poverty. Francisco stood in the centre of the room, his jaw flexing, emotions simmering. Ernesto handed him a towel and he snatched it with only a flicker of gratitude.

'Funny I was going to tell *you* a secret and all along you had one about *me*,' he said.

'I'm so sorry, Francisco.'

'Are you?'

'Yes completely. I wanted to show them to you, but I couldn't. Not yet.' His words sounded pathetic.

'So show them to me now,' he said. Ernesto hesitated but he could see that Francisco was determined. 'Show me!' he repeated with the authority of someone badly hurt.

All afternoon they read; Ernesto passing each unopened envelope directly to the boy with no intention of intercepting the revelations taking place before him. To Ernesto's surprise, each time the boy finished a letter, he passed it back, so that Ernesto could read it too. Oh what joy, allowed to share Francisco's moment of discovery and to have their friendship restored like this, so gently, so revealing. And as they read together, Ernesto noticed how, letter by letter, Francisco's body changed from tight-jawed anger, laden with self-righteousness and blame, to a softening of his features, a dropping of the shoulders, a letting out of sighs, as he pieced together his mother's extraordinary life. He saw too how, with each letter, Emilia's hand writing became neater and the tone darker.

October'51, the one he had already opened, ended happily. '*Will you have a party? Save me some cake, little one*' and '52 showed the girl's increasing maturity. '*There's a man in your midst. His name is Juan – friend to my grandparents in the second republic. You must show him respect for, when all around us there is treachery, he is a true friend.'* But by '53 the tone had changed. *'Oh Javier, how I long to see you. There is talk that we have been discovered and that soon they will come. Perhaps we will have to leave.'* The next was even worse.

October 1954

Oh Javier, how can I bear to tell you? They captured your father whilst he was touring Valencia, dragged him into the countryside and shot him like a rabid dog. I cried Javier, of course I did, but not for long. We both knew the risks and we both took an oath not to mourn. If only you'd met him before it was too late. But he's gone now Javier and I don't know what to do. Maybe I'll carry on here, or perhaps I'll go to France to search for my grandfather. In any case, have a happy seventh birthday my love and may you find peace where I cannot.

Poor Francisco. What must he be thinking? These were just words written on thin insubstantial paper but they were thick, coagulating words, swollen with significance. The father he had never known, a stranger whose blood he shared, was now dead. The boy must be doing somersaults in his mind. One moment told an elevating, hopeful truth only to be plunged into perplexing despair the next. How could the poor boy come to terms with all this? Before passing the next envelope over Ernesto looked over at the boy waiting patiently for her message of love. With his shoes kicked off and one leg hanging over the arm of the chair, he seemed almost content. So how could Ernesto allow him to discover what he was now holding in his hand, evidence that his mother *had* gone away. A new postmark had appeared stamped 'October 1955 Pau, Aquitaine.' So she *had* gone. She'd travelled all the way to France and Francisco's mother, suddenly so close was now so very far away. Ernesto held the envelope to his chest unwilling to reveal this truth.

'Come on, let's read the next,' Francisco said holding out his hand. Ernesto couldn't bear it. He leant forward, reluctantly offering up the letter containing yet another betrayal within. How can I catch him when he falls? He thought, but at that moment Carlos barged in without knocking.

He spoke roughly. 'Don Anselmo's downstairs. He wants his boy.'

Francisco folded his arms and scowled. 'I want to stay,'

'Your father insists.'

'He's not my father,' Francisco snapped.

'Of course he's your father. Now come on.'

'No. I won't.'

Ernesto intervened. 'Look it's not his fault. He …' but Carlos was angry. He turned to Francisco. 'Look, I've been told to collect you, so come on!' Francisco let out an exaggerated sigh, picked up his trombone and left. Carlos stayed for a moment, turning to Ernesto with fire in his eyes,

'There's something's going on with you and Anselmo and we don't like it. You'd better come and swear your oath or else.'

Ernesto stalked the wooden boards of his room, back and forth, this way and that, making them creak and groan. What an idiot he'd been, too busy thinking about the boy to worry about his *own* safety. Now though, it hit him. The boy was bound to tell Don Anselmo about the letters, he was sure to challenge his grandfather's lie and demand to know about his real mother. Then what would Don Anselmo do? He would notify the authorities. He wouldn't need to mention the letters; just tell them that his son's trombone teacher was a member of the Maquis. They would take his word for it and escort him to the police station where the superintendent would interrogate him, probably with a cruel smile, and he would be black and blue like Jorge and they would force him to explain the chain of distribution starting with Juan, then Carlos, and the tavern with no name and where Manuel was hiding. The Monkeys would be flushed out and finished for good. Oh god, what had he done! Then after that, what would happen to him? After that he would almost certainly be dead.

26. Loyalty

Ernesto scooped up the letters and stuffed them deep into the pockets of his overcoat. He left the trombone sitting innocently on the shelf. If they raided his room, they would find nothing. Then he hurried down to tell Juan.

'We've got to get you off the streets. Come with me,' Juan said closing the shop and shuffling across to the bar. Ernesto heard him mutter something to the barman before beckoning him through the dark interior to the rear door then out into the bright street. They picked their way through narrow lanes, Juan's slippers slowing him down and Ernesto's heart racing as they passed through dark alleyways and bright-lit squares and round sudden corners where excited children splashed in shallow puddles. Ernesto sighed. Oh to be free like that, he thought. They passed long warehouses where the dank smell of fermentation oozed from the stonework, and along narrow pavements with rows of cottages, doors open, people peering, nodding their consent. Despite his ancient slippers, Juan was faster now; head down, unstoppable, until they reached their destination. Ernesto recognised it at once, the bar *Los Cinco Vientos* where he'd met the musicians and where they'd hidden Manuel. Juan swerved, Ernesto followed, down an alley, through a door, up some stairs - the same stairs - the same attic.

Wait here,' Juan said. 'I'll be back as soon as I have news.'

Ernesto slumped in a low chair and tried to control his breathing. Francisco would be home now, sitting in his grandfather's study, telling him about the letters, asking why he'd lied, maybe demanding to meet his mother. Don Anselmo would be furious and perhaps he'd deny it, but in the end, the secret would be exposed and Francisco would know the truth. Ernesto sighed again. Maybe that would be a good thing. Maybe when the dust of revelation had settled, Don Anselmo would be freed from his mendacious past, free to repair the lies and start again. But what about him? How could he escape this situation? By now Don Anselmo would have sent out a search party and they'd show him no mercy when they found this place. Perhaps Don Anselmo already knew its location. After all he seemed to know everything else about the Monkeys. Perhaps that superintendent was on his way there now. His stomach lurched. He didn't feel safe. He had to get out. He tried to stand, but the roof was too low. He bumped his head and a cascade of debris fell on his shoulders. He sat back down and stared at the ceiling. Most of the plaster had fallen away exposing the laths. It looked as if the entire roof could collapse if he stood again. So he remained seated, head down, blood pumping, not daring to move, compressed into the tiny space where he hardly dared breathe.

An old woman came up the stairs carrying bread and stew. He ate the bread, sipped the stew and felt her eyes watching him through milky, cataract eyes.

'Why are you here?' she asked and her voice was so soft he could hardly hear her.

'Some people are after me,' he said.

'No, dear, I mean, why are you here in Andalucía? Why aren't you in your own country surrounded by those who love you?'

'People are after me there too,' he said, realising how pathetic it sounded.

'Did you do something wrong, dear? she asked.

'No, nothing. I did nothing.'

The old lady chewed the inside of her mouth as if she was thinking.

'Well doing nothing is doing *something*,' she said studying his face. Ernesto felt himself tense. What nonsense the woman was talking. But then she took his hands and held them cupped in hers. He felt the warmth of her palms and their softness, almost like jelly. She was so close to him that he could see her wrinkles and the fine brown age spots across her cheeks. She must be eighty at least. 'So what *should* you have done, dear?' she asked. Her eyes were gentle, her voice mesmerising. Ernesto let himself relax. She smiled and he smiled back, two strangers sharing a wafer of time, a sliver of space. Suddenly it seemed right. He lowered his guard. His story had weighed him down for far too long. He took a deep breath and started.

'I was in Havana. I heard voices in the toilets. They were shouting. Silvio was there.'

'Who is Silvio, dear?'

'My boss's son. A man was screaming and Silvio ran off. There was blood - a lot of blood. There was a knife. I called for help but by the time the ambulance arrived the man was dead.'

'So you did well then,' she said, but Ernesto shook his head.

'I said I would testify but Arsenio was on my back.'

'Who is Arsenio?'

'My boss, Silvio's dad.' He said I had to protect his son, said if I spoke out he's make sure I never worked again.'

'Could he do that?'

'Arsenio could make anything happen so it was best I kept my mouth shut. I needed the money you see. But then there was the dead man. Didn't he need justice too?' Ernesto stopped for breath. 'Look, I'm sorry, I shouldn't be telling you all this. It's not nice.'

'So you did nothing?'

Ernesto dropped his head. 'I ran away.' The woman touched his arm and her tenderness made him want to cry. 'I had a girl. Her name was Belle.' The old lady smiled.

'That's nice.'

'But I told her!'

'Told her what?'

'I told her that I'd seen the murder, and that was a mistake too because, poor Belle. She insisted I testify but I couldn't and I ran and now she thinks I'm a coward. And worse still I left her there laden with the burden of my knowledge. How can that be right? How can that be the behaviour of an honourable man?'

The old lady squeezed his hands gently. You must forgive yourself, dear. A time will come to put this right. You just need a little courage and the help of those who love you. But right now you need to rest.' She patted his arm. 'And don't worry about the police. Juan will find a way. He's a clever man.' Then she smiled again and her face took on an ageless glow.

Ernesto settled on an old mattress under the eaves, his feet extending over the edge, and pulled a threadbare blanket over him to keep out the cold. He closed his eyes trying to summon sleep. But the old lady's words had bewitched him. *Doing nothing is doing something* she had said. But what did that mean? He thought about her wrinkled face and her soft palms and that gentle voice. Why was she bothering to harbour him, and Manuel before that? Why was she doing this when she could be safely tucked up in her own bed dreaming of her grandchildren? She must be one of the Monkeys he concluded, after all this was their safe house for Manuel so she must be one of them. He tried to imagine what the woman might have been through in the past. Perhaps she had fought in the civil war and had many stories of brutality and cruelty to tell. He thought about Emilia far away in the hills too, transcribing testimonies. How brave and heroic these two women were. Not like him, he thought. Not like me. He closed his eyes and tried to sleep but the words kept coming *Doing nothing is doing something* she'd said but still he shook his head unsure of what her words could mean.

He woke at dawn, body shivering with the cold and now the questions kept coming, nagging him to stay awake. Had they searched his room yet? Was there a citywide hunt with posters on the street? Had Don Anselmo despatched the police superintendent to root him out? If so he was in for a very rough ride. He waited all day for Juan, sleeping, eating, talking to the old lady, hoping for a breakthrough, waiting for news. Finally Juan arrived late in the evening looking exhausted.

'I've been watching your building day and night and no one's been up. No policemen, no Don Anselmo, nobody. Then this afternoon Beatriz came to the shop with this.' He handed Ernesto an envelope addressed to him in Don Anselmo's unmistakeable handwriting. A letter? After all that has happened – just a letter? He ripped it open.

November 30th 1958

Ernesto Costa, Once again you have enquired about my family. Not only have you disobeyed my strict instructions but now my son is even more distressed. This is completely unacceptable so I have decided that Francisco will no longer attend your lessons. You must calculate the monies owed and Beatriz will come by next week to make payment. Do not try to contact Francisco again.

This matter is finished, but the other is not. I expect full cooperation

253

as discussed and will contact you next week to receive your first notifications.

Anselmo Jimenez

Ernesto frowned. Why was there no mention of Emilia's letters? And Don Anselmo had written *my son,* as if everything was normal. Did this mean Francisco hadn't told him? Hadn't disclosed the secret of his mother and her letters? If not, why not? He handed the letter to Juan and watched him frown with the same incomprehension. Eventually Juan sat back and laughed.

'Well I never! Young Francisco has held his tongue and fed his grandfather just enough information to deflect him from the truth. The boy is a triumph!'

'But why would he do that?'

'To protect you, of course. Seems he's realised the repercussions if he were to tell.'

'Surely he couldn't have been so devious?' Ernesto said.

'Or so clever?'

'Or so disloyal to Don Anselmo.'

'And so loyal to you.'

Ernesto gazed at the ceiling of this modest little house and suddenly the roof seemed sturdier and the space felt warmer than before. He was safe again, all because an eleven-year-old boy had grasped the situation Ernesto would be in if he told. He'd withheld the most important secret of his young life. Oh Francisco, how can I ever repay you for what you have done? But Juan wasn't quite finished. He waved the letter in the air. 'What does Don Anselmo mean *other matter* and *first notifications*? Ernesto sighed, considering if he should try to cover up his identity as Don Anselmo's informant. But Juan was keeping his gaze steady, waiting for his reply. How could he lie to this extraordinary man? He sighed again.

'He wants me to notify him of anything suspicious,'

'Suspicious? By whom?'

'The Monkeys of course. Don Anselmo threatened to expose us if I didn't comply. But I'm not an informant. I never was. You have to believe me. I'm still on your side.' Ernesto hung his head in shame, expecting disapproval but Juan was smiling again.

'This could be useful, Ernesto. Go home. Act as though nothing has happened. Keep your cool. If you really are one of us you will have to prove it.' He waved the letter in front of him. 'And don't worry. This is between you and me. For now.'

Ernesto returned home, hopeful that Juan would not expose him before he'd had a chance to prove himself. After all he really was on their side. He said it again to check that he was right; that he *was* on their side? Is that what he had just said to Juan? Well it must be true. He searched his mind for thoughts to the contrary, remembering how he used to think of Franco as a strong leader of a great nation - well he'd been wrong about that. And that Spain was a respectable society full of citizens who towed the line –he'd been wrong about that too. Or that the union syndicates were following the law of the land – wrong again. And what about that crowd waving handkerchiefs in the square? According to Manuel that was pure theatre. And all those articles in *The Chronicle* telling its readers how their society was stable and content? It was all propaganda and lies. He scoffed. What a fool he'd been. Perhaps he'd half-seen it in the back his mind, incubating like a pupa in its chrysalis waiting to fully form but now he saw it in a glorious colour-stained revelation. He was a Monkey, he was a socialist and he was a rebel against the regime. Why hadn't he seen this before? Why hadn't he understood his own convictions? Why had this life been concealed from him for so long? And for once the answers came to him, swift and sharp. Because people are terrified of being denounced by their neighbours, of being seen to step out of line, terrified of mentioning their civil war for fear of repercussions, terrified by fear itself. Yet behind the scenes, the Monkeys were working to put all this right. Manuel with his union, Juan with his chain of contacts, Jorge studying law, Emilia collecting evidence, the old woman harbouring rebels on the run, the barman in the square. All this was going on behind the scenes and one day all this effort would sweep away the communal anxiety that plagued this nation. One day democracy would be restored. So yes, he *was* on their side and suddenly it felt right to say so. Then he remembered the old lady's words. *Doing nothing is doing something*, and now he understood. By sitting on the fence he had allowed all sorts of iniquities to occur. A murderer had escaped justice; he'd left his homeland, maybe lost Belle too. He'd lost the trust of his friend Paco. Perhaps he could have stopped him before it was too late. He'd agreed to spy for Don Anselmo and put his friends in danger and most of all, by concealing a mother's letters, he'd let down Francisco too. Now though, he didn't feel guilt. Now everything had changed. He had taken sides and it felt good. He smiled a big expansive smile, recognising his commitment, accepting his choice. He rushed to the corner of the room, picked up his trombone and strode back to the window. He leaned out into the street and started to play *Trombones Triumphant* just as he had after Paco's funeral. It was a march full of vigour and hope, a sound to lift the spirits. He played it loud, he played it bright and all the time he was thinking of Francisco and how strong the boy had been protecting him, and of all the people sheltering out there in their tiny apartments. They deserved better. When he'd finished and had lowered his trombone, there was a kind of rumble in the street, and as he listened more carefully he realised it was the steady clapping of applause coming from the apartments in his block and from the pavement too, rippling all the way down the street like molten brass, to reach the cascading fountain.

All day he waited for Beatriz to arrive with his final payment. But she didn't. Perhaps Don Anselmo was punishing him for upsetting the boy. He stayed in his room, hardly playing his trombone, hardly daring to imagine a happy outcome to current events. Thanks to Francisco he had escaped exposure, torture and death, but in some ways his problems were only just beginning. Carlos had demanded an oath of allegiance, a commitment to kill. But was this really what he wanted?

The big old doors of the meeting hall slammed shut and an iron bar was padlocked into place. Jorge fetched drinks from the bar and wafts of alcohol and tobacco closed in as several men settled around Ernesto.

In Manuel's absence Carlos took the lead. 'Where have you been? You were supposed to come yesterday.'

'I err... Francisco was upset about something and I forgot,' he said.

'Well stop messing us about, Nesto. Anyway, never mind. Something's come up. Don Anselmo was ranting in the car about that wretched Cuban. What did you do? Why is he so furious with you?' Ernesto hesitated. How should he answer? The men waited. Ernesto coughed into the silence, stalling for time. He couldn't reveal the truth. He daren't. Then he realised. Francisco's lie would do instead.

'I ignored his instructions and asked Francisco about his family, that's all. As a result, he's cancelled all my lessons.'

'Is that it?' Carlos said. 'Well the man's rattled that's for sure and if he hates you that much, then that's good enough for us.' The men nodded and Jorge slapped him on his back. The lie was satisfactory. 'No need to pledge your allegiance, Nesto. We trust you.' Thank goodness for that, Ernesto thought, although he couldn't decide if being an enemy of Don Anselmo was better or worse than upsetting these fanatical men here in this closed-off, fetid room.

'Now down to important business,' Carlos said splaying his long athletic legs and puffing out his chest. He spoke slowly, with a newly-found gravitas that didn't suit his impetuous character. 'Manuel has appointed me second-in-command. He wants me to coordinate our strategy from here.' Ernesto frowned. Really? Carlos a strategist? A chauffeur who is told where to drive and what to do, making vital decisions on Manuel's behalf? But there was something different about Carlos today; that same streak of madness in his eyes that Ernesto had witnessed in Manuel's. Carlos continued. 'Comrades, at this very moment our leader Manuel is hidden in a secure place, planning our next move to restore a communist republic to our land. When he has completed his plan we owe it to him to see it through. So are you with me?' Carlos raised his brandy. The men muttered in agreement and raised their sherries above their heads. Ernesto watched them, so determined, so sure that what they were doing was right. In his mind he knew that murder was never right but what else could he do now that his heart was broken? No more Francisco, no more sharing his love of trombone, no more innocence in the face of life's convolutions. And with his income gone there was no chance of getting back home soon. In the last few days his life had been turned upside-down and he needed a place to rest his heart. And here it was; a ready-made family who'd accepted him into their midst. It made him feel safe, made him feel wanted, made him feel secure. Besides, he still doubted their ability to carry off some half-baked plan to assassinate the Head of State, the Generalissimo, the Caudillo, his Excellency General Francisco Franco, or whatever else they called him. How in heavens could Manuel organise a plan of such complexity stuck up there in the mountains? It was all too ridiculous to be true. So he raised his rum and grunted a quiet

'Yes'

And there it was; that one word, that one small expiration, with a thousand repercussions. The decision had been made. He was in whether he liked it or not.

Carlos was in his stride. 'Under the light of an old oil lamp Manuel has studied the maps of the area surrounding Cádiz, and from these humble headquarters, his plans will be sent to us, passing through the cork forests, across the fields of cotton and wheat, past the bulls and the horses, and the straddle of settlements on the south side of town, until they finally reach me at this meeting hall.' His words reminded Ernesto of their journey across the countryside to Sauce de Valle, and of the massacre that was so wrong, so wretched, so cruel. He began to feel better about their intentions as Carlos continued. 'Then from here I will work with you, planning and agreeing in this dark and private place, until finally everyone knows exactly what to do.'

'And what *are* we going to do?' Jorge asked. Carlos looked pleased for the opportunity to expand. Again he seemed rehearsed, as though Manuel's careful plans had been reassigned from puppet-master to puppet and the puppet had memorised his master's words.

'General Franco is scared of flying so he's decided to develop the nation's roads instead. He's coming to Cádiz on 22nd December to discuss our road transport system across the bay. As you know, there are no bridges at the moment. The only access in and out is that single highway - more of a causeway than a road, with the Atlantic Ocean on one side and the trapped waters of the bay on the other. So Franco will attend morning mass in the Cathedral, then he and the mayors of the two regions will drive out of the city to view the location where a new bridge will unite both sides. Then on this narrow strip of road, General Franco will encounter a group of terrorists – that's us, men!' They all sniggered. '…who will blow up his car, and just to make sure we get him, we'll dynamite those in front and behind as well. Then, with the dictator dead, we Monkeys will retake the country and turn it into the communist state of which we all dream.'

According to Carlos it was as simple as that.

Ernesto stared into the middle distance. Could he really be part of this? It sounded like mass murder. It sounded insane. 'I'm no warrior,' he said quietly.

'Me neither,' said Jorge.

'We know that. Just leave it to us.'

Jorge was frowning. 'Then why ask us here? Why do we have to be involved?'

'Manuel insists. Says the more involved with the present plan, the more useful you will be to our future.'

'What do you mean?' Ernesto asked.

'He reckons you two are the thinkers. Says you're the ones who will plan our steps into government. You will coax the new regime into place.' Ernesto raised his eyebrows. He'd never thought of himself as a thinker. Jorge yes, but not him.

27. The Informant

Ernesto watched from his window as two men with identical moustaches and dark suits, approached his building. Below, he heard the door pull open and their footsteps clumping up the stairs. He froze. Had Francisco finally exposed him? He waited for the knock on the door, for the men to barge in and haul him away to some dismal place to face the consequences of Emilia's letters. But no. Instead, an envelope was pushed beneath the door. Thank god for young Francisco, still loyal, still on his side. He heard the footsteps fade away, grabbed the envelope and ripped it open. Inside was a simple instruction.

GENTLEMEN'S OUTFITTERS. TEN MINUTES.

He had known this was coming, summoned sooner or later as Don Anselmo's informant. But please, not now. He wasn't ready, hadn't managed to think of any news to spill – a speck of information that could satisfy Don Anselmo and make the man think he was an active spy. He'd spent hours wondering whose name he could expose to the light, but each had a link to the next; the barman, Juan, Manuel, Dolores, Jorge, the men in the meeting room. They would all be in danger if he spoke their names. Besides, Don Anselmo already had them on his list so he probably wanted something fresh and surprising. He pulled on his overcoat, stepped into the cold and lumbered down the street, his head empty of ideas.

The shopkeeper twisted the door sign from open to closed and pointed towards a platform at the back of the shop.

'Up there,' he snapped.

Ernesto followed the man's jabbing finger towards two broad steps that led up to a platform containing the changing cubicles. The central one was sealed by a curtain and in the gap between the hem and the floor Ernesto glimpsed a pair of well-polished, old-fashioned brogues. He stared, waiting hopefully for the shoes to move and for a customer to emerge with clothing draped over his arm ready to make a purchase. But the shoes did not move. They were stationary as if the wearer was sitting down - as if the wearer was waiting. Ernesto sighed. There was no escape from this reckoning, so he placed his foot on the first step, his head full of unholy images; Carlos in the meeting room describing how to blow up General Franco, Jorge in his dimly-lit room studying illegal incriminating documents, and the little attic where the old lady had sheltered him from the police. He could taste her delicious stew on his dried-up tongue. What would they do to her if he named her? His stomach churned. On the second step he thought he was going to vomit. How could he control his words? How could he stop himself from blurting out the truth?

He reached the platform, raised his arm, pulled back the curtain and gasped. Dressed in a bulky dark overcoat, Don Anselmo filled the space. Ernesto shivered and another image flashed through his mind. That of Manuel crammed up in the old lady's attic – another big man in a very small space and another person with demands he was unable to meet. Ernesto stepped in, squeezing himself into the corner, holding his breath. He was so close to Don Anselmo that he could see the slight stubble on his chin, his

262

eyes red with fury and his face as cold as stone. Behind him he heard the screech of metal rings running along the brass rail as the curtain was pulled shut and the shopkeeper's footsteps retreated. Ernesto scanned the bulk of the man, running his eyes down the expensive coat sleeve to the insignia on his gold cufflinks. *AJ* he said to himself, taking his time, stalling the moment when he would have to speak. But what was he going to say? He had no idea, and this must have shown because Don Anselmo was staring at him, waiting. Ernesto tried to stare back, but he couldn't hold the man's gaze. Instead he diverted his eyes to the mirror behind and saw the reverse image of Don Anselmo's broad-shoulders, the smoothed-down Macassar-oiled hair on the back of his head and a row of shiny curls gathered in the nape of his neck. But then beyond that and slightly above, Ernesto saw his own reflection, gaunt and desperate, staring back at him with wild eyes, exposing the weasel informer he was expected to be. He began to sweat. Don Anselmo shifted his weight.

'Speak up, man! What have you got to tell me?'

'I err... I don't know.'

'Of course you do.' Don Anselmo tapped his fingers on the arm of the chair. The gold paint was chipped. 'Well?' Ernesto ransacked his mind trying to think. Who could he name? Who should he betray? Don Anselmo raised his voice. 'Come on man, give me someone.' Ernesto bit the inside of his mouth. Whom could he implicate without condemning them to disaster? Someone anonymous? Someone who couldn't be traced? But who could that be?'Spit it out!' Don Anselmo shouted and Ernesto jumped as if lightening had pierced his body, and this seemed to illuminate his path to a convincing lie. The fat housekeeper that Dolores had mentioned, the one who was at Don Anselmo's house when baby Javier arrived, the child re-named Francisco.

'Well...there is...one person,' he said slowly, searching for an authentic sounding name.

'Well then?'

'I overheard something about your old housekeeper. Apparently she's still complaining about being sacked.'

'Don't be ridiculous. Servants come and go. Give me the name of someone who is actively working against me.' Ernesto ignored him, dreaming up the details.

'About eleven years ago I heard.'

Don Anselmo went white.

'Eleven years?' Don Anselmo repeated the words. His eyes narrowed, scrutinising Ernesto's face.

'Yes, sir.'

'And her name?'

'Err...Maria I think.'

'Her full name, you fool.'

'Err...Maria Moreno,' he said swallowing hard to hold in his lie. Don Anselmo coughed as if he was about to speak. But then he didn't. Ernesto held his breath. Had Don Anselmo realised he was being deceived? Did he already know the correct name of that housekeeper from all those years ago? Surely a man like him didn't notice servants who came and went from his dusty old house? But what if he *did* remember? What if the arrival of a baby grandson on his doorstep had cemented every detail of that day into his memory? If so, then he would know that Ernesto was lying. He stared at the floor, waiting, hoping that his invention had worked.

Finally Don Anselmo spoke. 'Huh! That silly woman.' he scoffed.

Ernesto could see a twitch in his jaw, sense the disorientation this information had achieved.

'So where is this Maria Moreno now?' Don Anselmo asked. Again that twitch.

'She doesn't live here anymore. Gone back to, err... Malaga, where she came from. It's just gossip anyhow.'

'Well that's something I suppose,' Don Anselmo muttered as he stood up. There was no space. Their chests bumped together, shoving Ernesto against the wall as the man steered his way around the cubicle, desperate, it seemed, to get out as fast as possible. Ernesto watched him hurry down the elevated platform and out of the shop and he left too, pleased with his hasty fabrication and grateful that Don Anselmo hadn't asked for more. The man was on the back foot, probably off to telephone the authorities in Malaga right now, ordering them to find this woman Maria and stop her reporting on the arrival of a baby on his doorstep. Perhaps to silence her for good. Ernesto grinned. How clever he had been without realising it!

He reached the safety of his room and threw himself into the chair. Once again he had been saved from disaster, just as before; twice at the police station, then by Francisco's silence, and again in the old lady's attic. And now this. Did he have a guardian angel? Was someone or something on his side, watching over him? If so, perhaps things would turn out alright after all. Perhaps his problems would disappear without him having to lift a finger.

December 22nd, the day of the proposed attack, was still weeks away and how slowly time passed. Without Francisco to keep him occupied, there was nothing for Ernesto to do. There'd been no further contact with Don Anselmo after their meeting in the changing room, no further demands to pass on information however false or thin. Perhaps Don Anselmo was too busy trying to find Maria from Malaga or maybe he'd forgotten about his new spy altogether. Ernesto began to relax. By mid-December, the cotton-boll weevil was in hibernation and somewhere in a mountain cave, a bat's heartbeat had slowed almost to a halt. Ernesto pushed old newspapers into the grate and thought of Manuel alone in that old house in Sauce del Valle, probably sitting by a fire just like this, with barely enough heat to warm the space around his chair. Would his assassination plan really come to fruition? Or was it just the fanciful idea of a madman forced into unproductive exile?

Jorge came by looking anxious.

'I've been thinking, Nesto.'

'Yes?'

'I'm not sure Manuel's plan is a good idea.'

'What do you mean?'

'This is murder on a huge scale. I'm not sure I want to be involved.'

'But your pact with Paco? Isn't this what you both wanted? Revenge.'

'I did, yes, but…'

'Look if you ask me, it's never going to happen.'

Jorge sighed. 'Perhaps you're right,' he said and smiled as if his conscience had just been cleared. Ernesto smiled too, recognising their simultaneous thoughts, that maybe this was an impossible plan created by a group of obsessive men who were quite incapable of seeing it through. If so, then they could go along with it knowing that it would come to nothing, knowing there would be no consequences. So with good conscience they could set aside their fears, trepidations and doubts, and he changed the subject.

'What am I going to do with these?' Ernesto said spreading Emilia's last letters onto the table.

'Let's open them, Nesto.'

'I can't. It wouldn't be right.'

'Don't tell me you haven't thought about it.'

'Yes but they are someone else's secret, not mine. I haven't even told Carlos, so Manuel doesn't know about them either. If he did,

266

he might do something stupid.' They both laughed. Their leader was too obsessed, and his sidekick Carlos too impetuous to be trusted with something as delicate as this.

'Come on, Nesto. What harm can it do?' Finally Ernesto nodded and picked up the tenth letter with its new French postmark.

October 1956

My dear boy,

I've gone, abandoned our encampment before we were exposed. First I travelled north to a town near Valencia where they murdered your Papa. The locals showed me where it happened and I stood there on the roadside next to a ditch full of nettles. The place was enchanting, with views of the mountains and I was surprisingly calm. All around was a feeling of hope because in the adjacent field, someone had planted endless rows of olive trees, so tender and new that they were still supported with stakes and their immature branches were bending in the breeze. I thought of you my love and the youthfulness of your arms, the softness of your legs, and your surely handsome face. I seem to know you, even though I don't, and I felt you close even though you are so far away. And your Papa too, concealed as he was beneath the earth. He too was with me in that wild and lovely place. I know this because, as I stood there, a warm wind came up making the trees quiver and moan. Moisture welled in my eyes and although we'd told each other not to mourn, those tears came not only from the wind but also from my heart.

Javier, now I am even further away in a town in France searching for my grandfather – your great grandfather. You never know, there is just a chance he has survived. So I send you my best wishes and hope with all my heart that one day the three of us will be together. Happy ninth birthday son.

Your loving Mama

Emilia.

Jorge sighed. 'This girl Emilia has a beautiful way with words,' he said. 'I wonder what she's like in person.'

Ernesto sighed too. 'Francisco should have been the first to read this, not me. If only he could.'

'Well let's ask Carlos to arrange a meeting. He doesn't need to know about the letters. Just say you want to check if Francisco's all right.' Ernesto considered it briefly. What a good idea.

They met down an alley off the main square, tucked away from curious eyes. Halfway along was a small tourist café with wine barrels outside and geraniums in hanging baskets moving gently in the December breeze. It was good choice of venue where hesitant tourists tasted sherry for the first time and tried out tapas with strange-sounding names. No one there would notice an adult and child having breakfast together. To keep Carlos away, Jorge suggested he stand at the end of the alley observing passers-by whilst he sat close by at another table, watching for anyone who might threaten the secret conversation between a man and a boy.

Francisco was wearing long trousers and an overcoat to keep out the cold. He looked grown up but his face was as anxious as a child. Ernesto went to shake his hand but the boy threw his arms around him instead.

His voice was muffled against Ernesto's coat. 'I didn't tell,' he said.

'I know you didn't, Francisco. You were very brave.'

'And I still won't. I promise'

Ernesto's heart was bursting 'Thank you,' he said, 'thank you for what you have done.' As they pulled apart, Ernesto saw the moisture in Francisco's eyes. The boy was distraught. 'I miss our lessons,' he said.

'Me too,'

The letters sat between them on the table and when the moment felt right, Ernesto pushed the tenth envelope with its French address, over to Francisco. He read it slowly, and then read it again. He studied the postage mark to confirm what Emilia had told him inside. Ernesto guessed what he was thinking. Throughout his childhood he'd thought that his mother was dead but then he'd discovered that she was not, that she was living somewhere close by. But this letter was telling him that she had moved away. How confusing and upsetting must that be. And not just that. His father - his real, rebellious father – was dead in a ditch somewhere in the north of the country. How could he make sense of all that too?

Ernesto studied Francisco's face for signs of upset, but instead his eyes had turned blank and his mouth was set firm. He threw the letter back onto the table.

'My father told me that family business is personal and no one should be asking questions, especially you.'

'Father? Don't you mean grandfather?' Had the boy learned nothing?

'How can I stop thinking of him as my father, after everything he has done for me?' Ernesto didn't like the way this was going but Francisco was in his stride, eyes wet and wild, his words full of indignation. 'My father told me that all rebels are enemies of the people and that I must have nothing to do with them. That means *you* I suppose.' Ernesto was shocked. He wasn't expecting this. 'He says your friends are traitors.' Tears began to fall down Francisco's cheeks as he grappled with his conflicting emotions. Ernesto sighed. Poor boy. He'd held it all back, hiding his newly-found discoveries from Don Anselmo even when he realised that his mother must be a traitor too. But now it was pouring out, every twist and turn rotating in his mind like a knife forced into tender flesh. It was all too much, and now he was retreating, backing away from a truth that hurt too much to accept. Ernesto rested a hand on Francisco's arm.

'My dear friend, life is complicated. One day you will understand.' But he could see that Francisco had shut down completely. The boy's mind had been altered. Don Anselmo's words had turned him, and this meeting, this letter, had been the last straw. He ransacked his mind for what to say, what to do, but Francisco was talking again.

'Remember that secret I was going to tell you?'

'Yes, but I told you not to tell.'

'But I want to.'

'No Francisco…' but the boy interrupted.

'I'm to be presented to El Caudillo next week in Cádiz.'

'What?' Ernesto's heart jumped. 'No you can't!'

'Of course I can. I'm old enough.'

'But the General…'

'My father says it is a great honour. There will be lots of dignitaries there and my father is an important man. It means a lot to him.' Ernesto tried to speak but the words wouldn't come. The boy would be in the entourage. The boy would be in danger. The boy would be dead.

'Look, it isn't a good idea.'

'Why not?'

'It's for grown-ups.'

'I *am* grown up.' Francisco looked offended.

'I'm sorry. I didn't mean…' but Francisco interrupted again.

'Of course I'm going to Cádiz. I will be seen alongside our leader just like my father has asked me to. I am going and that is that.' He folded his arms across his chest.

'Francisco, you can't.' But there was nothing he could say or do to make a difference. Defiance was part of Francisco's character. Like his mother, defiance was in his blood.

270

Carlos dropped the boy home and rushed back to join Ernesto and Jorge in the bar.

'What's going on? The boy wouldn't speak in the car.'

Ernesto tried to explain but it took some time for Carlos to grasp the situation.

'So Don Anselmo will attend the event with Franco?'

'Yes that's right.'

'That means I'll be driving the K6.'

'Yes that's right too.'

'In the entourage we've planned to blow up!'

'Correct.'

Carlos sat back wide-eyed as if watching a glass falling off a table in slow motion.

'So…' But he couldn't finish his sentence. Instead he put his hand over his mouth to stop the words from emerging. Ernesto watched him processing the information. Despite all his planning, Carlos hadn't thought it through. At last he spoke, and his eyes seemed wild with fear. 'Don Anselmo will attend mass so *of course* I'll be there. Then he'll be at the meeting with the two mayors, so I'll be driving down that causeway. I'll be caught in the blast.' He began to shake. 'Why didn't I think of this before? Ernesto ordered him a drink.

'Let's cancel it.' Ernesto said. You can send a message to Manuel to say it's off.'

But Jorge disagreed. 'Manuel would never allow it - not now. It's too late.'

'Not even with a child involved?'

'And me! Don't forget I'll be there too,' Carlos said.

For a moment there was silence until Jorge said 'Maybe there's another way,'

By the end of their frantic discussions, they had a plan. Ernesto would travel into Cádiz - first by bus and then by boat – just as he had last time he'd travelled to the city. He would attend mass in the cathedral whilst Carlos would drive Don Anselmo and Francisco in the K6 as expected. After the mass when all the dignitaries set off for the causeway, Carlos would hang back, making sure the K6 was at the rear of the procession. That way Carlos, Francisco and even Don Anselmo himself would be at a safe enough distance to avoid the blast. If there was any problem Ernesto would ring Jorge from the phone box in the square and he, in turn, would ring Manuel and warn him not to continue with his plan.

'Yes but let's not tell Manuel about this unless we have to,' Jorge suggested and they all agreed this was best.

Back in his room, Ernesto looked in the mirror and saw a tall thin man pinched with fear and buried in self-delusion. What a fool he'd been. For weeks now he'd been squeezing his worries into a tiny ball, pressing the life out of them in active suppression, convincing himself that Manuel and Carlos were madmen and this whole plan was a charade. *It's never going to happen* he'd said to Jorge and *I don't need to lift a finger*, he'd said to himself. *Perhaps I have a guardian angel,* he'd wondered. How foolish that seemed now, because the worst thing *was* happening. Not only was Manuel's plan about to be realised, but Francisco was in danger too. He hung his head, unable to gaze at the man in the mirror, the man who sat on the fence, the undecided man, the beige man, the one who couldn't say yes and who couldn't say no. He shook his head. 'This has to stop. It has to stop right now,' he told the room. 'It's now or never. I have to act.'

28. The storm

On the morning of 22nd December 1958, Ernesto took the first bus out of the city and travelled south towards the coast, then embarked on the ferryboat that would take him across the bay to the city of Cádiz. It was packed with travellers holding white handkerchiefs presumably to salute General Franco. He settled himself on a wooden bench inside the cabin and looked out on deck where many more passengers were clutching the deck rails and watching the waves hit the prow. The engine whirred in a super-high pitch, struggling to transport its additional weight, but as it launched out into open waters, it soon settled into a vibrating murmur that calmed Ernesto's anxious heart. After a few moments he noticed the windows filling with cascades of water as showers began to fall and a slight wind darted across the surface of the ocean, flipping the water into ruffles of brisk, white foam. If anything the sea seemed calmer as the ferryboat approached the city's towers, glimmering in the December sun. Perhaps the water swelled against the harbour wall with more force than usual. And perhaps undercurrents caused the boat to heave a little as it turned to dock. But if these were hints of disruption to come, Ernesto didn't notice. He stepped off the boat and onto the jetty and made his way, in the spitting rain, to the exit where he saw a large hoarding advertising berths on the Urania, the ship that could take him away from all this intrigue and maybe into the arms of Belle. For a moment it seemed tempting but then common sense prevailed. He couldn't afford a ticket. Besides he had no luggage, his passport was in his room, and he'd made promises he was expected to keep. But what were these promises if not complicity to slaughter? For a moment he faltered but then he held his nerve. Francisco was in danger. He had no choice. He took a deep breath and strode out towards the centre of the city, long legs pounding in rhythm with his racing heart and his mind released from uncertainty as a multitude of clouds gathered over the turrets of the city and seagulls disappeared from the sky.

The cathedral was set in a large square with shallow steps leading to the main door. El Caudillo's security men were standing in the portico, demanding identity documents and whisking away anyone who looked suspicious. Despite his tall frame and goatee beard, they scanned his identity card, saw the recent endorsement stamped across his visa, and with no weapons on him, was allowed to enter. It was cool inside, and the grey stone walls and vaulted ceiling made it feel even colder. He pulled up his collar and looked at his watch. It was early. He would have to wait, so he sat on a pew at the back, re-imagining what Carlos had explained would be happening out there on that causeway. A tavern stood half-way along where Franco was scheduled to take lunch and opposite that, out on the salt flats, was an ancient refuge that nobody used anymore. The roof was sound. Someone had checked it. So the explosives were safe from damp and the detonators had been lifted off the ground to avoid vibration. Someone had had the foresight to attach lightning deflectors too, and the exclusion zone had been clearly marked. So despite Ernesto's early doubts, he had to admit that Manuel's plan was impressive. He'd even installed a telephone.

The cathedral was filling up. Ernesto heard the buzz of

274

lightweight talk as the congregation found their seats, arranging their hats, gloves and handbags ready for Mass to begin. Ernesto closed his eyes imagining Manuel's men. About now they would be crawling across the salt flats and attaching explosives along the stretch of road preceding the tavern. Manuel's snipers would be in position too, just in case someone came across the flats either by mistake or design. Manuel had given instruction to shoot first and ask questions later, and since everyone knew he was a great leader, no one questioned his judgement. Ernesto looked at his watch. It was almost done.

A wind started to whine through the stained glass and Ernesto felt a pressure on his ears as if the air around him was swelling and pushing inside his head. A bird flew in and headed to the chancel where it found a beam and perched there grooming its feathers. Everyone waited, watching the bird, listening to the stained glass windows vibrating, hearing the sound of expectancy. A surge of cold wind burst through the open doors making everyone shiver. Ernesto could hardly bear the wait. The order of service leaflet trembled in his hands. Oh god, let's get this done!

Then from outside came the deep hum of car engines drawing up to the cathedral step - one, then another, then more. Guards stood to attention. The congregation turned their heads. No one spoke. Someone coughed. Ernesto held his breath. El Caudillo appeared at the doorway in military dress followed by Carmen Polo wearing a black mantilla and those soft white pearls he'd seen before. The couple dipped their hands in the stone stoup, made moist signs of the cross on their foreheads and moved slowly down the central nave. The mayors of the two districts followed, each wearing their respective chains of office, tricorn hats, and capes that flapped raggedly in the draught. Behind them was a file of military men in full dress and local dignitaries in plain dark suits. Don Anselmo came in last, walking unsteadily, as if his recent discussions about Maria the mysterious housekeeper, had rendered him old before his time. Ah! There was Francisco accompanied by Beatriz looking pale and windswept behind her black lace veil. Carlos was nowhere to be seen. Good. He should be waiting with the K6 at the back of the queue.

The doors slammed shut. Mass began. In slow and measured motion the priest performed his rituals and the congregation performed theirs, kneeling, chanting, responding and bowing in supplication. Ernesto could hardly bear it. Let's get this nightmare over, but the priest droned on and the queue for Holy Communion was everlasting. The General and his wife went first, walking solemnly towards the altar rail, kneeling, hands together and offering their mouths to receive the host. Others followed, Beatriz and Francisco came last, joined by Don Anselmo. They knelt. They bowed. They made the sign of the cross. It was all so elaborate, so ornate. Poor Francisco, pulled into all this. And why was it taking so long? When their communion was done, the three ambled back, palms together, down the aisle, slowly, oh so slowly, and as they reached their seats, the light outside dimmed as if someone had turned down a switch. The cathedral fell into semi-darkness. Only a tiny ray of sunlight from a single window fell on the congregation like a shaft of light in a prison cell. Then rain began to hit the lead roof in a syncopated clatter. 'Hailstones,' someone whispered. And a flash of lightning lit the space, followed by a crack of thunder, so loud that several women shrieked. The priest looked to the heavens and continued speaking but Ernesto couldn't hear him for the noise. Soon an odour of damp rose from the flagstones and someone sneezed. There was movement in the pews as people consulted their watches no doubt wondering if they were going to get home before the storm got worse. Ernesto looked at his watch too. How much longer was this going to take?

Then it was over, pious solemnity released, as the great doors opened to a cascade of rain. Ernesto was first to leave, sheltering in the vaulted space under the portico and hiding behind a pillar

276

where he couldn't be seen. He peered out into the square. Franco's J12 was parked next to the steps. Other cars were positioned behind and the K6 had manoeuvred to the far end. Well done Carlos. Everything going to plan. Under the protection of the portico the congregation gathered in groups, reluctant to go to their cars, as they waited for the downpour to ease. But the rain wasn't easing. It was getting worse and the cacophony of hailstones hurt his ears. Out in the square, the line of vehicles waited, their overheated engines throwing up plumes of steam into the saturated air. Drivers emerged, opening umbrellas for their guests. General Franco peered impatiently through the barrier of rain towards his car. Everyone was watching. No one dared leave before their leader. Drivers looked at their watches, wipers flapped, birds gathered under eaves. Franco stepped forward, scurrying down the steps towards his car. His driver went to meet him, umbrella raised. But Franco strode past him, past the J12, and through the rows of parked cars towards something else, and Ernesto had seen it too. A car he'd only read about in magazines - the Pegaso Z-102, with a V8 engine, wearing its hardtop to protect it from the rain. Even in this haze it was a beauty.

Franco peered into the interior. He looked impressed. Then one of the mayors came over shaking his keys. The two men exchanged looks of admiration and Franco patted the mayor on his back. Rain became a torrent but they didn't seem to care, standing there soaked to the skin. The mayor opened the passenger door. Franco nodded and called over to Carmen Polo. What did he say? Then Franco got into the Pegaso. *No don't do that.* The mayor was in the driver's seat. What was going on? The V8 engine roared. *No! Get out. Go to your own car.* But now the Pegaso Z-102 was moving off and everyone was cheering through the rain. Franco waved from the passenger seat. No. This wasn't meant to happen. He should be in the J12. He should be in the centre of the blast. But already the little sports car was leaving, turning away from the cathedral and out of the square. Ernesto looked over at Carlos, but he was busy wiping the condensation from inside the windscreen. He hadn't seen the General going off in the wrong car. Carmen Polo was still in the portico and now she was chatting to Don Anselmo and Francisco. She was bending down to shake the boy's hand. She was putting her arm around his shoulder. She was smiling and Francisco was smiling back. Ernesto screamed inside his head. No that's not right either, because now she was steering Francisco down the steps and towards the J12. *Don't get in Francisco, don't!* But it was too late. The boy slid along the back seat next to the first lady and the car moved slowly away. *No Francisco. No!* Ernesto squinted through the rain. He had to stop them. He ran down the steps but the J12 was already turning the corner. Now the other engines were fired up too, people running, doors closing, lights on, Beatriz and Don Anselmo in the K6, Carlos up front, engine thrumming. Ernesto was desperate. He called out to warn them but a gust of wind robbed the words from his mouth. Now the whole entourage was in motion, one car after the other, moving smoothly through the downpour like ships on manoeuvres across an even wetter ocean. The K6 was at the rear as they all turned the corner and left the square heading for the causeway.

He was alone. The world had deserted him. No more people, no more engines, only the sound of thunderous rain bouncing off the cobbles onto his legs, making the fabric of his trousers cling to his calves. He looked up at a sky heavy with more rain to come. The wind was vicious, tearing through him, forcing his clothes against his body so that he could hardly move. Behind him a lamppost crashed to the ground. He jumped. Glass shattered. What should he do? The J12 was gone. Francisco inside. He'll be blown to pieces. He had to do something. He looked about. A taxi was parked in a side street.

'Take me out of town,' Ernesto screeched hearing the desperation in his voice.

'What! In this storm?'

'I have money,' Ernesto said urgently. The man sighed and ignited his engine. Ernesto threw himself in the back.

'Catch up with those cars,' he said.

They scuttled through the rain and it was only then that Ernesto remembered that he was supposed to telephone Jorge if there was a problem and Jorge would call Manuel at the refuge and they would cancel their plans. But it was far too late for that. The entourage would already be close to the causeway. He had to solve this himself. He stared forwards through the windscreen as a curtain of rain rolled down making everything blurred. Why hadn't Carlos stopped Francisco from getting into the J12? 'Faster please.' The driver pressed his foot to the accelerator. Surely Carlos knew the boy would be in danger. Why didn't he act?

A minute later they reached the causeway and the savagery of the storm lay before him. Waves were rising on both sides, hovering momentarily before crashing down on the road in a violent assault that launched the shingle through the air like bullets from a machine gun. Ernesto peered forwards. The K6 was still some way ahead with Carlos holding back as agreed and beyond them the rest of the entourage moving cautiously ahead. Perhaps there was time to catch them up and save Francisco. But then the wind caught the taxi sideways. The driver snatched at the wheel. A telegraph pole lurched across their path, its cables pulled tight, then, as it swung back, they relaxed into great loops swinging back and forth as the pole regained position.

'I don't like this one bit,' the taxi driver said.

'Nor do I,' Ernesto mumbled putting his hands together as if to pray. Manuel doesn't know that Francisco is in the J12. He doesn't know that he's going to blow up my boy. Waves were swelling on either side, rising like a snarling beast above the height of the cars then withdrawing back into the ocean. In the distance an oil tanker listed on the sea. Ahead, an array of brake lights lit up, creating a red blur cascading down the windscreen. The cars had stopped.

'Can't see a damn thing,' the driver said and for a moment there was an unsettling silence. Then a loud crash as a wave fell like lead onto the taxi roof. The car tipped sideways. Ernesto was flung across the seat, face pressed against the side window. For a second the car hovered, balancing on two wheels. Ernesto held his breath, waiting for it to plunge into the sea. But the taxi fell back, bouncing onto the shingle. They were upright again. The driver shook his head. 'That's it, I've had enough. I'm going back.'

'No you can't, not now.' Ernesto could see the tavern up ahead.

'Yes I can. Get out here if you want.' He pulled the car over, ready to turn. Ernesto threw money on the seat, opened the door and staggered out.

He fell, knocked over by the force of the wind. Sand swirled around him, stabbing his cheeks like needles. He pushed wet hair from his face and stared ahead. Red lights gone. Cars moving. He saw the K6 with Carlos, Don Anselmo and Beatriz inside and, some way off, six other cars before the J12. He couldn't see the Pegaso. Perhaps it had already accelerated away. He struggled to his feet and started to run. Somewhere on his left, Manuel's snipers were ready with their rifles. They wouldn't know it was him. They would shoot for sure. He kept moving. The wind pushed against his chest, his coat flapped in the gale. Ocean spray stung his cheeks and entered his eyes. His boots were heavy and the thud of his footsteps echoed in his brain. He reached the K6 and saw through the rear window the silhouettes of Beatriz upright and Don Anselmo asleep beside her. He came alongside and banged on the rear side window. Beatriz wound it down. He saw Don

Anselmo dozing. 'Francisco's in danger!' he shouted over the roar, but Beatriz frowned and Carlos just shrugged. Did they hear him? Surely they did? But there was no time to explain. He shook his head and started to run again, along the open road as fast as he could until he reached the rear of the entourage. No sign of Manuel or his snipers. Keep going, keep running. He passed cars, one - two – three. The occupants stared at the madman running alongside. Four - five - six. He had to get to Francisco before the J12 got to the tavern. A flash of lightning illuminated the causeway. Ahead, a car stopped. Someone was getting out. It was Franco's bodyguard. He was raising a gun. On the salt flats, a sniper was raising his too. Thunder roared. Lightning filled the sky and for a second Ernesto stood illuminated in its light. A bullet flashed, then another and another. Pain zipped through his calf. He was down. The sky returned black. He got up. He didn't care. He limped forward. Warm blood ran down his cold leg. He reached the J12. Hammered on its roof.

'Get out! Get out!'

It wasn't enough. They weren't listening. He wrenched the door of the J12 open. Carmen Polo screamed. He grabbed Francisco and hauled him out. They fell together, rolling onto the shingle. Then strong, forceful arms were around him, hauling him to his feet. He felt a gun jammed against his chest.

A bodyguard put handcuffs around his wrists just as six cars back, the ocean was recoiling. It pulled and dragged against the causeway exposing the beach in an echo of clattering stones. Then a mighty wave pulled upright, soaring as high as a ship. It hovered, lingering, like a hunter waiting for its prey. Then, with a deafening roar, it dropped onto the K6, with Carlos, Don Anselmo and Beatriz inside and the car toppled over into the sea.

29. A wound is healed

The bodyguard had released him. The entourage had fled. Ernesto eased himself into a chair by the tavern fire. His calf was wrapped in a bandage. It felt like stone, but they said it was only a graze and that he should rest. Through the window he saw a rescue party on the causeway and a security team dismantling the bombs. He imagined Manuel and the rest of the rebels retreating across the salt flats, disappearing into the rain. The landlord came over.

'Idiots,' he muttered. '? Don't they know explosives don't detonate right when they're wet?' He offered Ernesto some rum, and hot chocolate for the boy. Francisco pulled up his trouser legs and showed Ernesto his grazed knees where they'd fallen together on the harsh sand.

'You're my hero,' he said. But Ernesto shook his head.

'No, not me.' He sighed. 'I'm just pleased you're alright. And Beatriz? Where is she? And Carlos? And your...?'

'Divers are searching for them now,' Francisco said wrapping his arms around Ernesto and burying his face into his chest. Poor boy, was he going to lose even more people he loved today? Ernesto dropped his chin onto the top of the boy's head and gave it a gentle kiss. His hair was shining with health. He smelt of the sea.

An hour later, Ernesto was awoken from a deep sleep, first by an ambulance and then a hearse driving down the causeway to remove the just-living and the dead. The landlord came over.

'They've sent a car for you when you're ready.' Ernesto roused himself and looked around.

'Where's the boy?'

'They took him home.'

'What about the people in the K6?'

'They wouldn't say. State secret.'

Ernesto fetched his coat, still damp from his efforts, thanked the landlord and left. He rode home in comfort, dozing off in the back until it reached his street. Juan was on the pavement smiling, holding his papers.

'Hello, amigo. Saved you these,' he said with a friendly wink.

In his room Ernesto opened *The Chronicle*. A single photograph of a wet and windy Cádiz occupied the first page. The headline said it all,

STORM OF A LIFETIME 22nd December 1958

Our region of Cádiz suffered an assault from the ocean like no other this century. What started as a mild flurry of wind and rain, quickly gathered momentum, taking the inhabitants of the city by surprise. By mid-morning there were constant showers, followed by strong winds from the Southwest. By late morning water fell with such intensity that lakes formed in the streets making it impossible for pedestrians to pass. The wind worsened and within half an hour the gale had become a hurricane, blowing with such force that no one dared venture outside. The ceilings of numerous homes in the old town collapsed, and lampposts near the Cathedral were shot down by the wind. In some areas, electricity supplies were cut, rendering the city into darkness, and flood-water raided people's homes. At sea, the oil tanker Astorga had to be towed into dock.

Communications between Cádiz and the rest of the province have been cut off as telegraph poles fell across the city. Train services to Seville and Madrid are not expected to return to normal for several days. Travellers for Christmas celebrations are advised to make alternative arrangements.

Ernesto read the article again. There was no mention of the General's visit, or what happened afterwards. No words describing how he'd saved the boy. Oh well, he thought, at least Francisco was safe.

Yet in his neighbourhood, everyone wanted to talk to him. To some he was a hero and to others a villain. At the police station the superintendent took his statement, listening suspiciously as Ernesto explained that he had been attending mass in the cathedral when he overheard a plot to kill General Franco, but that he hadn't recognised the men and that he was just a trombonist who had rescued the boy. During their conversation there was yet another telephone call and once again the superintendent returned from his office disgruntled but reluctantly letting him go. If General Franco had commanded it, it was never mentioned, and Ernesto received no praise for trying to save the life of his wife Carmen Polo and that of the son of his right-hand man. At the meeting room Manuel's men were more direct, asking what he thought he was doing sabotaging their plans, but he managed to convince them of his best intentions to save the boy. And since the bombs were unlikely to have exploded, they backed off, perhaps realising the insanity of Manuel's plan or even relieved that their leader had left the area to fight his battles elsewhere. The loss of their comrade Carlos however, had been much harder to bear.

On Christmas Eve, Ernesto and Jorge met Beatriz and Francisco at a café in the middle of town, choosing an outside table where passing traffic would muffle their words. Beatriz and Francisco were dressed in black having just come from Don Anselmo's funeral, his body having finally been retrieved from the bay. Beatriz ordered a muffin for Francisco and settled herself in the chair. Ernesto smiled. How different she looked, eyes brighter, mouth softer. Had she changed the colour of her hair?

'You were lucky to survive,' Ernesto said.

'I'm a strong swimmer. Besides, I'd opened the car window, remember?'

'Why wasn't the incident reported in the papers? Ernesto showed Beatriz *The Chronicle* that Juan had given him.

'They came to see me in hospital. Told me not to say anything about the rescue and the bombs,' she said. 'I suppose they thought it would do the General's reputation no good to know that dangerous rebels had nearly killed him.' Jorge and Ernesto agreed. 'I suppose that's why they're not calling you a hero for stopping it either,' she added.

'I wasn't a hero. I had no interest in saving El Caudillo.'

'I wouldn't say that out loud, if I were you,' Jorge said, looking around the café, and they laughed. Birds had assembled at Francisco's feet, waiting for crumbs to fall. Jorge leaned towards him.

'Francisco, why did you get into the General's car?'

'Dona Carmen invited me, said she felt lonely because the General had gone off in that sports car.'

'*I've* got a question now,' he said. 'Why did my grandfather change my name?'

Jorge seemed to know the answer. 'Your grandfather named you after the General: Francisco Franco or El Caudillo or His Excellency, or whatever else they choose to call him.' Francisco frowned.

'I think I prefer Javier.' They laughed again and it felt good to feel so light and free.

'Did you enjoy reading the letters I gave you?' Ernesto asked.

'Yes. We went through them one by one. Beatriz explained everything and I'm beginning to understand why my mother abandoned me.' He dug his hands into his pockets to retrieve Emilia's photograph. 'Juan, the newspaper man gave me this, isn't she beautiful.' Ernesto studied Emilia's face. She didn't look like a fighter, or a rebel, or a passionate chronicler of evil deeds. With her sweet expression and pretty floral dress, she seemed innocent and calm, as if the world loved her and she loved it back. Jorge took the photo from him and studied it for a while. 'Pretty girl,' he said passing it back.

'Beatriz is going to help me find her, and we won't stop until we do.' Francisco announced.

'And the last two letters? Have you read those too?' Ernesto asked.

'I saved them so we could read them together.' A lump came to Ernesto's throat. He couldn't speak. How the boy must love him, if he was willing to wait before opening them. Beatriz removed them from her handbag.

'Here, 'she said. 'Let's see.' The three adults huddled over the table as Francisco read out his mother's words.

October 1957

My dearest Javier,

I've settled here in Pau. The people are friendly and I'm learning to speak French. It is a truly wonderful thing to see how open and tolerant the people in this country are compared to the deathly paralysis in our own. But there are many Spaniards here too, released from the internment camps years ago.

I am still hopeful of finding my grandfather. He is always in my thoughts and even if all I discover is a stone plaque with his name on it, I will be content. He taught me to look for the good in people and not to hate, even when his son was his enemy. They had so many rows when I was a child and in the end my father left and didn't come back. That's how I ended up with my grandfather and I wouldn't have it any other way.

Juan (remember the man I told you about) informed me that someone tried to assassinate El Caudillo on the Dominguez estate and that they captured the man responsible and killed him without trial. Some say it was my father who ordered it. So you see Javier, your grandfather is not a nice man and one day his devotion to the General will bring him down.

How are you my love? Ten years old today! I try to imagine what you look like and hope it is like your father. He had the thickest and shiniest hair you have ever seen and I am sure that you will have that too. Anyway have a good birthday, Javier, and one day we will meet. Be sure of it.

Your loving mother Emilia.

Ernesto sighed remembering again his dear friend Paco, sitting beside him, bragging about his imaginary conquests. Poor man, arrested then tortured. What a way to meet his death. Francisco must have understood. His voice faltered but his words were firm.

'She is right. My grandfather was not a nice man,' he said, and Ernesto nodded gently at the boy's new understanding.

Jorge lightened the mood. 'Emilia sounds like the kind of woman I'd like to meet,' he said, cheeks flushed. 'After all I've been reading her documents for years, haven't I?'

Ernesto smiled to himself. What a match that would be. A chronicler and an academic, both on the same side, both passionate about change.

'There's no address?' Beatriz asked, searching the envelope.

'She doesn't want to be found. She's an enemy of the people.' Jorge said.

Francisco opened the last letter.

October 1958

My dear son,

I've found him! My grandfather is very weak but he lives! Can you believe it? As soon as we met I decided to suspend my politics in order to give him the care he needs. Perhaps we only have a few years or months or even days, but all that matters is that we are together.

So now I have made a decision Javier. No more hiding in the shadows, no more shrouding of my past. Look on the back of this letter my love. You can write to me here and although right now I cannot leave my grandfather (your great-grandfather!) nor return to Spain, at least we can get to know each other on the page. Oh Javier how things have changed and so quickly. I cannot wait a moment longer to post this to you.

So it's not goodbye, my little one, but 'a bien tot.'

Your loving mother Emilia

Jorge took the letter, turned it over, and there it was. The address in a small village called Billère near Pau. There was a hand-drawn map too, showing a river and narrow tracks through woodland where residents could enjoy some peace.

'Looks like Paradise,' Jorge said.

New Year's Eve passed without much celebration. Ernesto stayed in his room playing his trombone, happy to return to his usual routines. But events were still on the move. Juan appeared at his door, out of breath.

'Come downstairs, someone wants to talk to you.'

Standing on the pavement next to Juan's shop was the poor man from the steamship Urania - the Cuban with the twin teenage girls. Despite his grey complexion, his eyes were twinkling.

'Roberto's got news for us,' Juan said slapping the man on the back. 'But first let's buy him a drink.' They crossed over to the bar where they asked for sherry and rum. Ernesto ordered a sandwich, and when it arrived he pushed it across to Roberto, just as he'd done last time they'd met. Juan explained. 'Every month Roberto sends me a telegram from the harbour, but this time he's come up here with his news and I thought our Cuban friend should be the first to hear it.' They waited for Roberto to finish eating. He swallowed then grinned.

'Batista's gone - left on New Year's Eve - scurried out of the country with his tail between his legs.' Roberto raised his rum above his head. 'Here's to our revolution!'

'Are you absolutely sure?' Ernesto said, wanting certainty.

'Here, if you don't believe me take a look at this.' Roberto handed Ernesto a ship's telegram sent by the man himself.

I resign my powers as President of the Republic and beg the people to maintain law and order and avoid any changes that could jeopardise our Cuban nation.

Signed Fulgencio Batista Zaldívar, President of the Republic. Havana, January 1, 1959.

Roberto was talking, but Ernesto wasn't listening. He was thinking, dreaming, imagining. Would she be there at the port in Havana? Would she wave and smile as she always did? Oh my Belle I'm coming home.

Next day he and Jorge met at the bar.

'Funny how things we thought would never change, suddenly seem more fluid and open,' Ernesto said.

'I thought you hated change.'

'I did once. But some change is good.'

290

'Well here's to your communist Cuba, Nesto.'

'Maybe,' Ernesto replied. 'But the Castro brothers are intellectuals not revolutionaries.'

'Don't underestimate the academics and the philosophers my friend. Once these evil regimes are gone, it's the thinking bastards like you and I that will make things happen.'

'Well then, here's to the thinking bastards, be they in Spain or Cuba.'

'You're going back then?'

'Yes. Got the ticket here.' He tapped his pocket. 'Juan organised a collection to pay my fare.'

'So this Belle woman - will she have you?'

'I sent her a telegram and she sent me one back.'

'Well? Come on - tell.'

'It said "You made me wait, mulatto," so I think she'll have me.'

'Really? Is that what that means? Well you know her best.'

'I'm not sure I know her at all.'

'And Beatriz?'

'Not interested.'

'You or her?'

'Both really. You were right. I need a real woman not a fantasy.'

He'd met Beatriz for lunch - he in his best clothes and she in a dark fur coat with her hair all soft and brown.

'You look lovely,' he'd said.

'Thank you. Blonde was never a good look.'

They spoke for an hour and there was so much Ernesto wanted to know. For a start, what had she said to Francisco to help him change his mind about his grandfather and his mother? 'I told him about the cruelty, and the killings and the corruption and that his grandfather had been part of all that.'

'But I thought you were part of that too.'

'I was. Well my husband was. He served under Don Anselmo in Morocco as a young recruit. But as soon as the Civil War started, he saw what was going on, the cruelty, the shame.'

'I thought he died fighting the communists.'

'No. He *became* one, disobeyed Don Anselmo's orders once too often, and in the end they shot him as a traitor.' Ernesto was shocked.

'But the bicycle? You were spying on us weren't you?'

'No. The other way round. When Dolores took Emilia's letter to Juan, he was worried that the Monkey operation would be exposed. So he suggested that I went to work for Anselmo to see how things evolved.'

'But you were the wife of a rebel. Surely he wouldn't employ you?'

'True, but it's surprising what a bit of feminine charm can do,' she said grinning. Ernesto smiled. He already knew that.

'So you intercepted those letters?'

'Yes. It was easy. I was his secretarial assistant after all and saw all his correspondence. And of course I pretended to spy on Juan but nothing ever got back to Don Anselmo, at least not from me. The man in the gentlemen's outfitters is the real informer.'

Ernesto nodded. He already knew that too.

'But wasn't spying for Don Anselmo like surrender?'

'Not at all. The man was terrified that people would find out that his daughter was a rebel and Francisco was not his son. The sad thing is that despite loving Emilia and raising Francisco, the man just couldn't change. His loyalty to General Franco was as fixed as the moon and stars above our heads.' She gave him a hard look. 'I might have been able to save him though, me being a strong swimmer.' She paused and lowered her voice. 'But I didn't, and I'm not sorry about that.'

'And Carlos?'

'Trapped behind the steering wheel. In any case…' she paused, then whispered. 'He knew Francisco was in that car. He bloody knew, but did nothing about it. Well he made his choice and I made mine.' Ernesto sat back speechless in wonder. Dear lovely Beatriz. What a woman, administering justice in her own special way. He laughed and she laughed too. He offered her his hand and she held it firmly.

'You seem much happier,' he said.

'I am,' she answered without hesitation, then smiled and added, 'Look, sorry I teased you, but it was just too easy. I knew it wasn't right, but I couldn't help myself. You were besotted. Besides, I had to keep up the charade of the femme fatale didn't I?' She smiled again, a natural, pretty, and final smile. A truce had occurred between them. He knew it, and he could see that she knew it too.

30. Trees

Ernesto leans over the iron balustrade taking in the crystal clear Caribbean light streaming into his sitting room. A Cuban bolero is playing on the radio and he smiles. It's good to be back. The house had been requisitioned after the Americans left, and now it is divided into multiple living quarters for the deserving. And he is one of the deserving. A month has passed since he stepped off the Urania and been greeted like a hero. Roberto had seen to that. So now he has a proper home with its own bathroom and kitchen and a separate room to practice his trombone. He looks into the patio below, where the neighbours are preparing their meal and he hears the clatter and chatter of pans in the kitchen and children playing on the step. Oh that Caribbean lilt he's missed so much. A cool breeze runs through the building from the open front door right through to the back, releasing the fruity aroma of the lemon tree that grows in the central patio. He reaches over the canopy and pulls a fat lemon from its branch, twisting it gently to do the tree no harm. Then he walks barefoot along to the kitchen where Belle is preparing her mojo marinade.

'Just what I need, Mulatto,' she says and he grins. Then he wanders to the front of the apartment and opens the doors to their balcony overlooking the street. Music hits him from every side, voices too, animated and sharp. He sits at the balcony table and opens a letter that has arrived several days ago, but only now is he ready to read. Juan is an evocative writer, with not a hint of the rough speech patterns he used before. His news is welcome. The meeting room has gone quiet; all talk of politics abandoned, at least for now. But *The Monkey* is still published daily and the Monkey's Mouth is still gently sowing seeds of mutiny. Juan has received news from Beatriz in France that Javier has been united with his mother and that her face is as sweet and as round as her photograph suggests. The grandfather has rallied and declares that he has no intention of dying for at least another ten years now that he has his family to care for. Jorge has travelled up to France too, and now he and Emilia are collaborating with Juan, laying the blueprint for some time in the future when Spain will once more be free. There is a message at the bottom of Juan's page written in Jorge's hand. *You never know, Nesto. The thinking bastards might just save the day.* And on the back Javier has written a note saying he is practising his trombone every day and will write his own letter soon. Inside the envelope Juan has enclosed a clipping from *The Monkey*. Gone are the bad spelling and grammar this publication is famous for, and in its place is the writing of an articulate man., Ernesto smiles as he finally realises. No wonder all those subversive commentaries escaped censure. Juan had carefully edited his newspaper with all those terrible errors so that the authorities would dismiss it as incoherent rubbish. *You clever man, my friend.*

FROM THE MONKEY'S MOUTH Comrades, let us congratulate our brothers on their successful revolution in Cuba. They have shown us there is another way; that no matter how downtrodden we may feel, no matter how weak we may be, courage is the answer, not just on a national level but personally too. There was a foreigner amongst us who thought he was weak. Yet he showed kindness when others were cruel, and he showed love when we were full of hate.

Above all he showed courage when it really mattered. So comrades take comfort knowing that we are stronger than we think and that one day humanity will prevail.

Ernesto shrugs. Belle doesn't need to know about my life over there, he thinks throwing the paper into the grate. It had taken ages for her to open up. She was moody and quiet when he first came back so he didn't ask about her life without him, and she didn't ask about his exile in Spain either. But yesterday she had suggested a walk in the countryside. They had walked out past the abandoned American golf course and the sprawling mansions once lived in by the rich, and on towards the sugar cane fields on the outskirts of town. They stood on a rise looking out across the tree-soaked horizon.

'Did you know that trees communicate underground?' she'd asked. 'They spread their roots until they touch.'

Ernesto had smiled - typical of Belle knowing something like that. She continued quietly as if she were, all of a sudden, shy.

'Well that's how I thought about us, when you were away. As if the undercurrents of the ocean were moving as one, searching the seabed for a connection, and that we were together even when we were so far apart.' Ernesto had stared at her. Any residual feelings for the crystalline Beatriz extinguished as he gazed at this beautiful, intelligent woman by his side. When they walked back home he told her that even with the Mafia gone – Arsenio too - he was going to the police station to tell them about the murder. She had smiled at him with what looked like admiration and when he took her hand she didn't resist.

Now Ernesto moves into his new practice room and stands with his feet slightly apart. Closing his eyes, he takes a deep breath, evoking a moment that had brought him such joy not so long ago. *'Imagine you're standing on the shore. Can you hear the waves?'* Francisco *nodded. 'You must breathe like the tide. First it draws back, pulled by the forces of nature. Breathe in. Then it returns unstoppable as it rushes across the sand. Breathe out.'* Ernesto stands rock steady and lifts the trombone to his lips. Change is all around him, arguments in the streets, a communist revolution only just born; differences of opinion and casualties of war. But change doesn't scare him anymore. Change is just a different journey yet to be travelled. Then he fills his lungs with air and makes his first virgin sounds of the day.

About the author

Patricia Román was born and raised in Oxford,
England and lives in rural Spain, drawing on her
Spanish heritage to create timeless stories about
ordinary people in extraordinary times.

Also by Patricia Román

Mothers Daughters Liars
A story from yesterday reflecting the #metoo
movement of today.

The Cuckoo and the Cuckquean
Spanish suffragettes and their fight for justice.